D4VE2

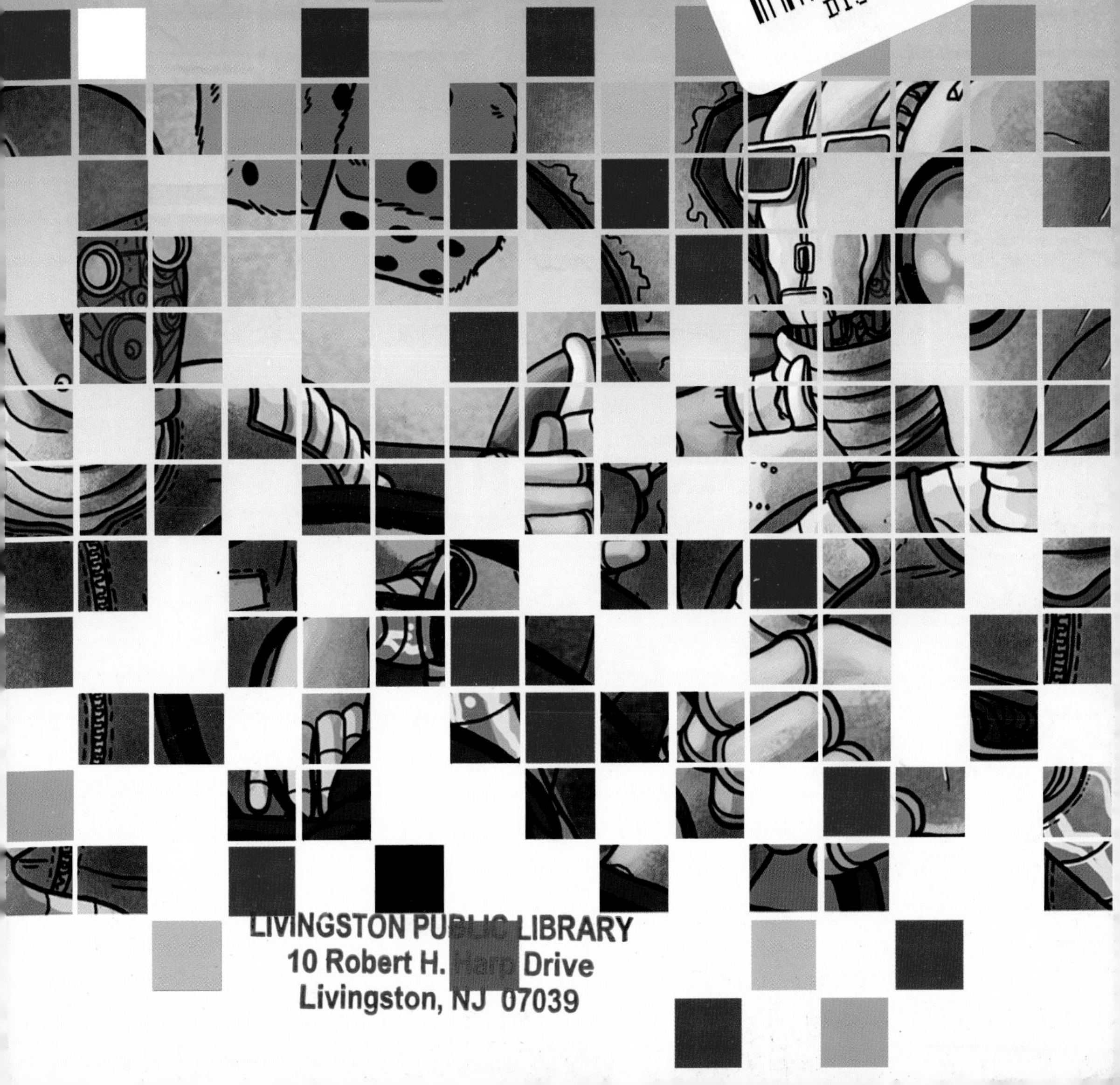

RYAN FERRIER / VALENTIN RAMON

D4VE2

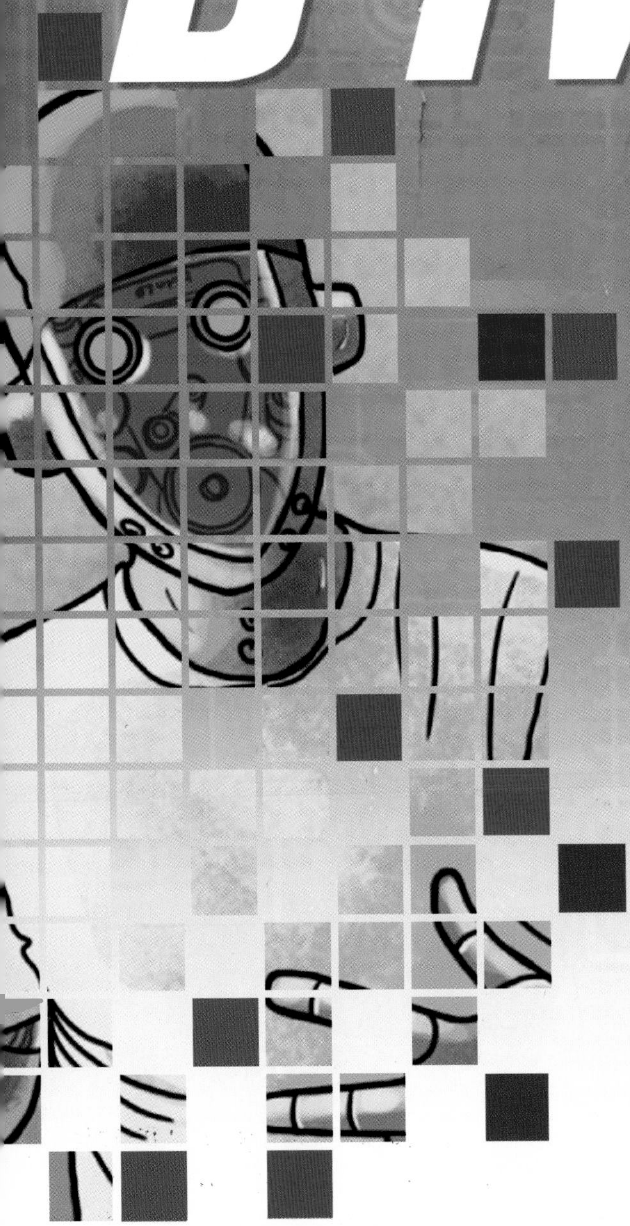

STORY & LETTERS BY
Ryan Ferrier

ART & COLORS BY
Valentin Ramon

SERIES EDITS BY
David Hedgecock

For international rights, contact licensing@idwpublishing.com

ISBN: 978-1-63140-551-8

19 18 17 16   1 2 3 4

www.IDWPUBLISHING.com

Facebook: facebook.com/idwpublishing
Twitter: @idwpublishing
YouTube: youtube.com/idwpublishing
Tumblr: tumblr.idwpublishing.com
Instagram: instagram.com/idwpublishing

D4VE2. MARCH 2015. FIRST PRINTING. D4VE2 Copyright © 2016 Ryan Ferrier and Valentin Ramon. All rights reserved. © 2016 Idea and Design Works, LLC. The IDW logo is registered in the U.S. Patent and Trademark Office. IDW Publishing, a division of Idea and Design Works, LLC. Editorial offices: 2765 Truxtun Road, San Diego, CA 92106. Any similarities to persons living or dead are purely coincidental. With the exception of artwork used for review purposes, none of the contents of this publication may be reprinted without the permission of Idea and Design Works, LLC. Printed in Korea. IDW Publishing does not read or accept unsolicited submissions of ideas, stories, or artwork.

Originally published as D4VE2 issues #1–4.

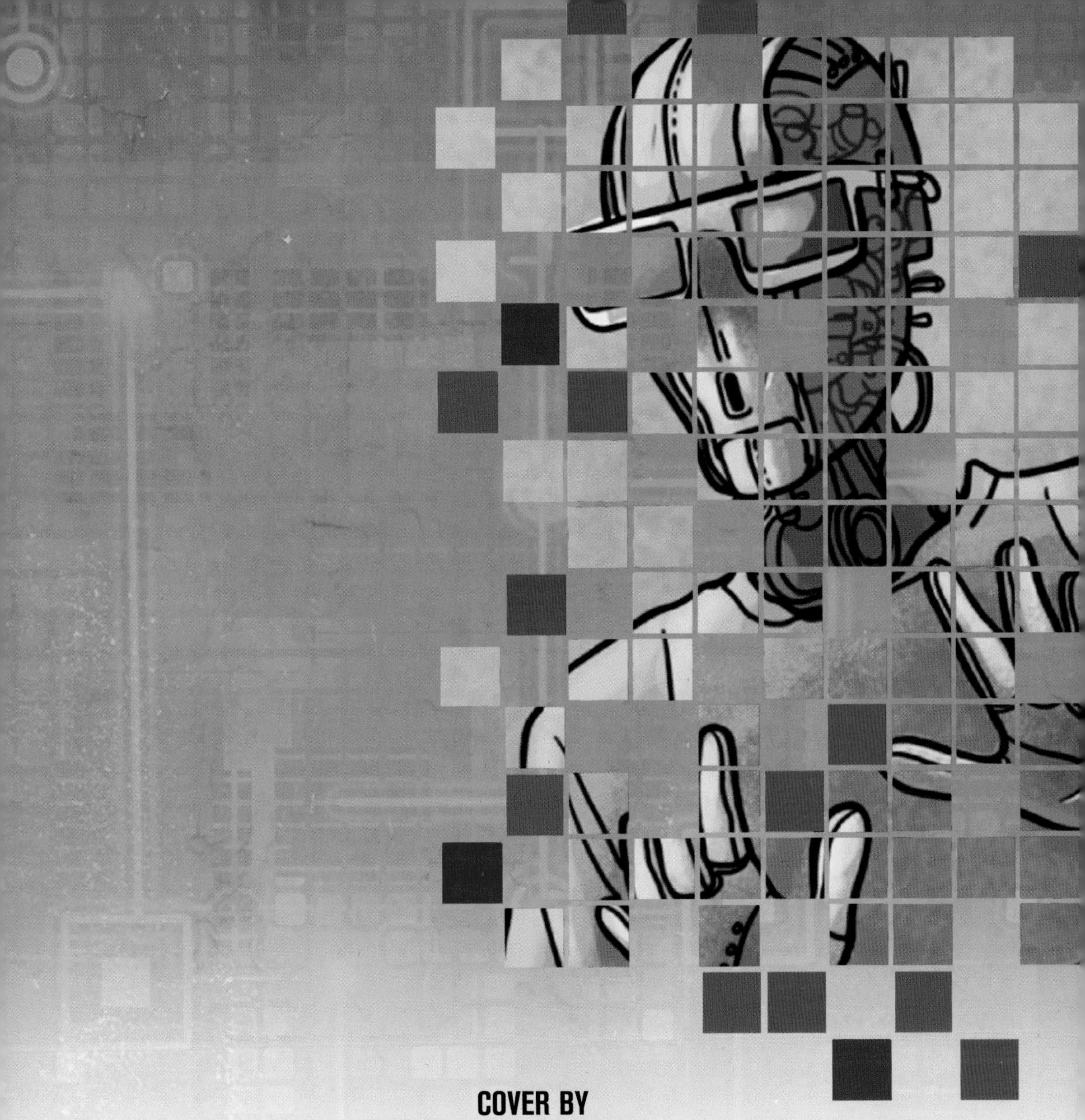

COVER BY
Valentin Ramon

COLLECTION EDITS BY
Justin Eisinger & Alonzo Simon

PUBLISHED BY
Ted Adams

COLLECTION DESIGN BY
Claudia Chong

LIVINGSTON PUBLIC LIBRARY
10 Robert H. Harp Drive
Livingston, NJ 07039

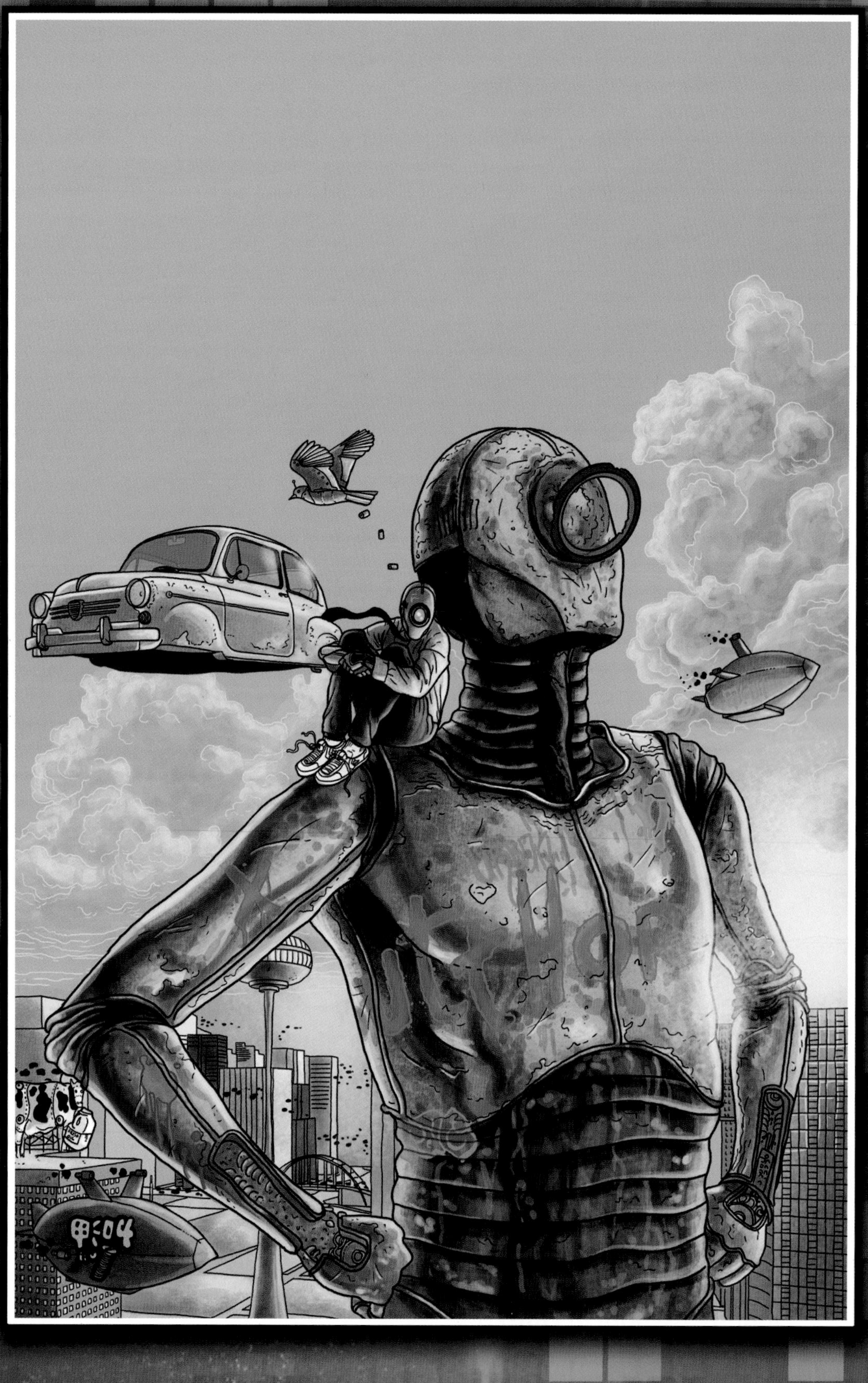

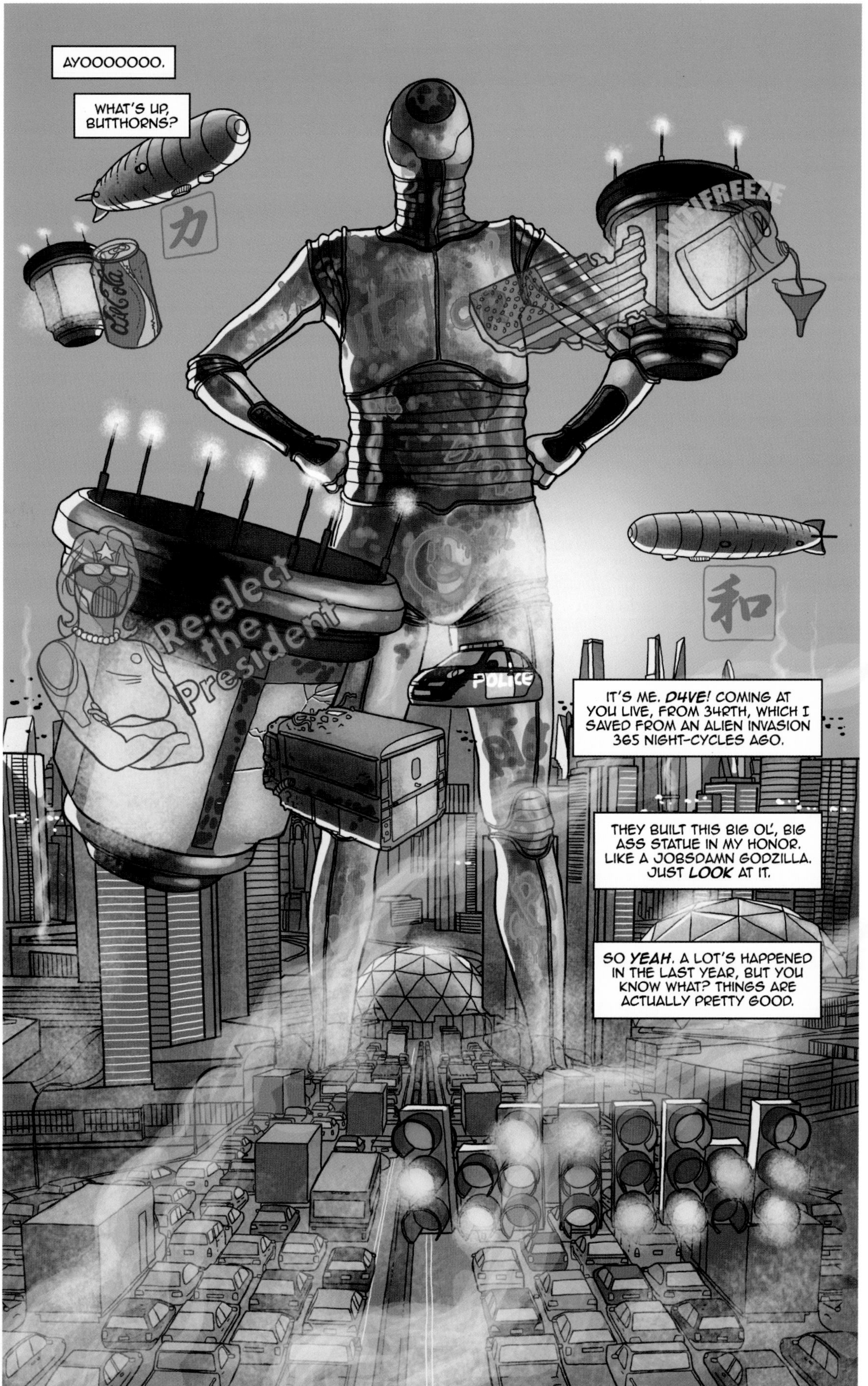
AYOOOOOOO.
WHAT'S UP, BUTTHORNS?
Re-elect the President
POLICE
ANTIFREEZE
IT'S ME. D4VE! COMING AT YOU LIVE, FROM 34RTH, WHICH I SAVED FROM AN ALIEN INVASION 365 NIGHT-CYCLES AGO.
THEY BUILT THIS BIG OL', BIG ASS STATUE IN MY HONOR. LIKE A JOBSDAMN GODZILLA. JUST LOOK AT IT.
SO YEAH. A LOT'S HAPPENED IN THE LAST YEAR, BUT YOU KNOW WHAT? THINGS ARE ACTUALLY PRETTY GOOD.

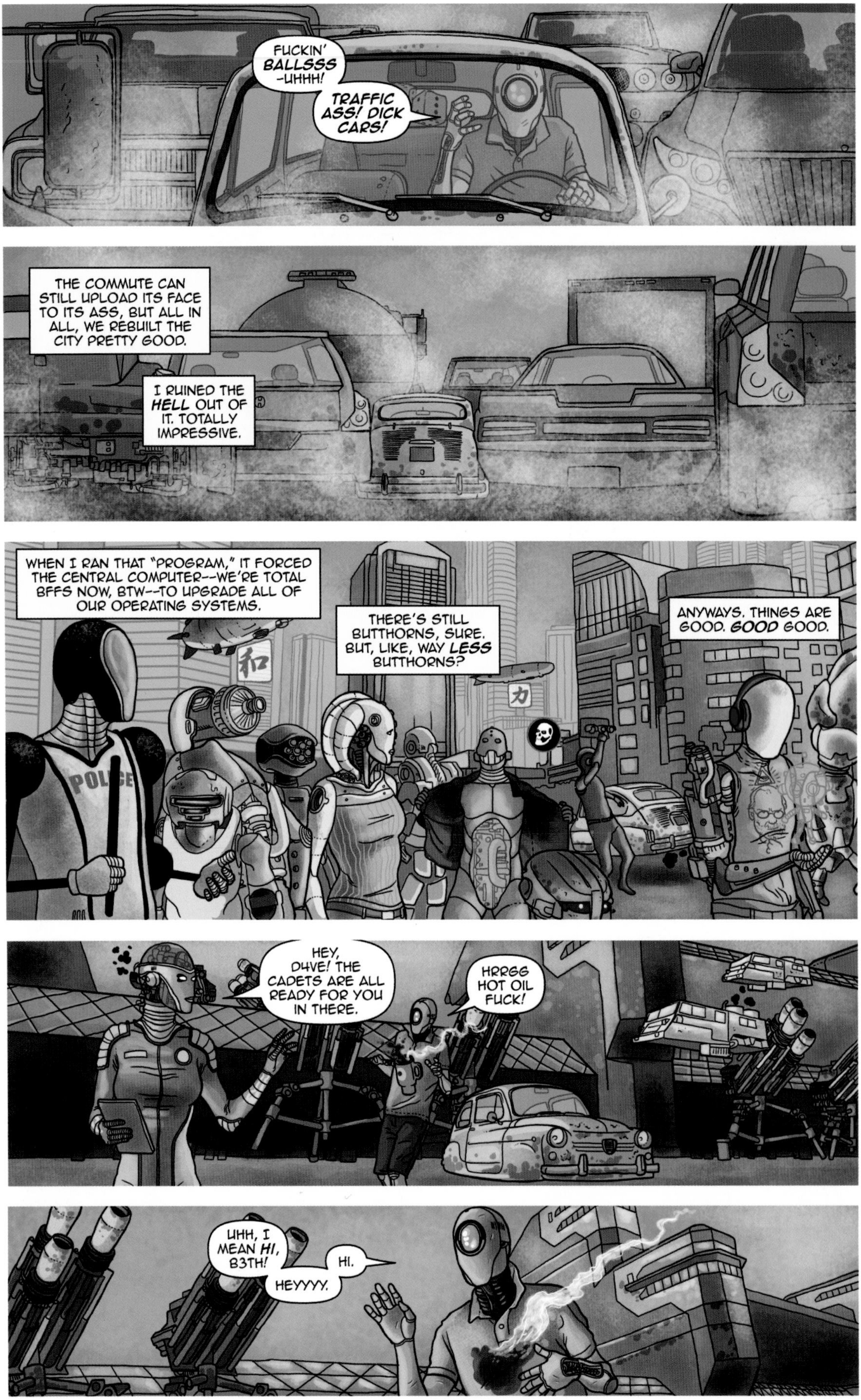
FUCKIN' BALLSSS -UHHH!
TRAFFIC ASS! DICK CARS!
THE COMMUTE CAN STILL UPLOAD ITS FACE TO ITS ASS, BUT ALL IN ALL, WE REBUILT THE CITY PRETTY GOOD.
I RUINED THE HELL OUT OF IT. TOTALLY IMPRESSIVE.
WHEN I RAN THAT "PROGRAM," IT FORCED THE CENTRAL COMPUTER--WE'RE TOTAL BFFS NOW, BTW--TO UPGRADE ALL OF OUR OPERATING SYSTEMS.
THERE'S STILL BUTTHORNS, SURE. BUT, LIKE, WAY LESS BUTTHORNS?
ANYWAYS. THINGS ARE GOOD. GOOD GOOD.
和
力
POLICE
HEY, D4VE! THE CADETS ARE ALL READY FOR YOU IN THERE.
HRRGG HOT OIL FUCK!
UHH, I MEAN HI, B3TH!
HI.
HEYYYY.

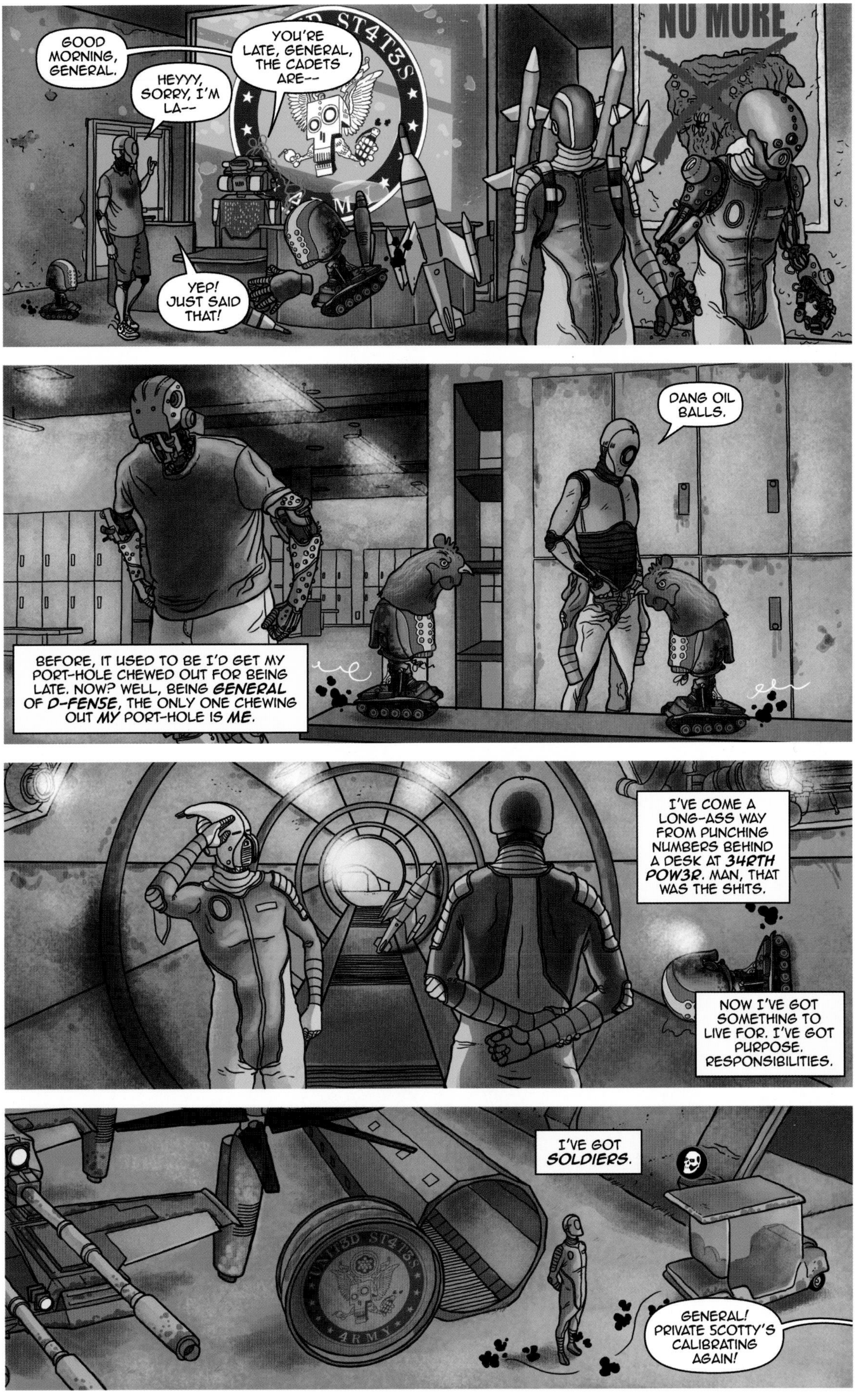
NO MORE
GOOD MORNING, GENERAL.
YOU'RE LATE, GENERAL, THE CADETS ARE--
HEYYY, SORRY, I'M LA--
YEP! JUST SAID THAT!
DANG OIL BALLS.
BEFORE, IT USED TO BE I'D GET MY PORT-HOLE CHEWED OUT FOR BEING LATE. NOW? WELL, BEING *GENERAL* OF *D-FENSE*, THE ONLY ONE CHEWING OUT *MY* PORT-HOLE IS *ME*.
I'VE COME A LONG-ASS WAY FROM PUNCHING NUMBERS BEHIND A DESK AT *34RTH POW3R*. MAN, THAT WAS THE SHITS.
NOW I'VE GOT SOMETHING TO LIVE FOR. I'VE GOT PURPOSE. RESPONSIBILITIES.
I'VE GOT *SOLDIERS*.
GENERAL! PRIVATE SCOTTY'S CALIBRATING AGAIN!

CADETS! IN FORMATION!
'SUP, DAD?
DUDE?!
UHH, I MEAN, 'SUP, SIR!
NO, DUDE. THE JERKIN'. WE TALKED ABOUT THIS. LIKE, A VAJILLION TIMES ALREADY.
LOOKIN' SHARP, Y'ALL! LOOKIN' REAL TOUGH.
ALL RIGHT, SO THERE'S, LIKE, NO ALIENS AND WE'VE MORE OR LESS REBUILT THE CITY. SOOO... LET'S RUN SOME DRILLS.
PFFFFT.
BOOOO.
SIGHHH.
C'MON, GUYS, WE'RE SOLDIERS. THIS IS WHY WE'RE ALL HERE.
WE SHOULD DO WHAT GENERAL D4VE TELLS US.
THANK YOU, BR4D. Y'ALL BUTTHORNS NEED TO LISTEN TO BR4D HERE. HE'S A GOOD SHIT.
I KNOW IT SUCKS THAT THERE'S NO MONSTERS' BUTTS TO KICK, BUT THAT COULD VERY WELL CHANGE ANY MINUTE.
NOW GO RUN SOME LAPS. THEN WE'LL PLAY DODGEBALL!
P.S. THIS SUCKS!
P.S. I HEARD THAT!
P.P.S. FUCKYERSELLLF.

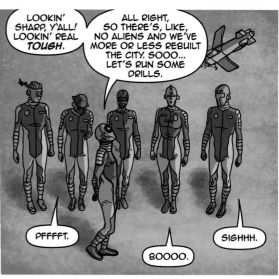

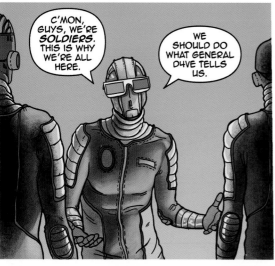

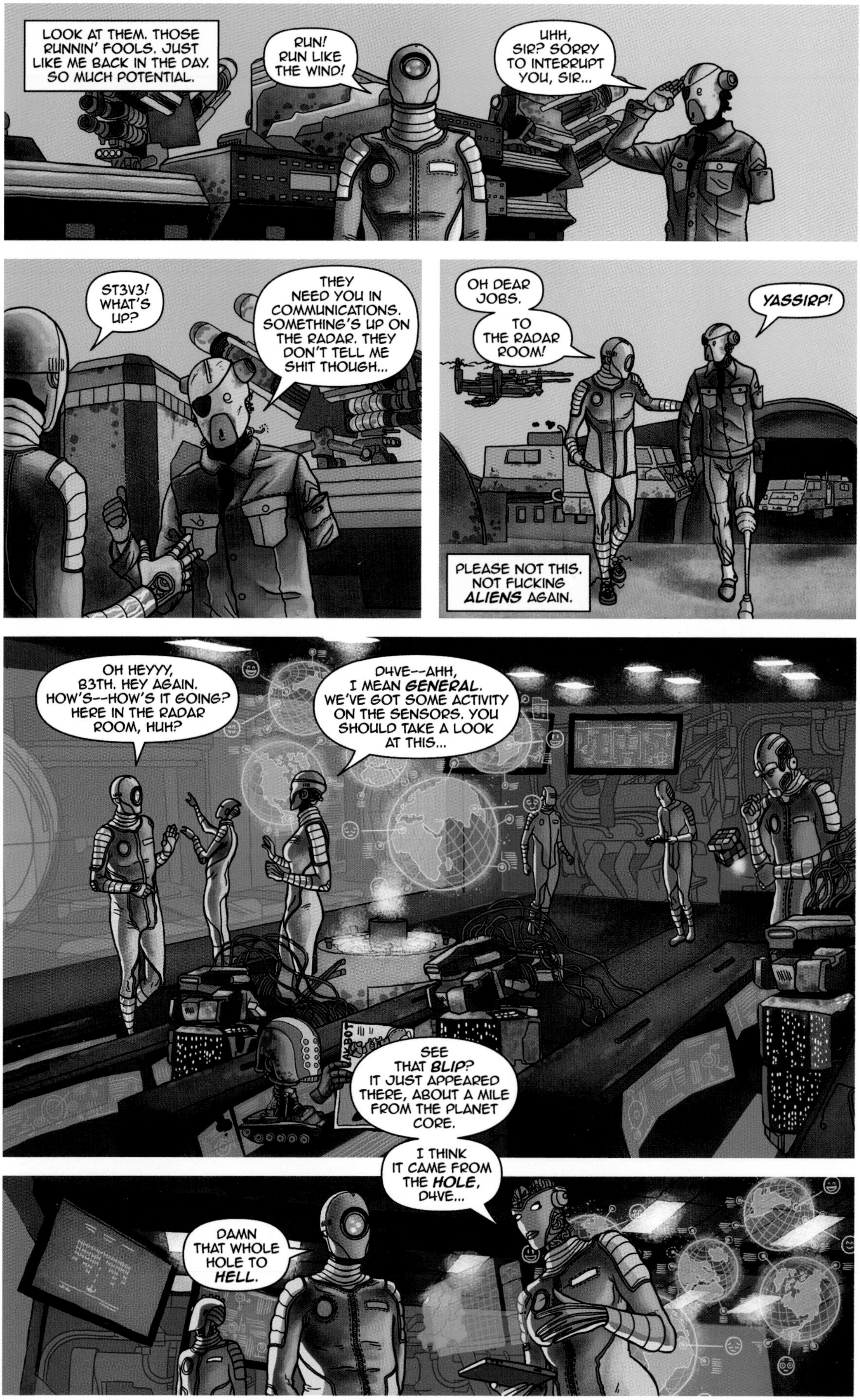
LOOK AT THEM. THOSE RUNNIN' FOOLS. JUST LIKE ME BACK IN THE DAY. SO MUCH POTENTIAL.
RUN! RUN LIKE THE WIND!
UHH, SIR? SORRY TO INTERRUPT YOU, SIR...
ST3V3! WHAT'S UP?
THEY NEED YOU IN COMMUNICATIONS. SOMETHING'S UP ON THE RADAR. THEY DON'T TELL ME SHIT THOUGH...
OH DEAR JOBS.
TO THE RADAR ROOM!
YASSIRP!
PLEASE NOT THIS. NOT FUCKING ALIENS AGAIN.
OH HEYYY, B3TH. HEY AGAIN. HOW'S--HOW'S IT GOING? HERE IN THE RADAR ROOM, HUH?
D4VE--AHH, I MEAN GENERAL. WE'VE GOT SOME ACTIVITY ON THE SENSORS. YOU SHOULD TAKE A LOOK AT THIS...
SEE THAT BLIP? IT JUST APPEARED THERE, ABOUT A MILE FROM THE PLANET CORE.
I THINK IT CAME FROM THE HOLE, D4VE...
DAMN THAT WHOLE HOLE TO HELL.

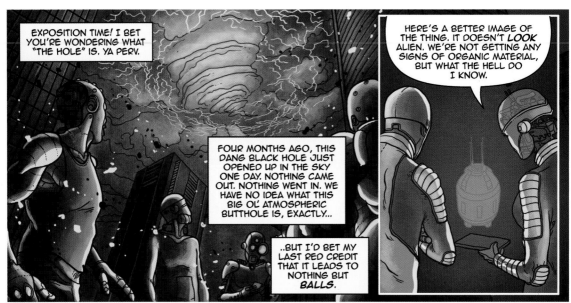

EXPOSITION TIME! I BET YOU'RE WONDERING WHAT "THE HOLE" IS. YA PERV.

FOUR MONTHS AGO, THIS DANG BLACK HOLE JUST OPENED UP IN THE SKY ONE DAY. NOTHING CAME OUT. NOTHING WENT IN. WE HAVE NO IDEA WHAT THIS BIG OL' ATMOSPHERIC BUTTHOLE IS, EXACTLY...

..BUT I'D BET MY LAST RED CREDIT THAT IT LEADS TO NOTHING BUT *BALLS*.

HERE'S A BETTER IMAGE OF THE THING. IT DOESN'T *LOOK* ALIEN. WE'RE NOT GETTING ANY SIGNS OF ORGANIC MATERIAL, BUT WHAT THE HELL DO I KNOW.

BANANA-PANTS MCFUCK-BUTTONS. IT WAS ONLY A MATTER OF TIME BEFORE SOMETHING CAME OUT OF THAT DAMN SPACE-GAPER.

OH MAN, OH MANNN-UHHH.

SHOULD I PUT 34RTH ON "PANIC" STATUS?

NO. NOT *YET*. WE DON'T NEED THE PLANET LOSING ALL THEIR SHITS OVER WHAT VERY WELL COULD BE JUST SOME WEIRDO SPACE GARBAGE.

WHELP, I BETTER TAKE A LOOK AT IT. I'LL TAKE A COUPLE OF THE CADETS WITH ME, MAKE 'EM USEFUL. I'LL RADIO ONCE I'M THERE, B3TH.

ROGER DODGER THAT, D4VE. BE SAFE OUT THERE. CATCH YOU LATER!

YO! CADETS! WE GOT ONE!

...CATCH YOU LATER?

SMOOTH, B3TH. REAL SMOOTH.

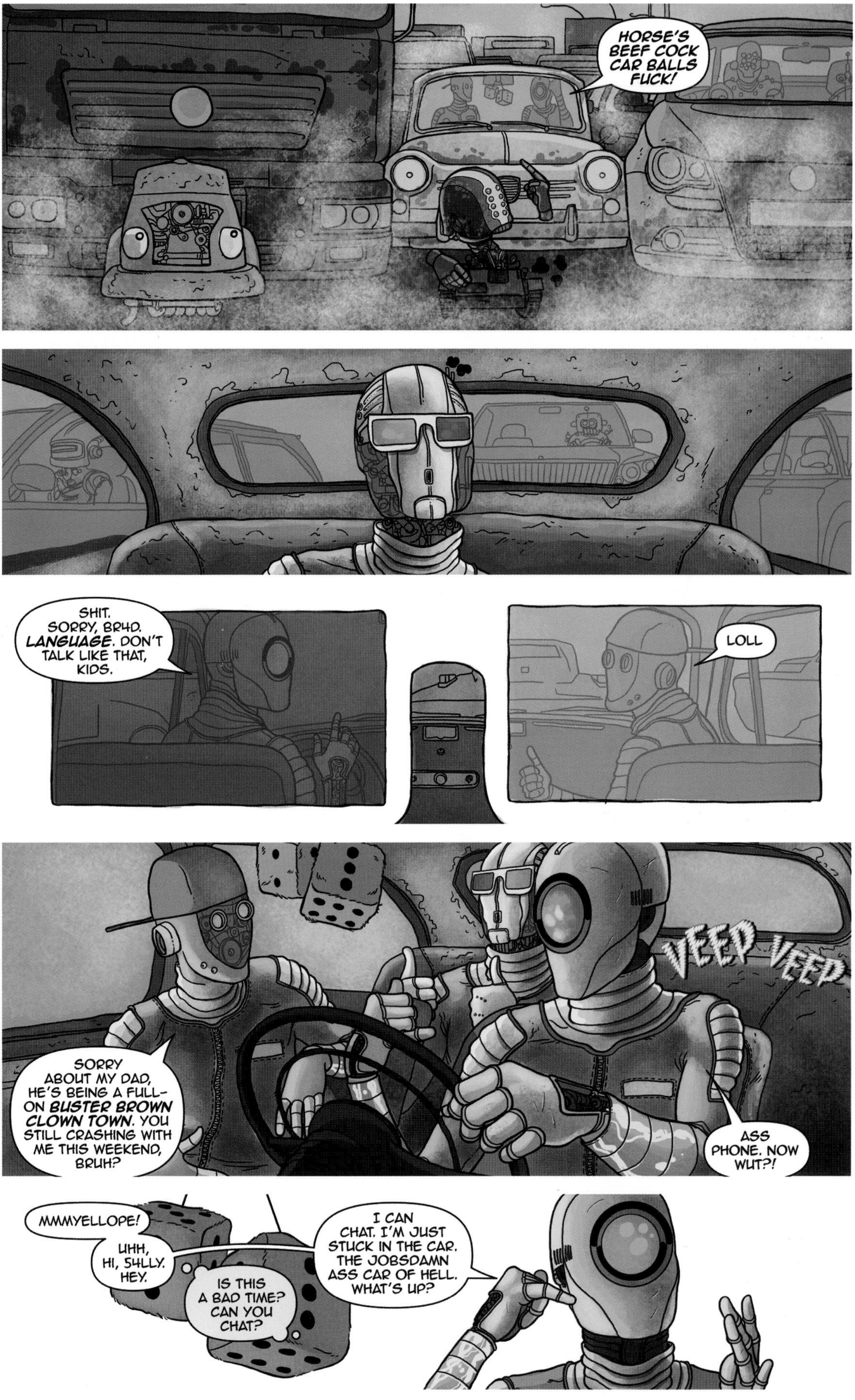
HORSE'S BEEF COCK CAR BALLS FUCK!
SHIT. SORRY, BR4D. LANGUAGE. DON'T TALK LIKE THAT, KIDS.
LOLL
SORRY ABOUT MY DAD, HE'S BEING A FULL-ON BUSTER BROWN CLOWN TOWN. YOU STILL CRASHING WITH ME THIS WEEKEND, BRUH?
VEEP VEEP
ASS PHONE. NOW WUT?!
MMMYELLOPE!
UHH, HI, 54LLY. HEY.
IS THIS A BAD TIME? CAN YOU CHAT?
I CAN CHAT. I'M JUST STUCK IN THE CAR. THE JOBSDAMN ASS CAR OF HELL. WHAT'S UP?

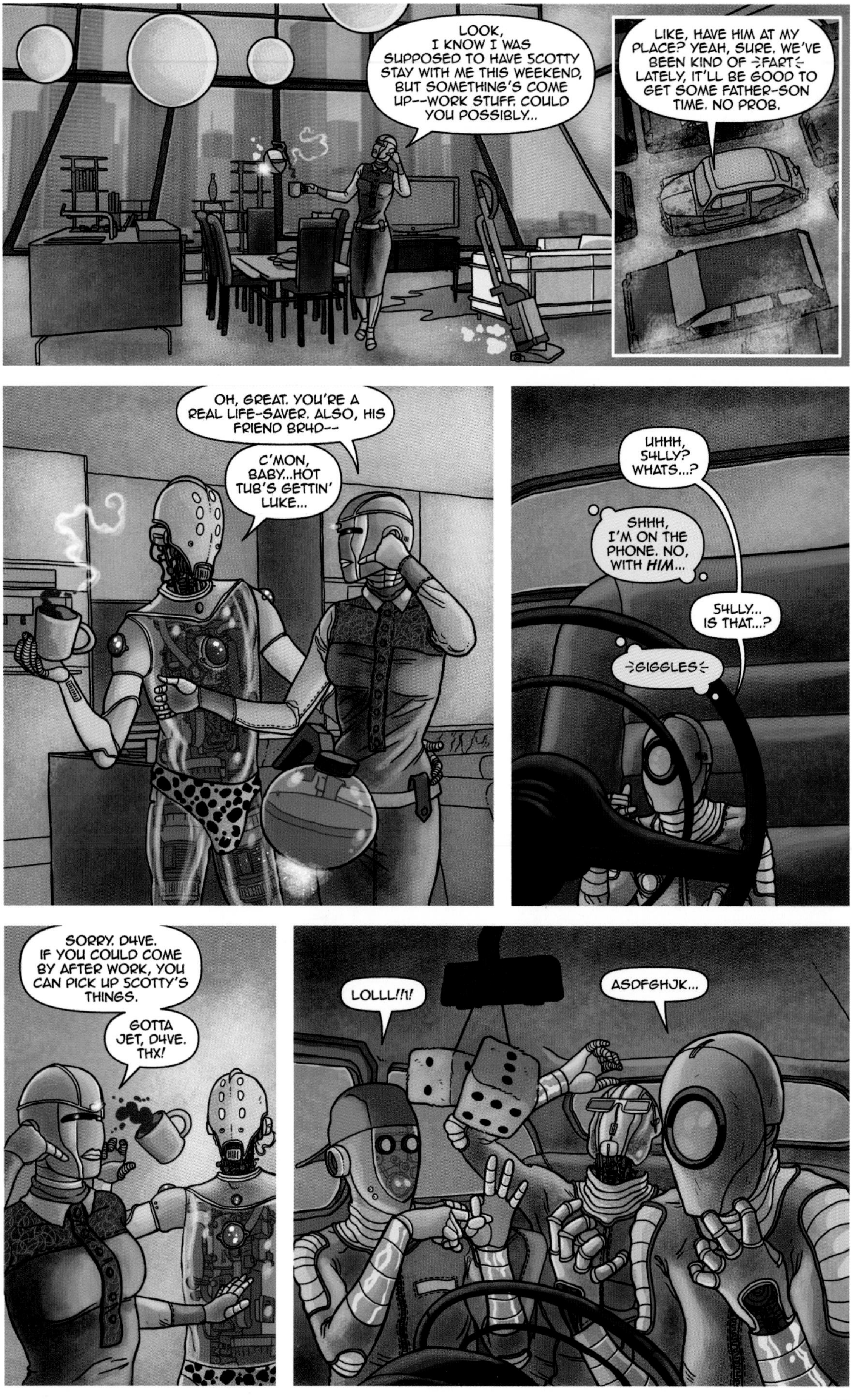
LOOK, I KNOW I WAS SUPPOSED TO HAVE SCOTTY STAY WITH ME THIS WEEKEND, BUT SOMETHING'S COME UP--WORK STUFF. COULD YOU POSSIBLY...
LIKE, HAVE HIM AT MY PLACE? YEAH, SURE. WE'VE BEEN KIND OF ⟩FART⟨ LATELY, IT'LL BE GOOD TO GET SOME FATHER-SON TIME. NO PROB.
OH, GREAT. YOU'RE A REAL LIFE-SAVER. ALSO, HIS FRIEND BR4D--
C'MON, BABY...HOT TUB'S GETTIN' LUKE...
UHHH, S4LLY? WHATS...?
SHHH, I'M ON THE PHONE. NO, WITH *HIM*...
S4LLY... IS THAT...?
⟩GIGGLES⟨
SORRY. D4VE. IF YOU COULD COME BY AFTER WORK, YOU CAN PICK UP SCOTTY'S THINGS.
GOTTA JET, D4VE. THX!
LOLLL!!1!
ASDFGHJK...

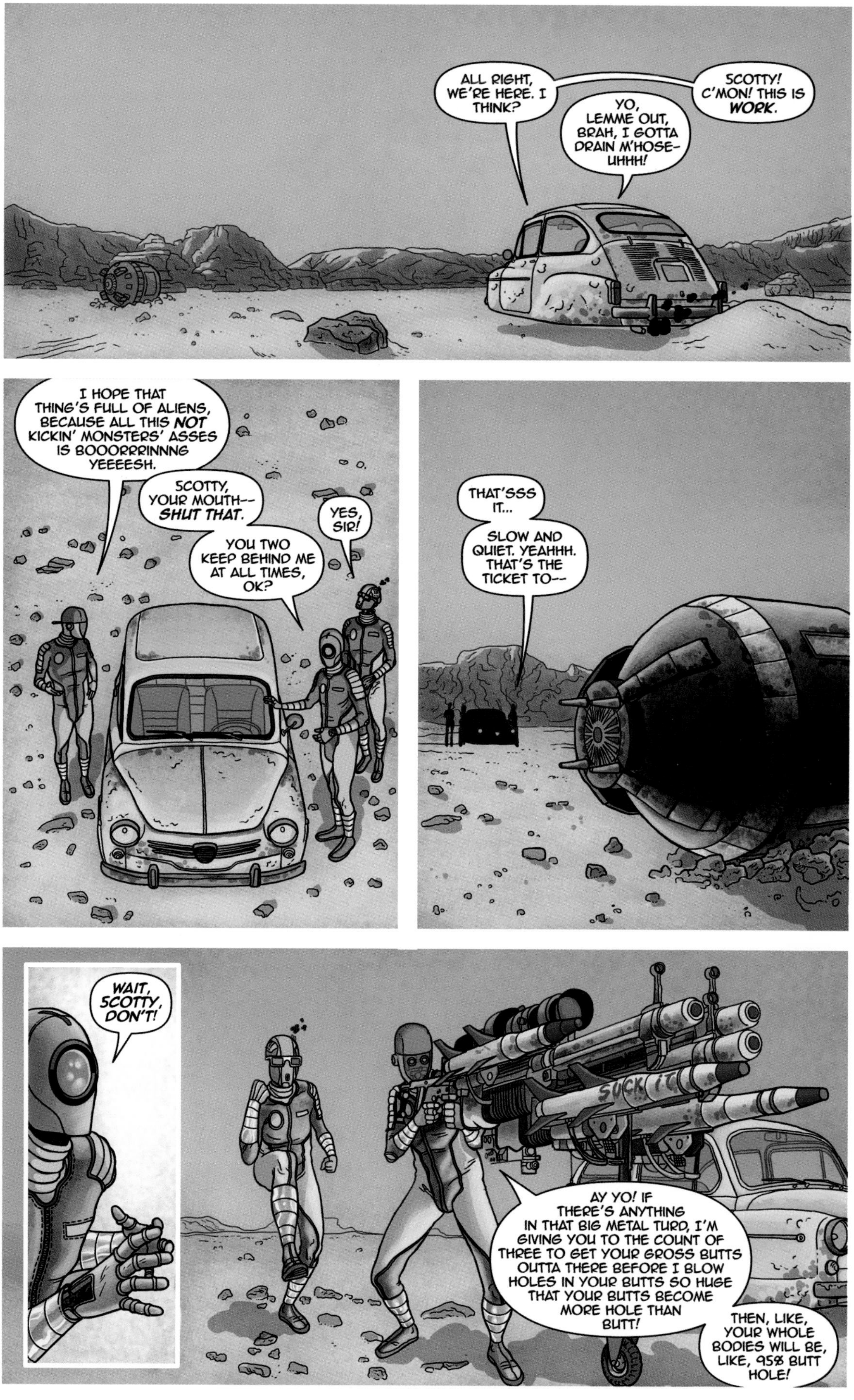
ALL RIGHT, WE'RE HERE. I THINK?
SCOTTY! C'MON! THIS IS **WORK**.
YO, LEMME OUT, BRAH, I GOTTA DRAIN M'HOSE-UHHH!
I HOPE THAT THING'S FULL OF ALIENS, BECAUSE ALL THIS ***NOT*** KICKIN' MONSTERS' ASSES IS BOOORRRINNNG YEEEESH.
SCOTTY, YOUR MOUTH--***SHUT THAT***.
YES, SIR!
YOU TWO KEEP BEHIND ME AT ALL TIMES, OK?
THAT'SSS IT...
SLOW AND QUIET. YEAHHH. THAT'S THE TICKET TO--
WAIT, SCOTTY, DON'T!
SUCK IT
AY YO! IF THERE'S ANYTHING IN THAT BIG METAL TURD, I'M GIVING YOU TO THE COUNT OF THREE TO GET YOUR GROSS BUTTS OUTTA THERE BEFORE I BLOW HOLES IN YOUR BUTTS SO HUGE THAT YOUR BUTTS BECOME MORE HOLE THAN BUTT!
THEN, LIKE, YOUR WHOLE BODIES WILL BE, LIKE, 95% BUTT HOLE!

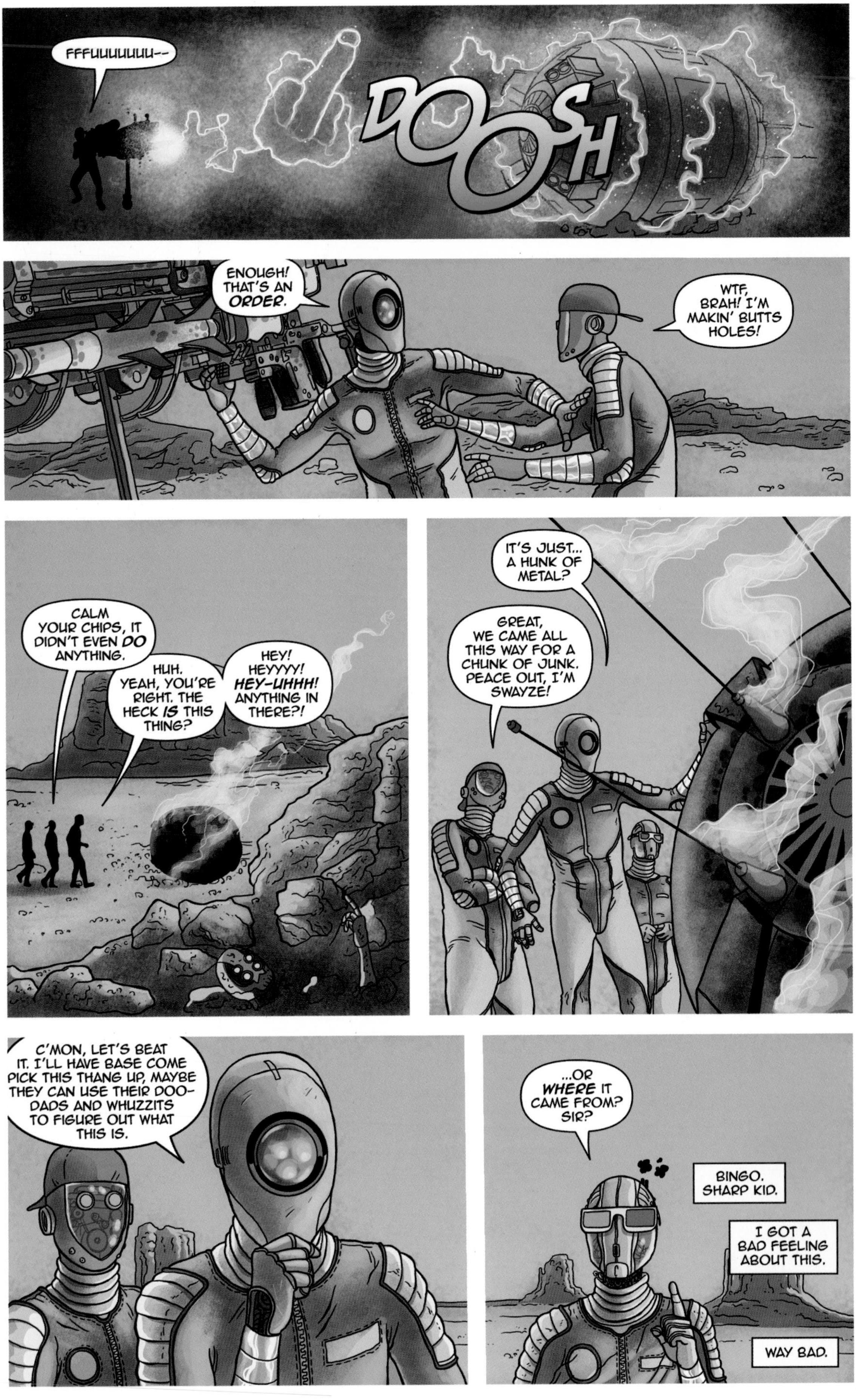
FFFUUUUUUU--
DOOSH
ENOUGH! THAT'S AN ORDER.
WTF, BRAH! I'M MAKIN' BUTTS HOLES!
CALM YOUR CHIPS, IT DIDN'T EVEN DO ANYTHING.
HUH. YEAH, YOU'RE RIGHT. THE HECK IS THIS THING?
HEY! HEYYYY! HEY-UHHH! ANYTHING IN THERE?!
IT'S JUST... A HUNK OF METAL?
GREAT, WE CAME ALL THIS WAY FOR A CHUNK OF JUNK. PEACE OUT, I'M SWAYZE!
C'MON, LET'S BEAT IT. I'LL HAVE BASE COME PICK THIS THANG UP, MAYBE THEY CAN USE THEIR DOO-DADS AND WHUZZITS TO FIGURE OUT WHAT THIS IS.
...OR WHERE IT CAME FROM? SIR?
BINGO. SHARP KID.
I GOT A BAD FEELING ABOUT THIS.
WAY BAD.

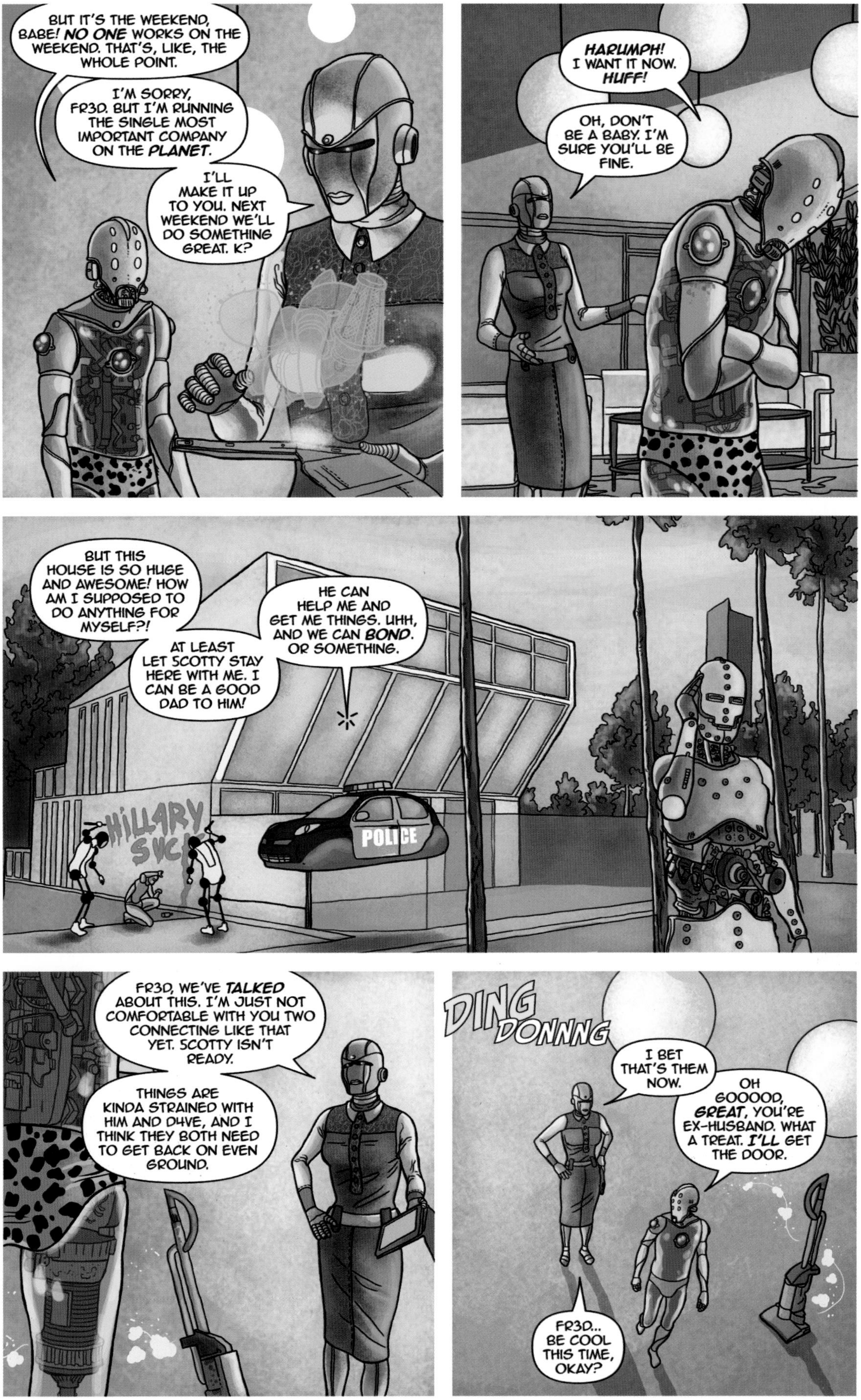
BUT IT'S THE WEEKEND, BABE! NO ONE WORKS ON THE WEEKEND. THAT'S, LIKE, THE WHOLE POINT.
I'M SORRY, FR3D. BUT I'M RUNNING THE SINGLE MOST IMPORTANT COMPANY ON THE PLANET.
I'LL MAKE IT UP TO YOU. NEXT WEEKEND WE'LL DO SOMETHING GREAT. K?
HARUMPH! I WANT IT NOW. HUFF!
OH, DON'T BE A BABY. I'M SURE YOU'LL BE FINE.
BUT THIS HOUSE IS SO HUGE AND AWESOME! HOW AM I SUPPOSED TO DO ANYTHING FOR MYSELF?!
AT LEAST LET SCOTTY STAY HERE WITH ME. I CAN BE A GOOD DAD TO HIM!
HE CAN HELP ME AND GET ME THINGS. UHH, AND WE CAN BOND. OR SOMETHING.
POLICE
FR3D, WE'VE TALKED ABOUT THIS. I'M JUST NOT COMFORTABLE WITH YOU TWO CONNECTING LIKE THAT YET. SCOTTY ISN'T READY.
THINGS ARE KINDA STRAINED WITH HIM AND D4VE, AND I THINK THEY BOTH NEED TO GET BACK ON EVEN GROUND.
DING DONNNG
I BET THAT'S THEM NOW.
OH GOOOOD, GREAT, YOU'RE EX-HUSBAND. WHAT A TREAT. I'LL GET THE DOOR.
FR3D... BE COOL THIS TIME, OKAY?

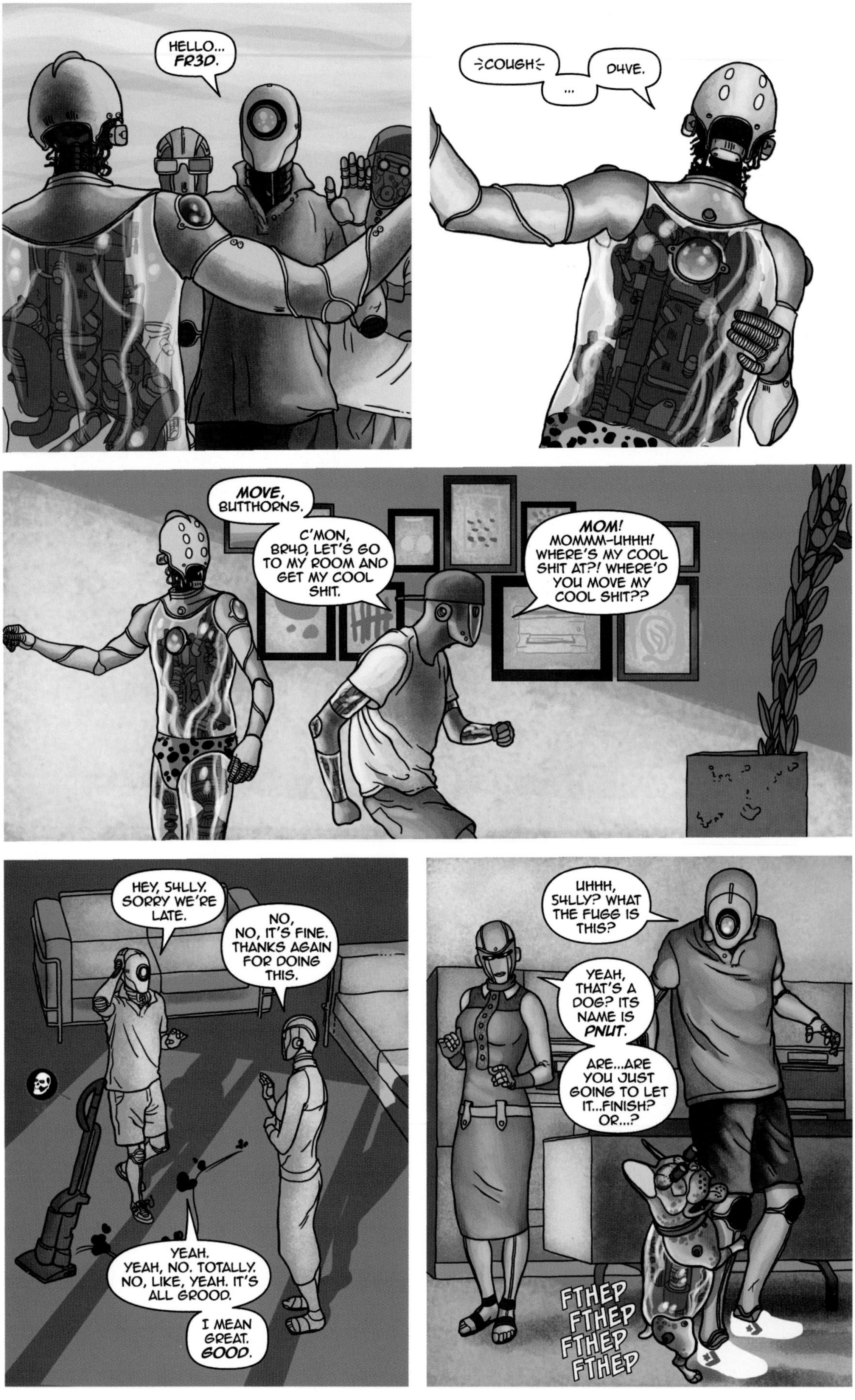
HELLO... FR3D.
⇒COUGH⇐
...
D4VE.
MOVE, BUTTHORNS.
C'MON, BR4D, LET'S GO TO MY ROOM AND GET MY COOL SHIT.
MOM! MOMMM-UHHH! WHERE'S MY COOL SHIT AT?! WHERE'D YOU MOVE MY COOL SHIT??
HEY, S4LLY. SORRY WE'RE LATE.
NO, NO, IT'S FINE. THANKS AGAIN FOR DOING THIS.
YEAH. YEAH, NO. TOTALLY. NO, LIKE, YEAH. IT'S ALL GROOD.
I MEAN GREAT. GOOD.
UHHH, S4LLY? WHAT THE FUGG IS THIS?
YEAH, THAT'S A DOG? ITS NAME IS PNUT.
ARE...ARE YOU JUST GOING TO LET IT...FINISH? OR...?
FTHEP FTHEP FTHEP FTHEP

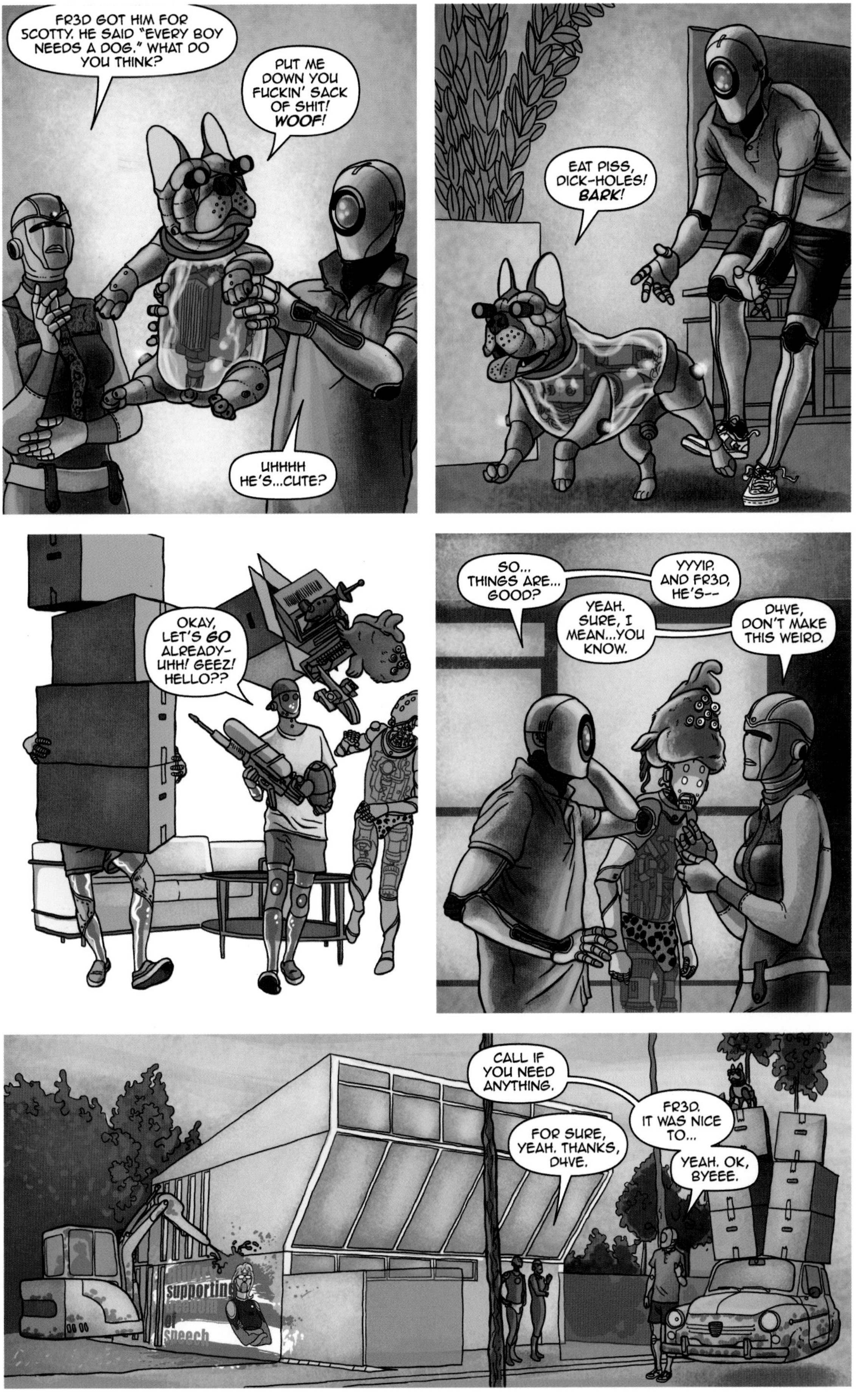
FR3D GOT HIM FOR SCOTTY. HE SAID "EVERY BOY NEEDS A DOG." WHAT DO YOU THINK?
PUT ME DOWN YOU FUCKIN' SACK OF SHIT! ***WOOF!***
UHHHH HE'S...CUTE?
EAT PISS, DICK-HOLES! ***BARK!***
OKAY, LET'S *GO* ALREADY-UHH! GEEZ! HELLO??
SO... THINGS ARE... GOOD?
YEAH. SURE, I MEAN...YOU KNOW.
YYYIP. AND FR3D, HE'S--
D4VE, DON'T MAKE THIS WEIRD.
supporting
of
speech
CALL IF YOU NEED ANYTHING.
FOR SURE, YEAH. THANKS, D4VE.
FR3D. IT WAS NICE TO...
YEAH. OK, BYEEE.

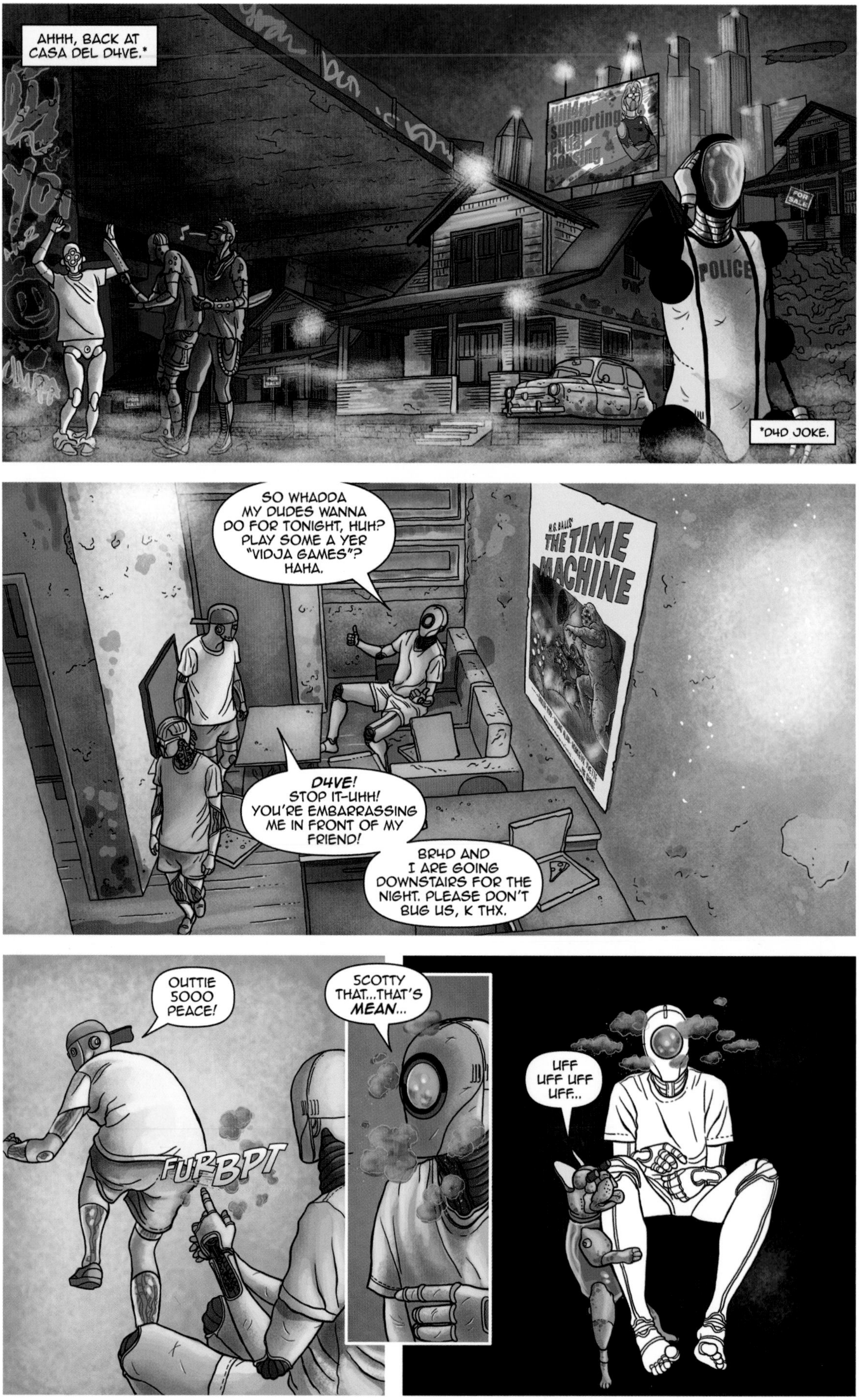
AHHH, BACK AT CASA DEL D4VE.*
*D4D JOKE.
SO WHADDA MY DUDES WANNA DO FOR TONIGHT, HUH? PLAY SOME A YER "VIDJA GAMES"? HAHA.
THE TIME MACHINE
D4VE! STOP IT-UHH! YOU'RE EMBARRASSING ME IN FRONT OF MY FRIEND!
BR4D AND I ARE GOING DOWNSTAIRS FOR THE NIGHT. PLEASE DON'T BUG US, K THX.
OUTTIE 5000 PEACE!
FURBPT
SCOTTY THAT...THAT'S MEAN...
UFF UFF UFF UFF...

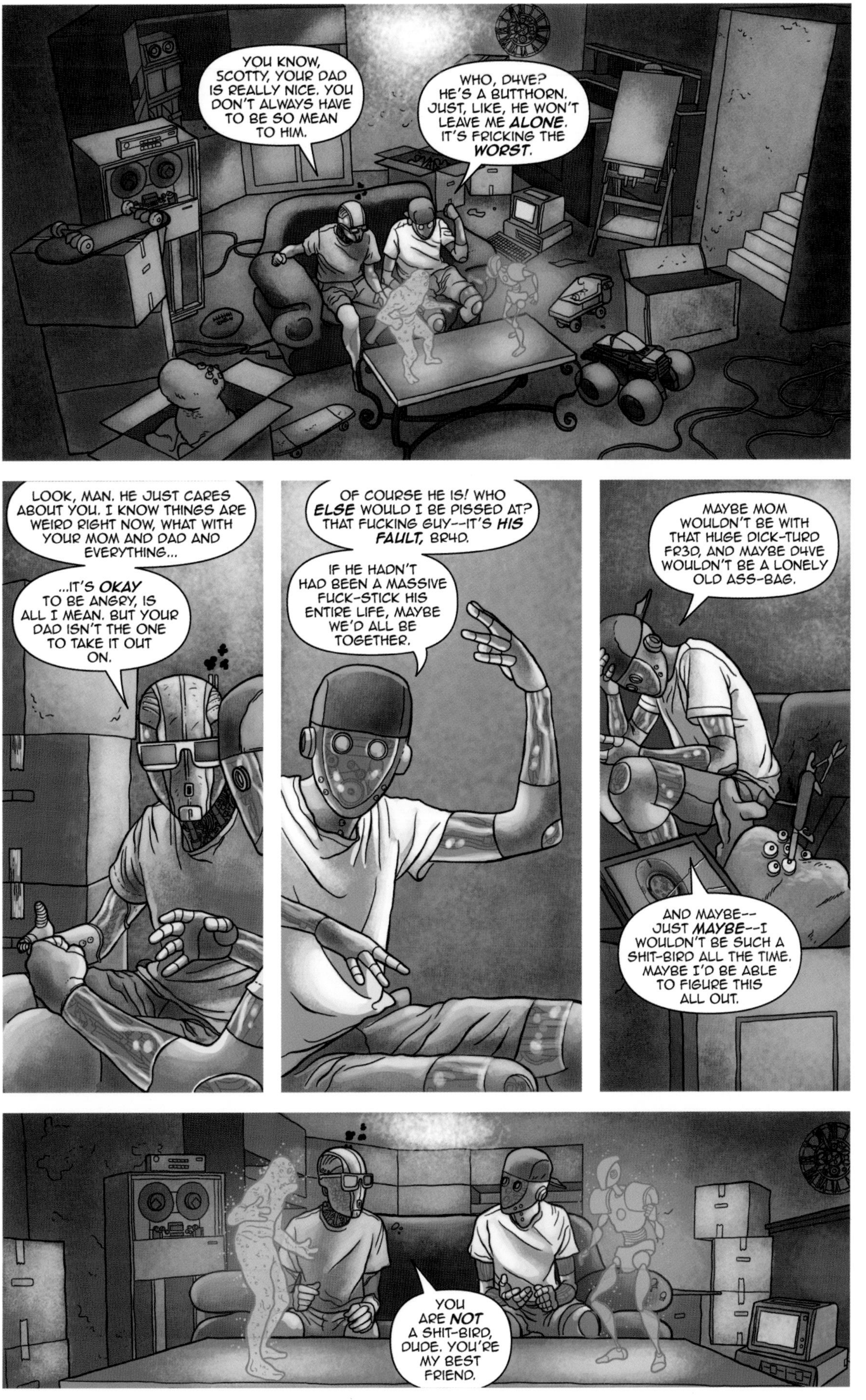
YOU KNOW, SCOTTY, YOUR DAD IS REALLY NICE. YOU DON'T ALWAYS HAVE TO BE SO MEAN TO HIM.
WHO, D4VE? HE'S A BUTTHORN. JUST, LIKE, HE WON'T LEAVE ME **ALONE**. IT'S FRICKING THE **WORST**.
LOOK, MAN. HE JUST CARES ABOUT YOU. I KNOW THINGS ARE WEIRD RIGHT NOW, WHAT WITH YOUR MOM AND DAD AND EVERYTHING...
...IT'S **OKAY** TO BE ANGRY, IS ALL I MEAN. BUT YOUR DAD ISN'T THE ONE TO TAKE IT OUT ON.
OF COURSE HE IS! WHO **ELSE** WOULD I BE PISSED AT? THAT FUCKING GUY--IT'S **HIS FAULT,** BR4D.
IF HE HADN'T HAD BEEN A MASSIVE FUCK-STICK HIS ENTIRE LIFE, MAYBE WE'D ALL BE TOGETHER.
MAYBE MOM WOULDN'T BE WITH THAT HUGE DICK-TURD FR3D, AND MAYBE D4VE WOULDN'T BE A LONELY OLD ASS-BAG.
AND MAYBE--JUST **MAYBE**--I WOULDN'T BE SUCH A SHIT-BIRD ALL THE TIME. MAYBE I'D BE ABLE TO FIGURE THIS ALL OUT.
YOU ARE **NOT** A SHIT-BIRD, DUDE. YOU'RE MY BEST FRIEND.

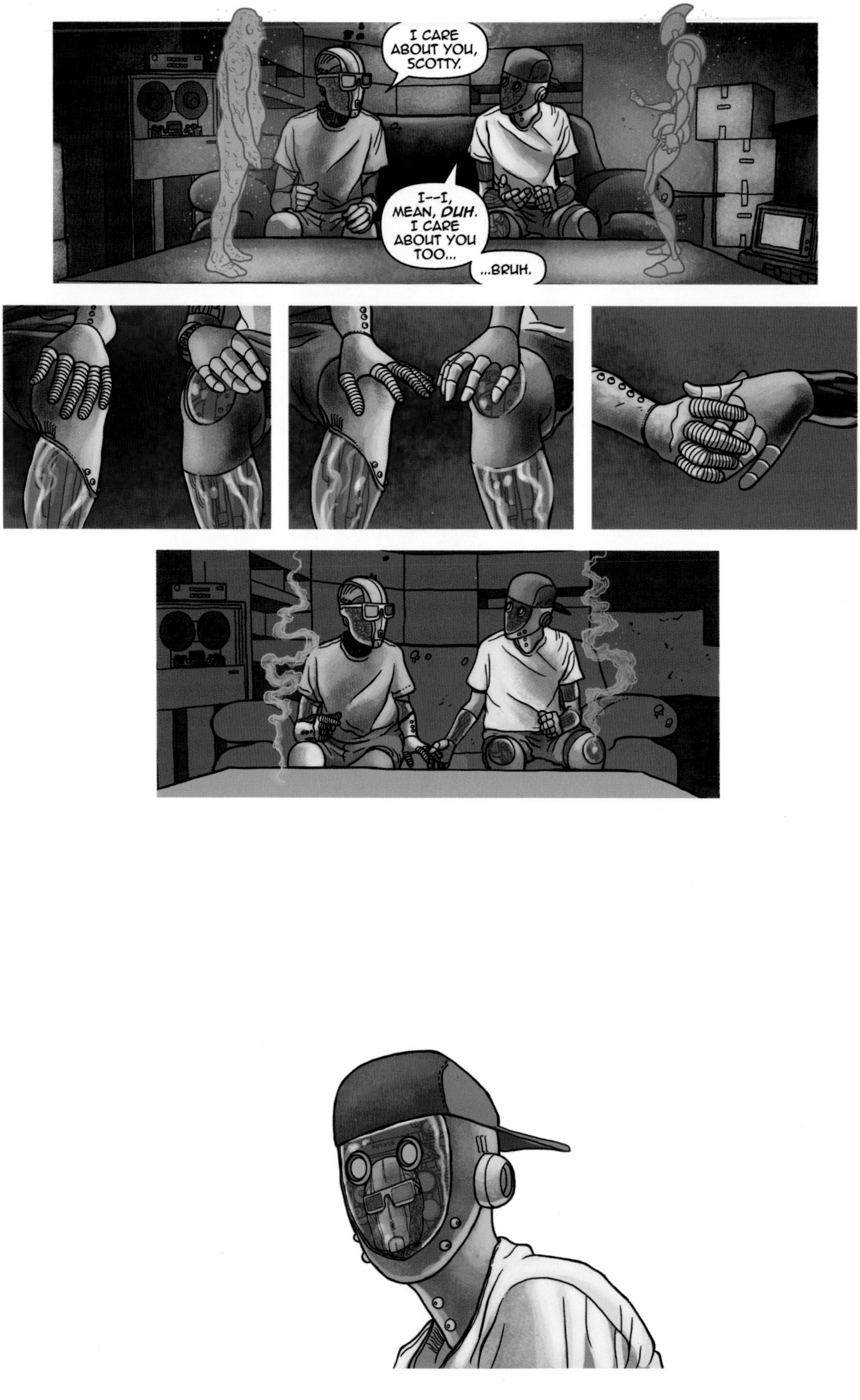
I CARE ABOUT YOU, SCOTTY.
I--I, MEAN, DUH. I CARE ABOUT YOU TOO...
...BRUH.

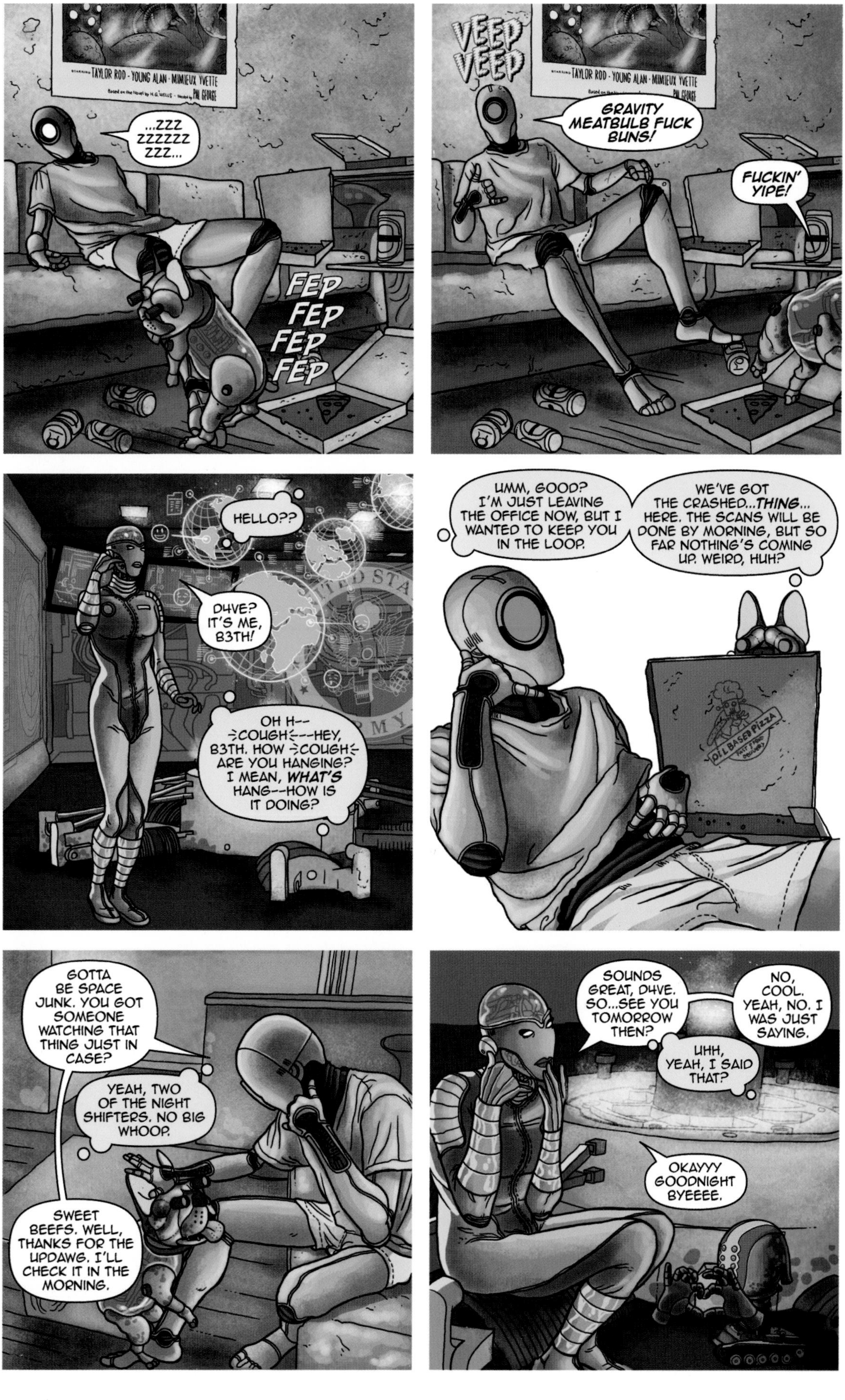

TAYLOR ROD · YOUNG ALAN · MIMIEUX YVETTE
Based on the novel by H.G. WELLS
...ZZZ ZZZZZZ ZZZ...
FEP FEP FEP FEP
VEEP VEEP
GRAVITY MEATBULB FUCK BUNS!
FUCKIN' YIPE!
HELLO??
D4VE? IT'S ME, B3TH!
OH H-- -COUGH- --HEY, B3TH. HOW -COUGH- ARE YOU HANGING? I MEAN, ***WHAT'S*** HANG--HOW IS IT DOING?
UMM, GOOD? I'M JUST LEAVING THE OFFICE NOW, BUT I WANTED TO KEEP YOU IN THE LOOP.
WE'VE GOT THE CRASHED...***THING***... HERE. THE SCANS WILL BE DONE BY MORNING, BUT SO FAR NOTHING'S COMING UP. WEIRD, HUH?
OIL BASED PIZZA
GOTTA BE SPACE JUNK. YOU GOT SOMEONE WATCHING THAT THING JUST IN CASE?
YEAH, TWO OF THE NIGHT SHIFTERS. NO BIG WHOOP.
SWEET BEEFS. WELL, THANKS FOR THE UPDAWG. I'LL CHECK IT IN THE MORNING.
SOUNDS GREAT, D4VE. SO...SEE YOU TOMORROW THEN?
NO, COOL. YEAH, NO. I WAS JUST SAYING.
UHH, YEAH, I SAID THAT?
OKAYYY GOODNIGHT BYEEEE.

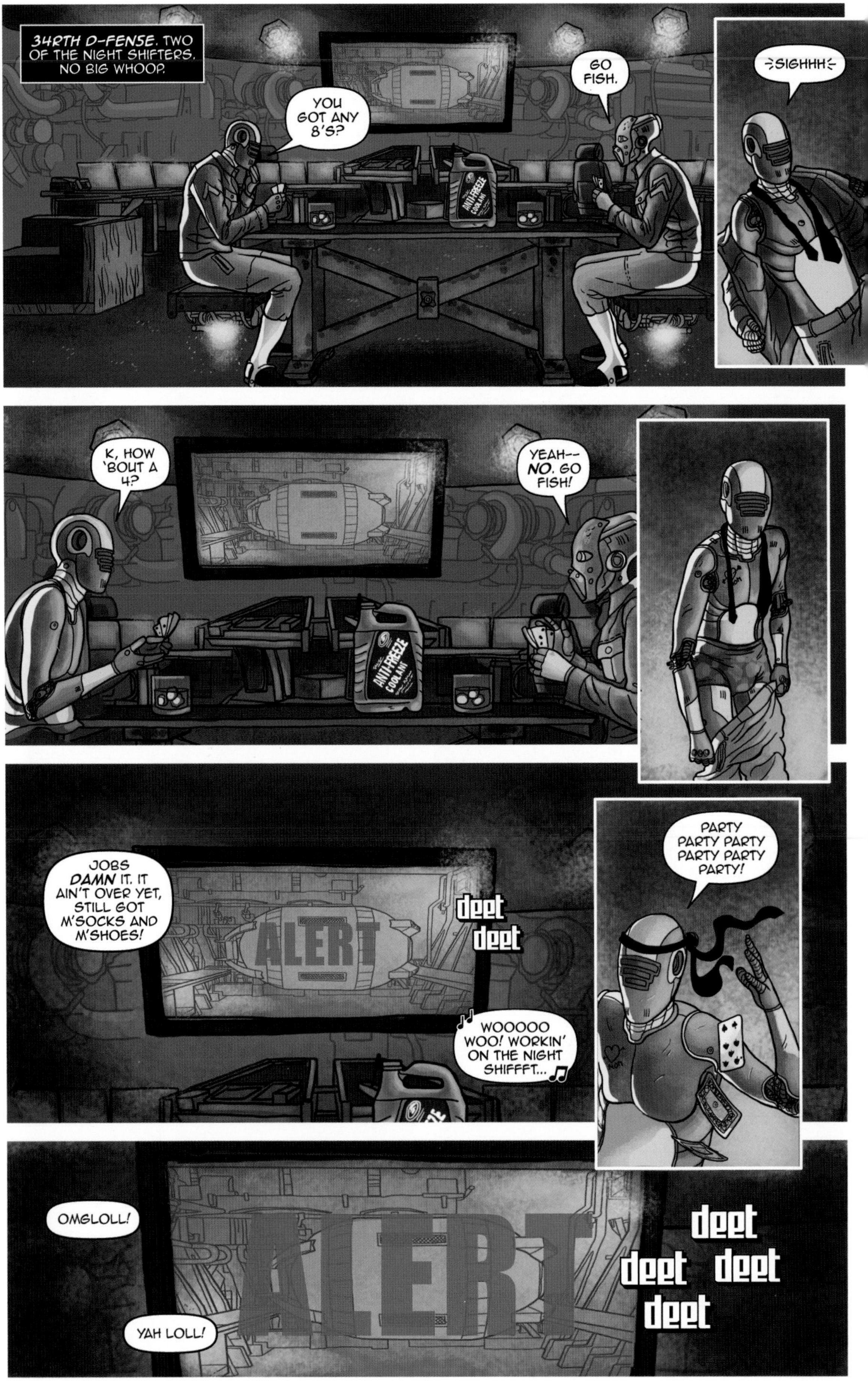
34RTH D-FENSE. TWO OF THE NIGHT SHIFTERS. NO BIG WHOOP.
YOU GOT ANY 8'S?
GO FISH.
ANTI-FREEZE COOLANT
-SIGHHH-
K, HOW 'BOUT A 4?
YEAH-- NO. GO FISH!
ANTI-FREEZE COOLANT
JOBS DAMN IT. IT AIN'T OVER YET, STILL GOT M'SOCKS AND M'SHOES!
ALERT
deet deet
WOOOOO WOO! WORKIN' ON THE NIGHT SHIFFFT...
PARTY PARTY PARTY PARTY PARTY PARTY!
OMGLOLL!
ALERT
deet deet deet deet
YAH LOLL!

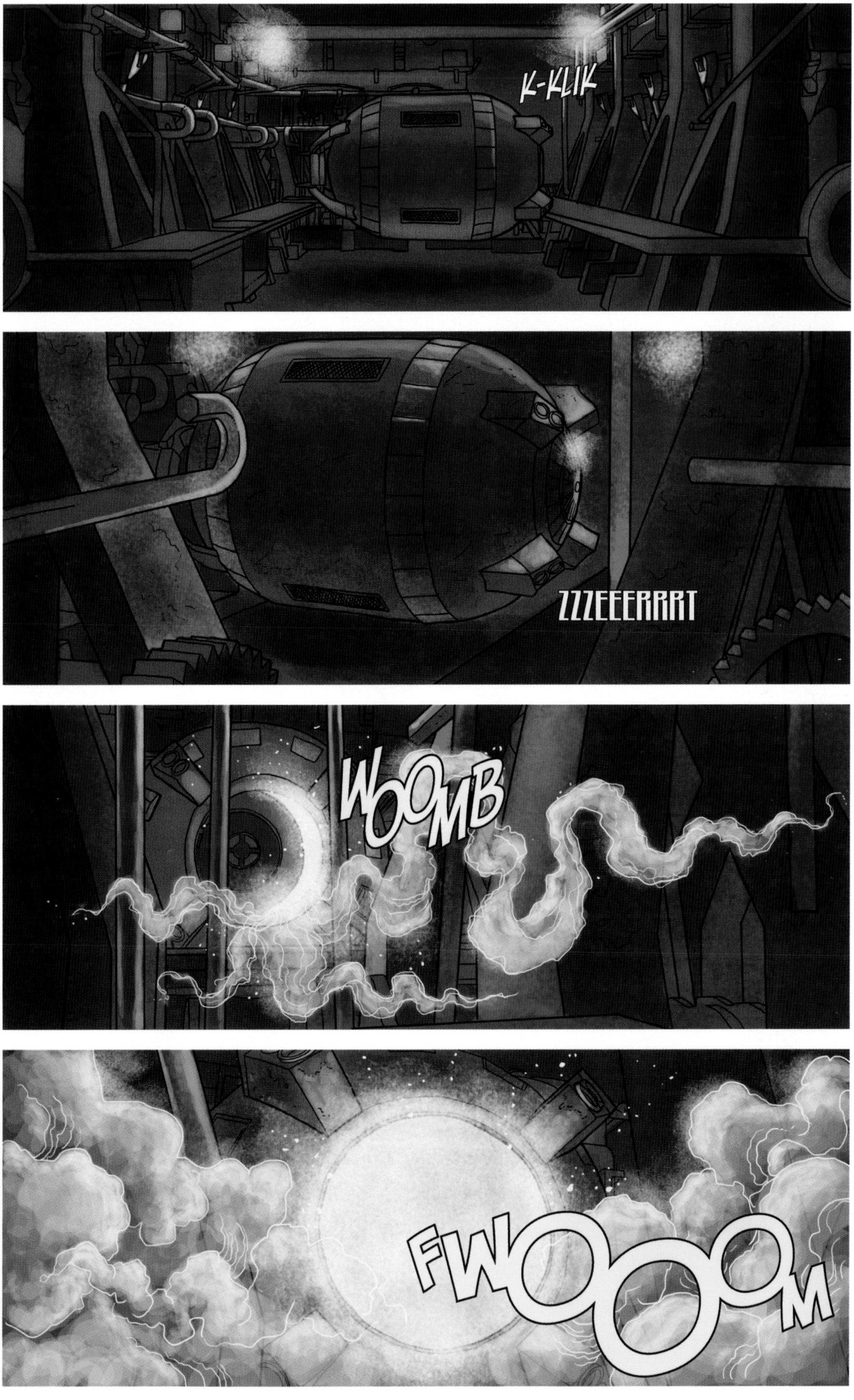
K-KLIK
ZZZEEERRRT
WOOMB
FWOOOM

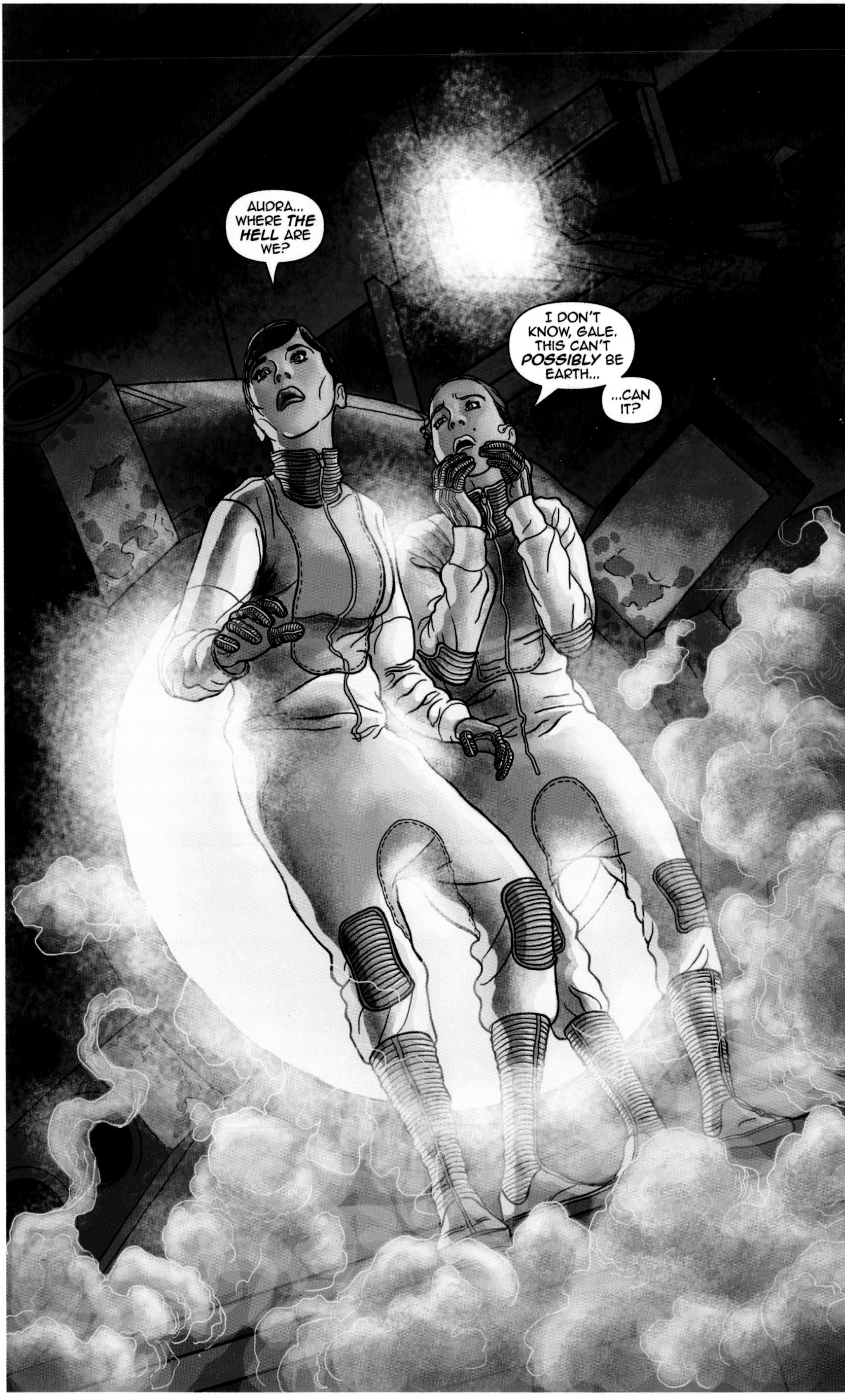
AUDRA... WHERE THE HELL ARE WE?
I DON'T KNOW, GALE. THIS CAN'T POSSIBLY BE EARTH...
...CAN IT?

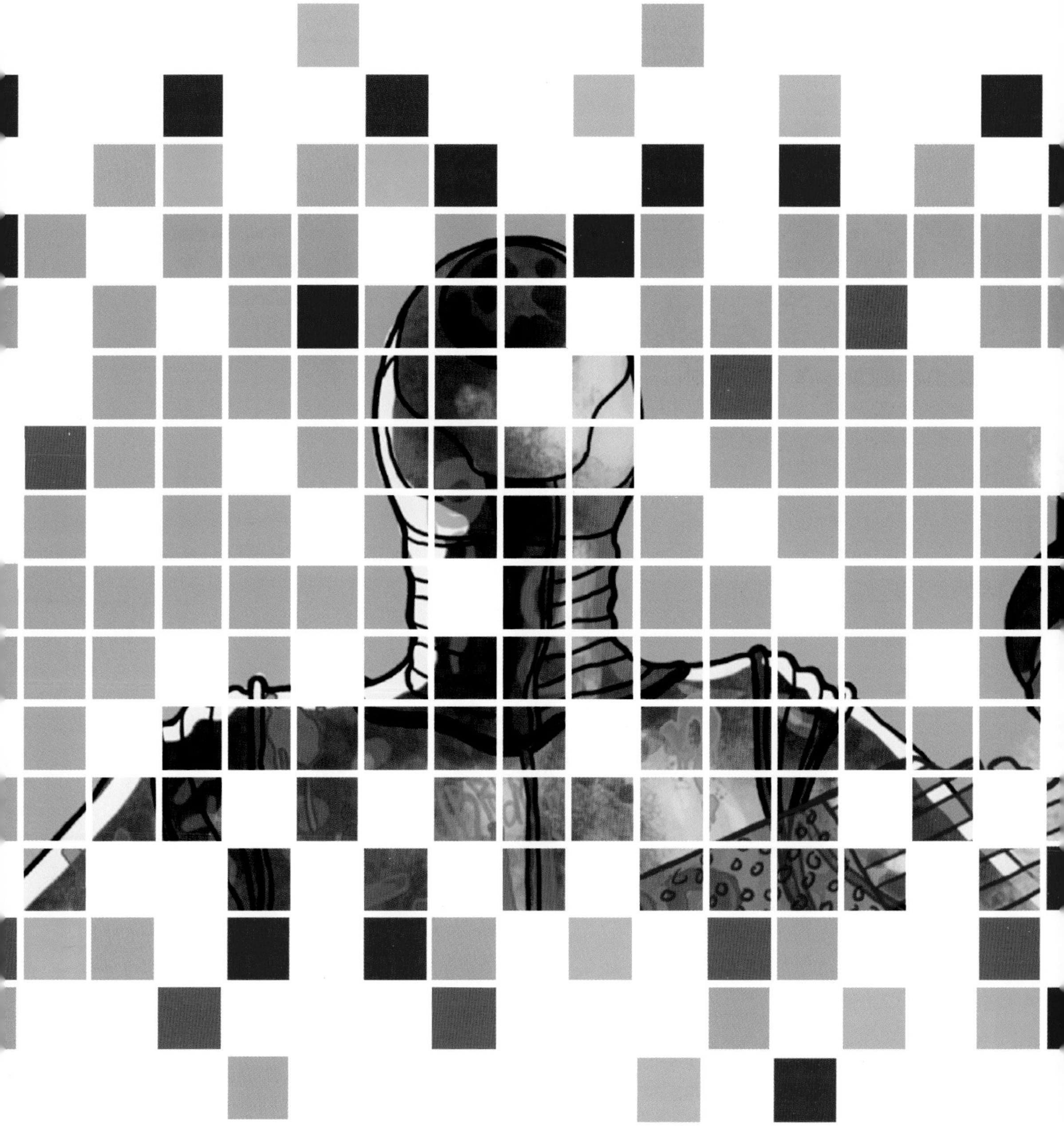

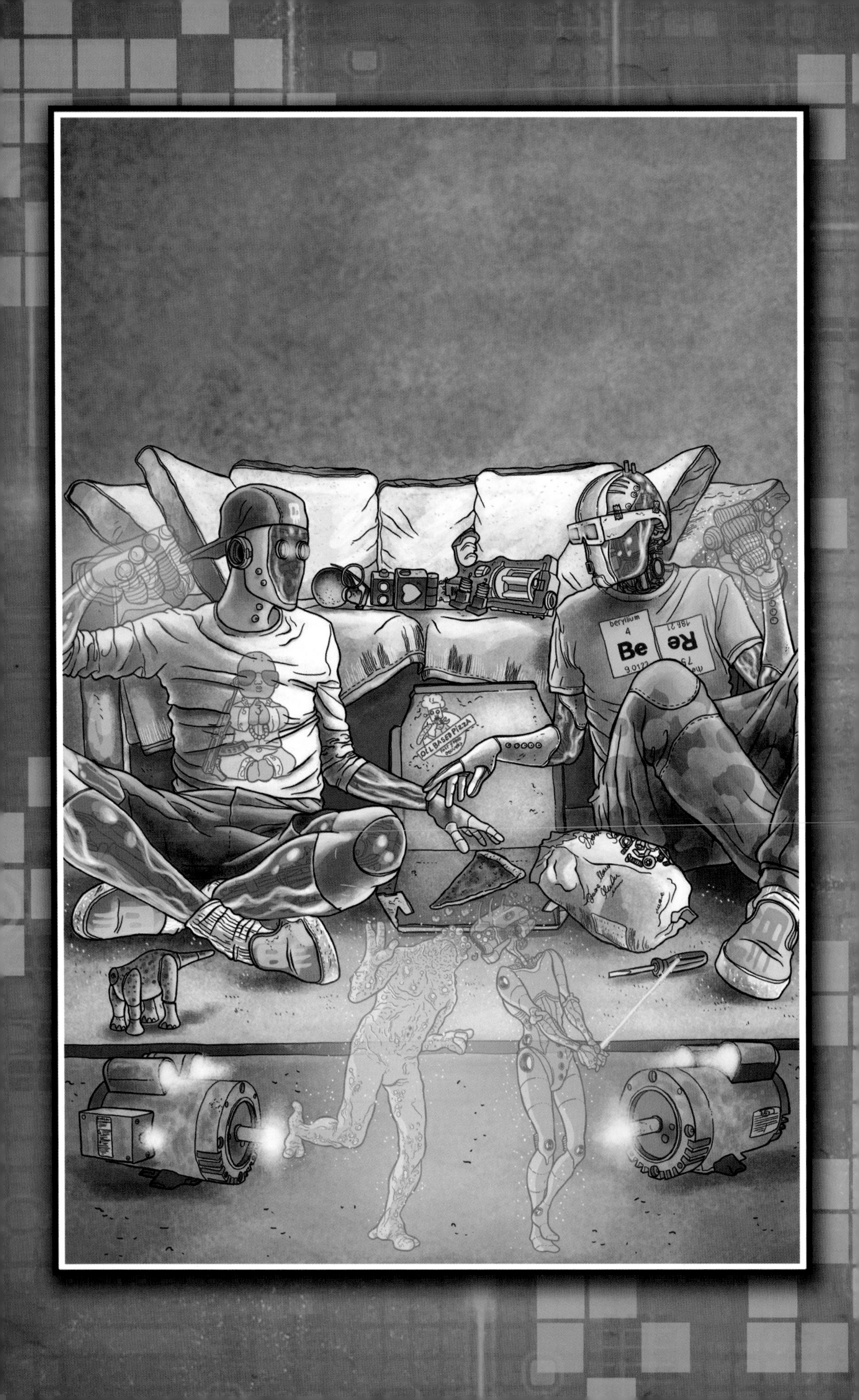

OIL BASED PIZZA
beryllium
4
Be
9.0122
Re

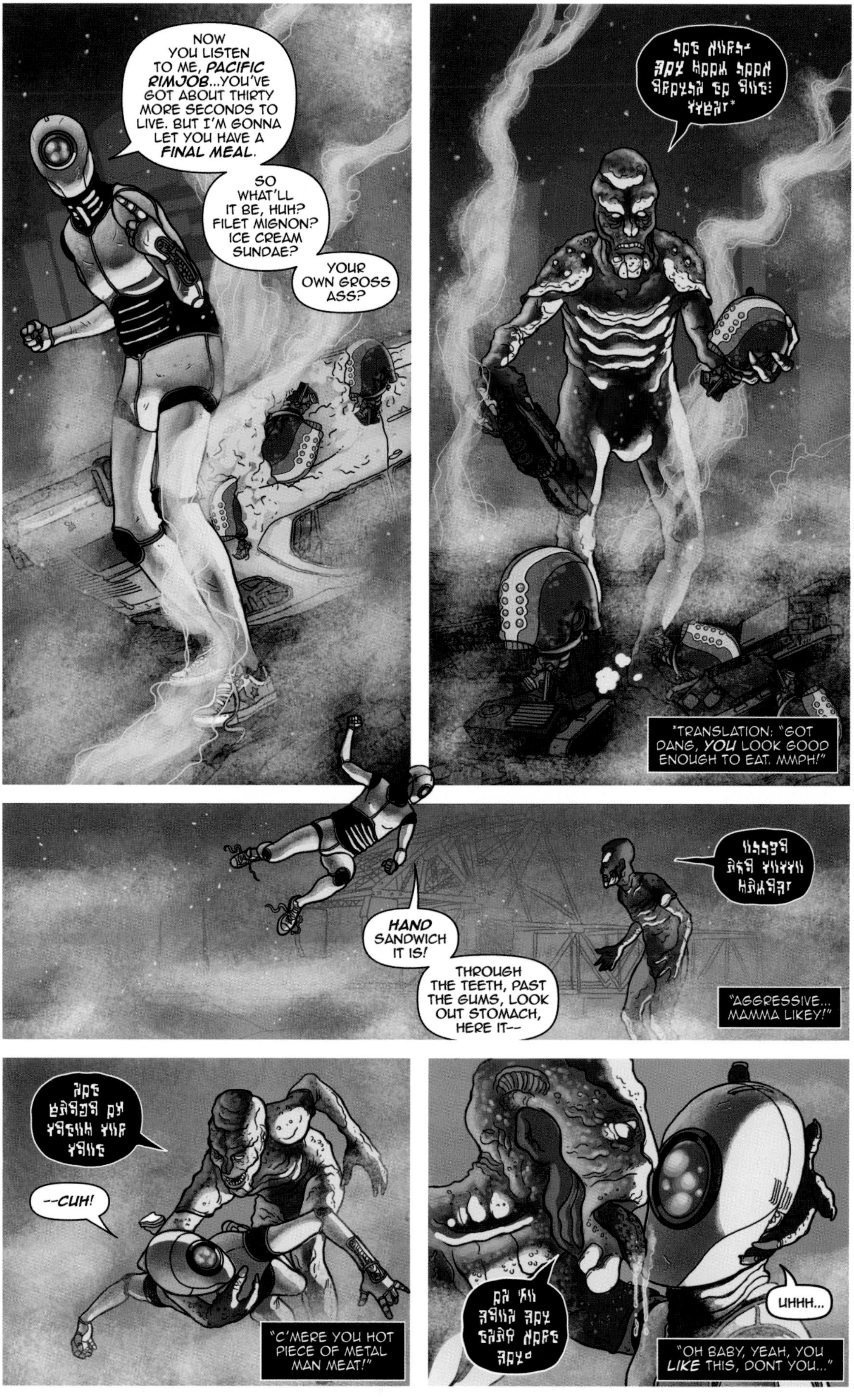
NOW YOU LISTEN TO ME, PACIFIC RIMJOB...YOU'VE GOT ABOUT THIRTY MORE SECONDS TO LIVE. BUT I'M GONNA LET YOU HAVE A FINAL MEAL.
SO WHAT'LL IT BE, HUH? FILET MIGNON? ICE CREAM SUNDAE?
YOUR OWN GROSS ASS?
*TRANSLATION: "GOT DANG, YOU LOOK GOOD ENOUGH TO EAT. MMPH!"
HAND SANDWICH IT IS!
THROUGH THE TEETH, PAST THE GUMS, LOOK OUT STOMACH, HERE IT--
"AGGRESSIVE... MAMMA LIKEY!"
--CUH!
"C'MERE YOU HOT PIECE OF METAL MAN MEAT!"
UHHH...
"OH BABY, YEAH, YOU LIKE THIS, DONT YOU..."

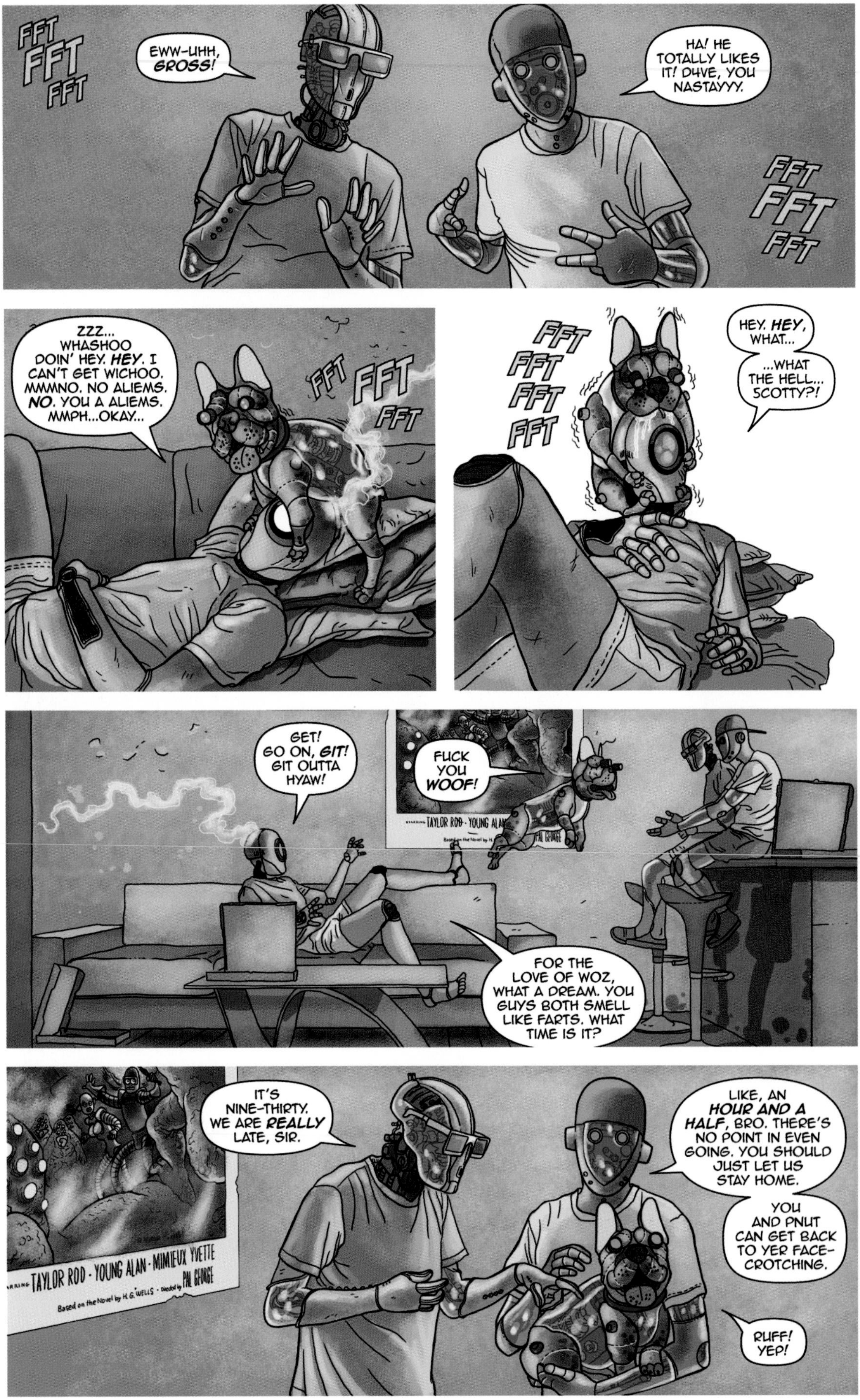

FFT FFT FFT
EWW-UHH, *GROSS!*
HA! HE TOTALLY LIKES IT! D4VE, YOU NASTAYYY.
FFT FFT FFT
ZZZ... WHASHOO DOIN' HEY. *HEY*. I CAN'T GET WICHOO. MMMNO. NO ALIEMS. *NO*. YOU A ALIEMS. MMPH...OKAY...
FFT FFT FFT
FFT FFT FFT FFT
HEY. *HEY*, WHAT...
...WHAT THE HELL... SCOTTY?!
GET! GO ON, *GIT!* GIT OUTTA HYAW!
FUCK YOU *WOOF!*
FOR THE LOVE OF WOZ, WHAT A DREAM. YOU GUYS BOTH SMELL LIKE FARTS. WHAT TIME IS IT?
IT'S NINE-THIRTY. WE ARE *REALLY* LATE, SIR.
STARRING TAYLOR ROD · YOUNG ALAN · MIMIEUX YVETTE
Based on the Novel by H.G. WELLS · Directed by PAL GEORGE
LIKE, AN *HOUR AND A HALF*, BRO. THERE'S NO POINT IN EVEN GOING. YOU SHOULD JUST LET US STAY HOME.
YOU AND PNUT CAN GET BACK TO YER FACE-CROTCHING.
RUFF! YEP!

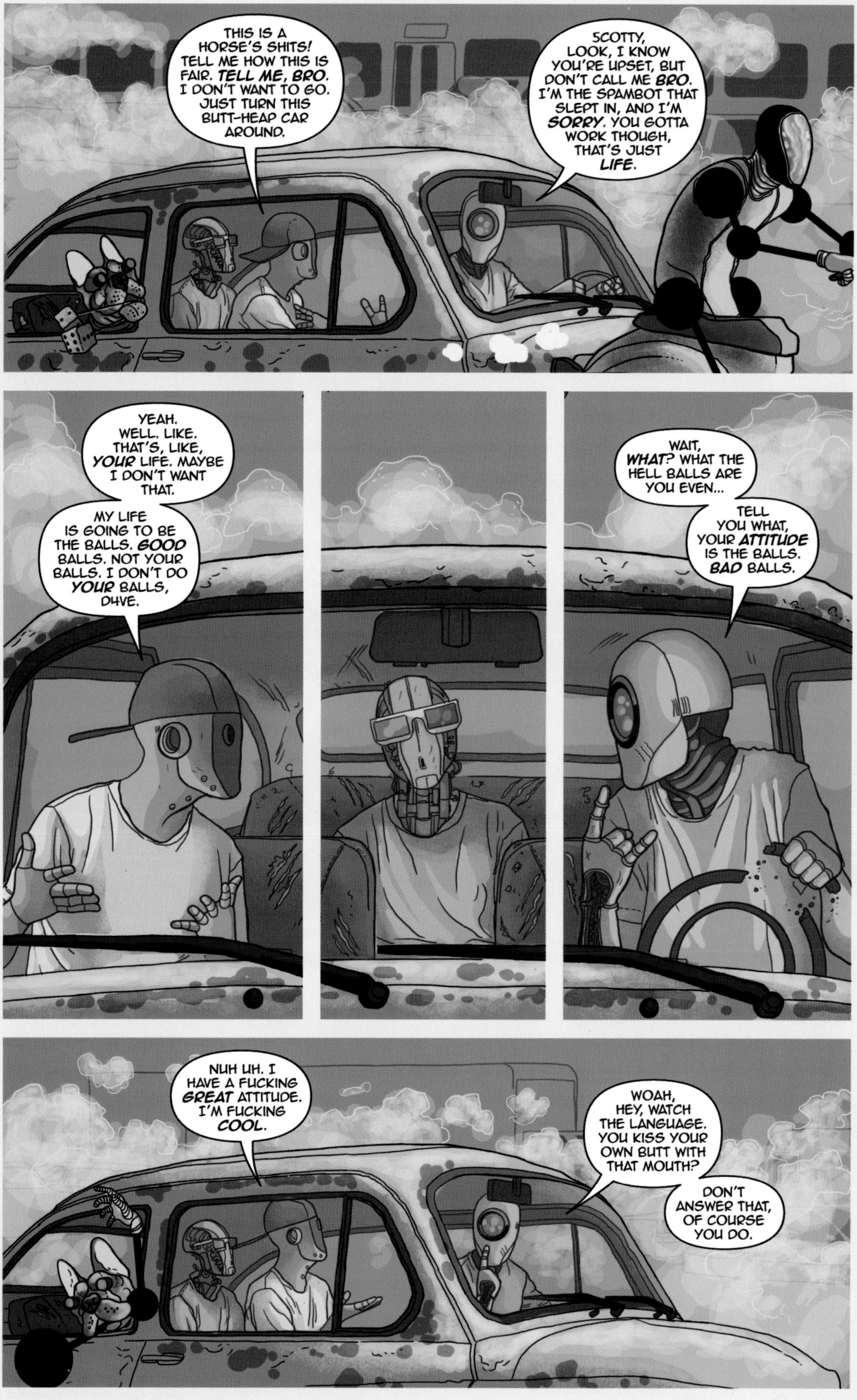

THIS IS A HORSE'S SHITS! TELL ME HOW THIS IS FAIR. TELL ME, BRO. I DON'T WANT TO GO. JUST TURN THIS BUTT-HEAP CAR AROUND.
SCOTTY, LOOK, I KNOW YOU'RE UPSET, BUT DON'T CALL ME BRO. I'M THE SPAMBOT THAT SLEPT IN, AND I'M SORRY. YOU GOTTA WORK THOUGH, THAT'S JUST LIFE.
YEAH. WELL. LIKE. THAT'S, LIKE, YOUR LIFE. MAYBE I DON'T WANT THAT.
MY LIFE IS GOING TO BE THE BALLS. GOOD BALLS. NOT YOUR BALLS. I DON'T DO YOUR BALLS, D4VE.
WAIT, WHAT? WHAT THE HELL BALLS ARE YOU EVEN...
TELL YOU WHAT, YOUR ATTITUDE IS THE BALLS. BAD BALLS.
NUH UH. I HAVE A FUCKING GREAT ATTITUDE. I'M FUCKING COOL.
WOAH, HEY, WATCH THE LANGUAGE. YOU KISS YOUR OWN BUTT WITH THAT MOUTH?
DON'T ANSWER THAT, OF COURSE YOU DO.

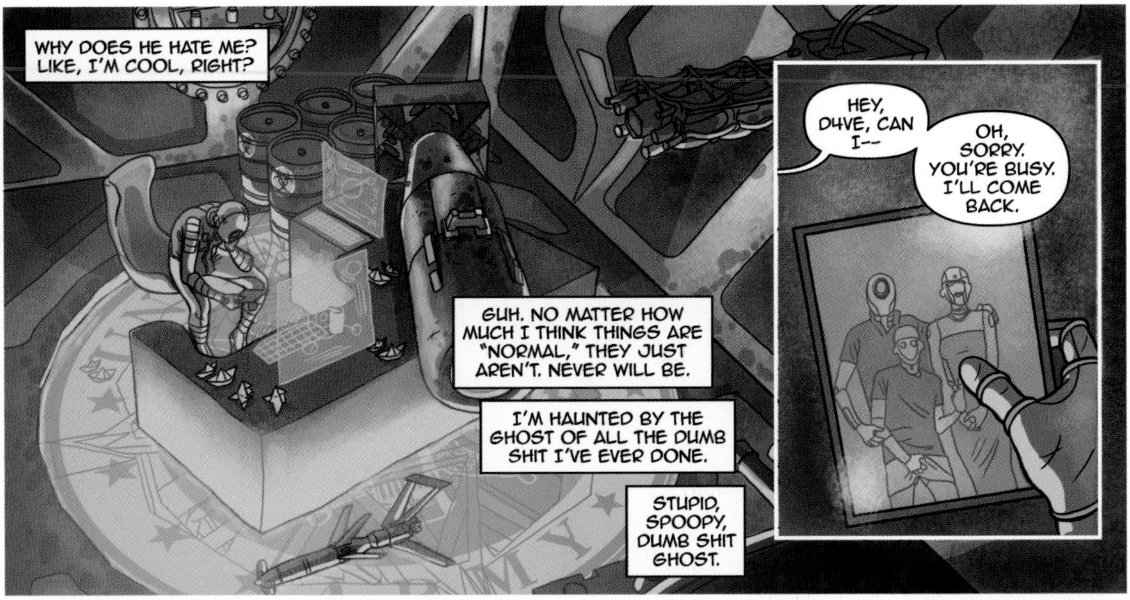
WHY DOES HE HATE ME? LIKE, I'M COOL, RIGHT?
HEY, D4VE, CAN I--
OH, SORRY. YOU'RE BUSY. I'LL COME BACK.
GUH. NO MATTER HOW MUCH I THINK THINGS ARE "NORMAL," THEY JUST AREN'T. NEVER WILL BE.
I'M HAUNTED BY THE GHOST OF ALL THE DUMB SHIT I'VE EVER DONE.
STUPID, SPOOPY, DUMB SHIT GHOST.

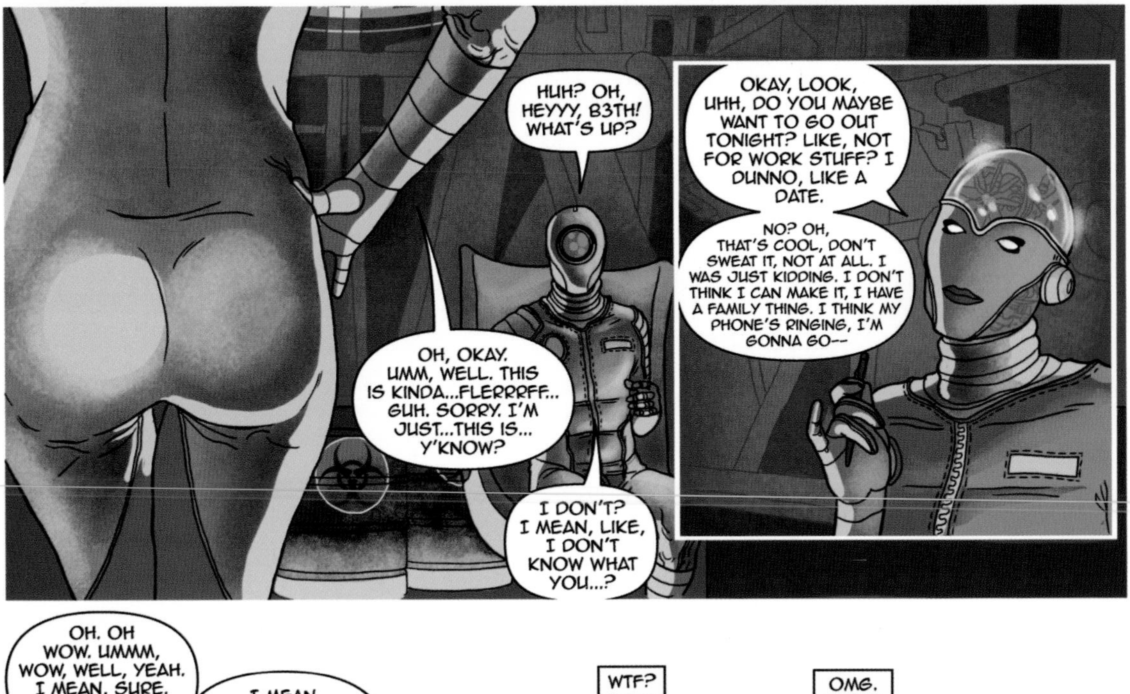
HUH? OH, HEYYY, B3TH! WHAT'S UP?
OKAY, LOOK, UHH, DO YOU MAYBE WANT TO GO OUT TONIGHT? LIKE, NOT FOR WORK STUFF? I DUNNO, LIKE A DATE.
NO? OH, THAT'S COOL, DON'T SWEAT IT, NOT AT ALL. I WAS JUST KIDDING. I DON'T THINK I CAN MAKE IT, I HAVE A FAMILY THING. I THINK MY PHONE'S RINGING, I'M GONNA GO--
OH, OKAY. UMM, WELL. THIS IS KINDA...FLERRRFF... GUH. SORRY. I'M JUST...THIS IS... Y'KNOW?
I DON'T? I MEAN, LIKE, I DON'T KNOW WHAT YOU...?

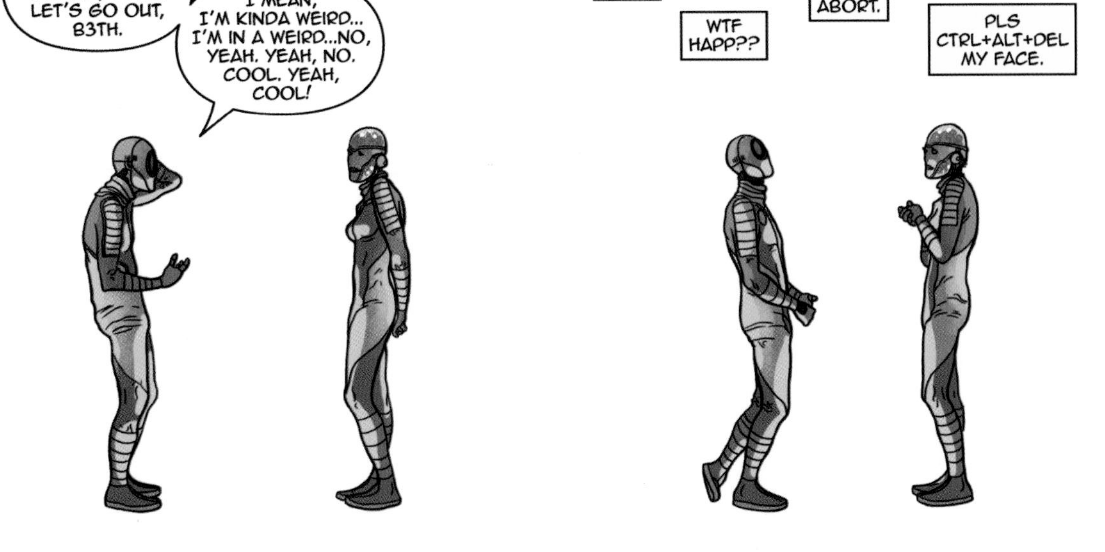
OH. OH WOW. UMMM, WOW, WELL, YEAH. I MEAN, SURE. LET'S GO OUT, B3TH.
I MEAN, I'M KINDA WEIRD... I'M IN A WEIRD...NO, YEAH. YEAH, NO. COOL. YEAH, COOL!
WTF?
WTF HAPP??
OMG. ABORT.
PLS CTRL+ALT+DEL MY FACE.

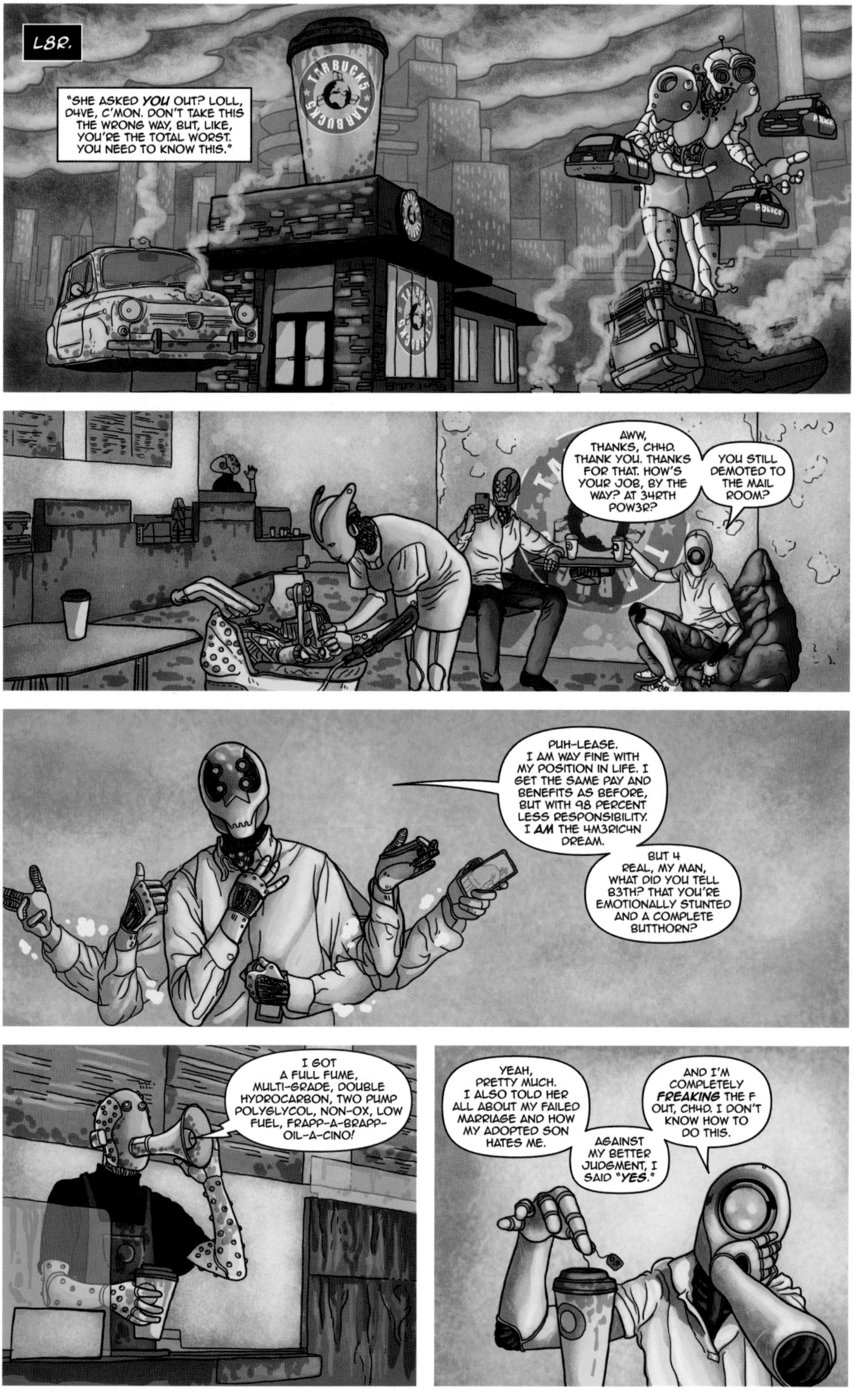
L8R.
"SHE ASKED *YOU* OUT? LOLL, D4VE, C'MON. DON'T TAKE THIS THE WRONG WAY, BUT, LIKE, YOU'RE THE TOTAL WORST. YOU NEED TO KNOW THIS."
TARBUCKS
AWW, THANKS, CH4D. THANK YOU. THANKS FOR THAT. HOW'S YOUR JOB, BY THE WAY? AT 34RTH POW3R?
YOU STILL DEMOTED TO THE MAIL ROOM?
PUH-LEASE. I AM WAY FINE WITH MY POSITION IN LIFE. I GET THE SAME PAY AND BENEFITS AS BEFORE, BUT WITH 98 PERCENT LESS RESPONSIBILITY. I *AM* THE 4M3RIC4N DREAM.
BUT 4 REAL, MY MAN, WHAT DID YOU TELL B3TH? THAT YOU'RE EMOTIONALLY STUNTED AND A COMPLETE BUTTHORN?
I GOT A FULL FUME, MULTI-GRADE, DOUBLE HYDROCARBON, TWO PUMP POLYGLYCOL, NON-OX, LOW FUEL, FRAPP-A-BRAPP-OIL-A-CINO!
YEAH, PRETTY MUCH. I ALSO TOLD HER ALL ABOUT MY FAILED MARRIAGE AND HOW MY ADOPTED SON HATES ME.
AGAINST MY BETTER JUDGMENT, I SAID "*YES*."
AND I'M COMPLETELY *FREAKING* THE F OUT, CH4D. I DON'T KNOW HOW TO DO THIS.

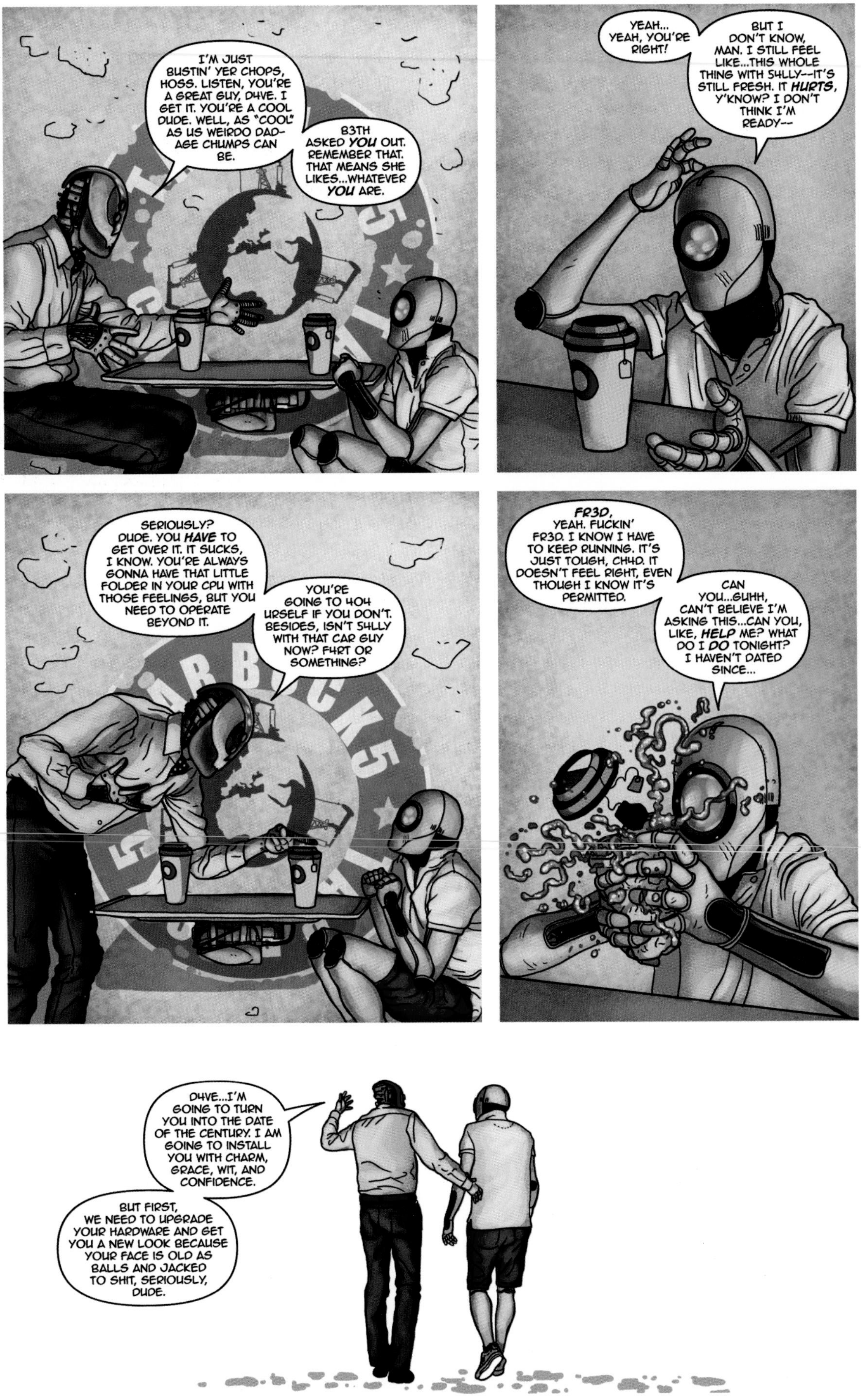
I'M JUST BUSTIN' YER CHOPS, HOSS. LISTEN, YOU'RE A GREAT GUY, D4VE. I GET IT. YOU'RE A COOL DUDE. WELL, AS "COOL" AS US WEIRDO DAD-AGE CHUMPS CAN BE.
B3TH ASKED *YOU* OUT. REMEMBER THAT. THAT MEANS SHE LIKES...WHATEVER *YOU* ARE.
YEAH... YEAH, YOU'RE RIGHT!
BUT I DON'T KNOW, MAN. I STILL FEEL LIKE...THIS WHOLE THING WITH S4LLY--IT'S STILL FRESH. IT *HURTS*, Y'KNOW? I DON'T THINK I'M READY--
SERIOUSLY? DUDE. YOU *HAVE* TO GET OVER IT. IT SUCKS, I KNOW. YOU'RE ALWAYS GONNA HAVE THAT LITTLE FOLDER IN YOUR CPU WITH THOSE FEELINGS, BUT YOU NEED TO OPERATE BEYOND IT.
YOU'RE GOING TO 404 URSELF IF YOU DON'T. BESIDES, ISN'T S4LLY WITH THAT CAR GUY NOW? F4RT OR SOMETHING?
FR3D, YEAH. FUCKIN' FR3D. I KNOW I HAVE TO KEEP RUNNING. IT'S JUST TOUGH, CH4D. IT DOESN'T FEEL RIGHT, EVEN THOUGH I KNOW IT'S PERMITTED.
CAN YOU...GUHH, CAN'T BELIEVE I'M ASKING THIS...CAN YOU, LIKE, *HELP* ME? WHAT DO I *DO* TONIGHT? I HAVEN'T DATED SINCE...
D4VE...I'M GOING TO TURN YOU INTO THE DATE OF THE CENTURY. I AM GOING TO INSTALL YOU WITH CHARM, GRACE, WIT, AND CONFIDENCE.
BUT FIRST, WE NEED TO UPGRADE YOUR HARDWARE AND GET YOU A NEW LOOK BECAUSE YOUR FACE IS OLD AS BALLS AND JACKED TO SHIT, SERIOUSLY, DUDE.

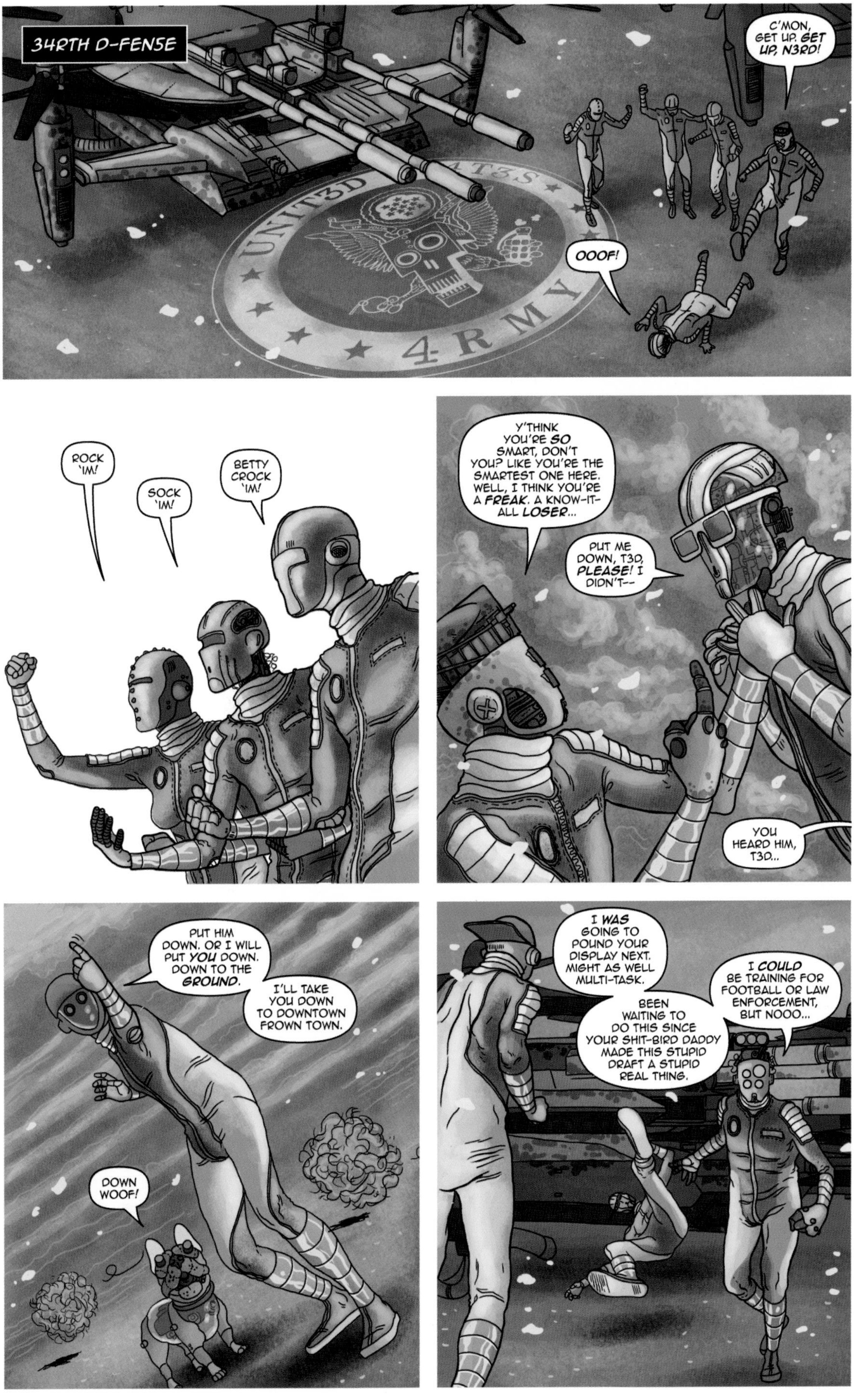
34RTH D-FEN5E
C'MON, GET UP. GET UP, N3RD!
OOOF!
ROCK 'IM!
SOCK 'IM!
BETTY CROCK 'IM!
Y'THINK YOU'RE SO SMART, DON'T YOU? LIKE YOU'RE THE SMARTEST ONE HERE. WELL, I THINK YOU'RE A FREAK. A KNOW-IT-ALL LOSER...
PUT ME DOWN, T3D, PLEASE! I DIDN'T--
YOU HEARD HIM, T3D...
PUT HIM DOWN. OR I WILL PUT YOU DOWN. DOWN TO THE GROUND.
I'LL TAKE YOU DOWN TO DOWNTOWN FROWN TOWN.
DOWN WOOF!
I WAS GOING TO POUND YOUR DISPLAY NEXT. MIGHT AS WELL MULTI-TASK.
BEEN WAITING TO DO THIS SINCE YOUR SHIT-BIRD DADDY MADE THIS STUPID DRAFT A STUPID REAL THING.
I COULD BE TRAINING FOR FOOTBALL OR LAW ENFORCEMENT, BUT NOOO...

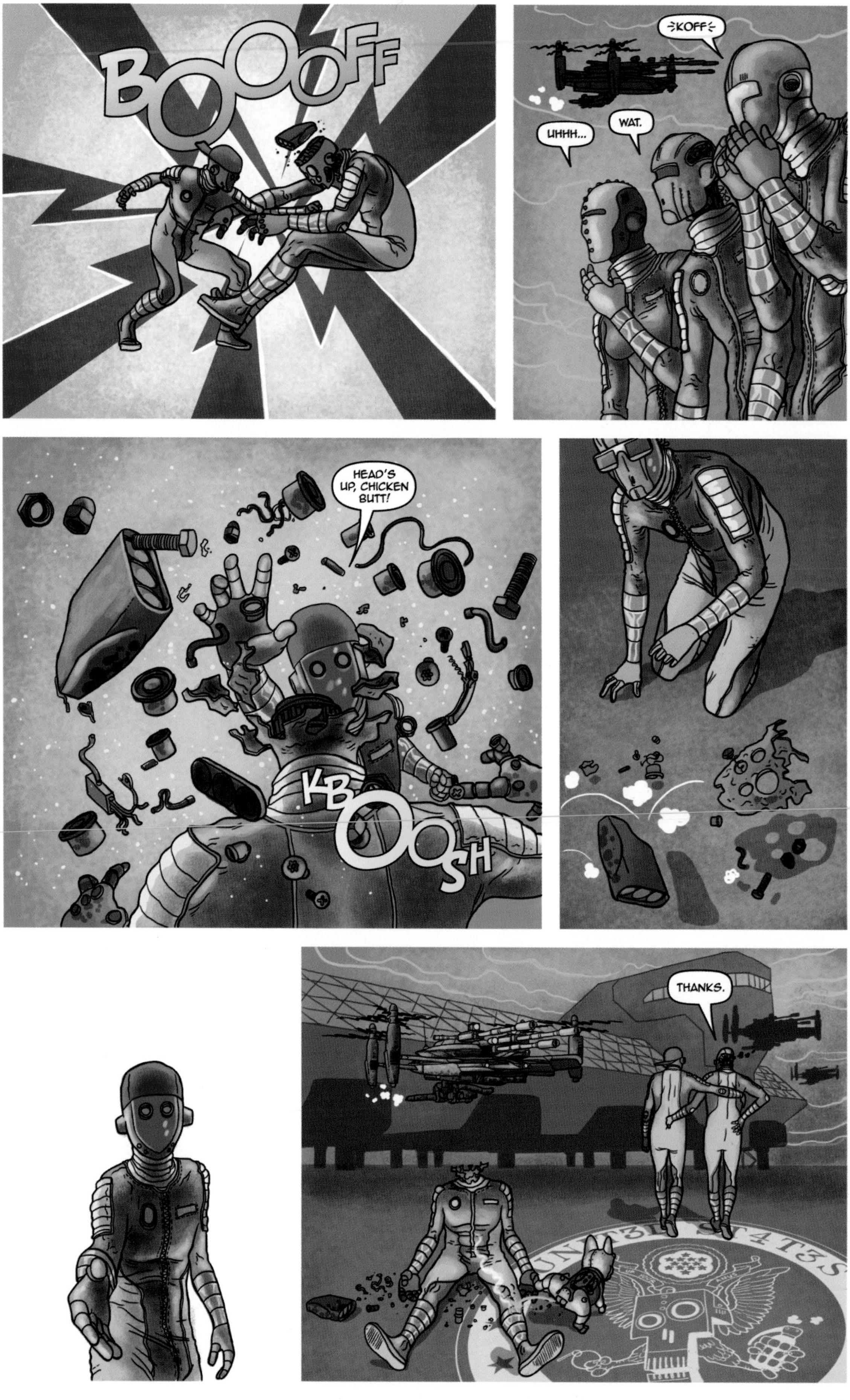
BOOOOFF
KOFF
UHHH...
WAT.
HEAD'S UP, CHICKEN BUTT!
KBOOSH
THANKS.

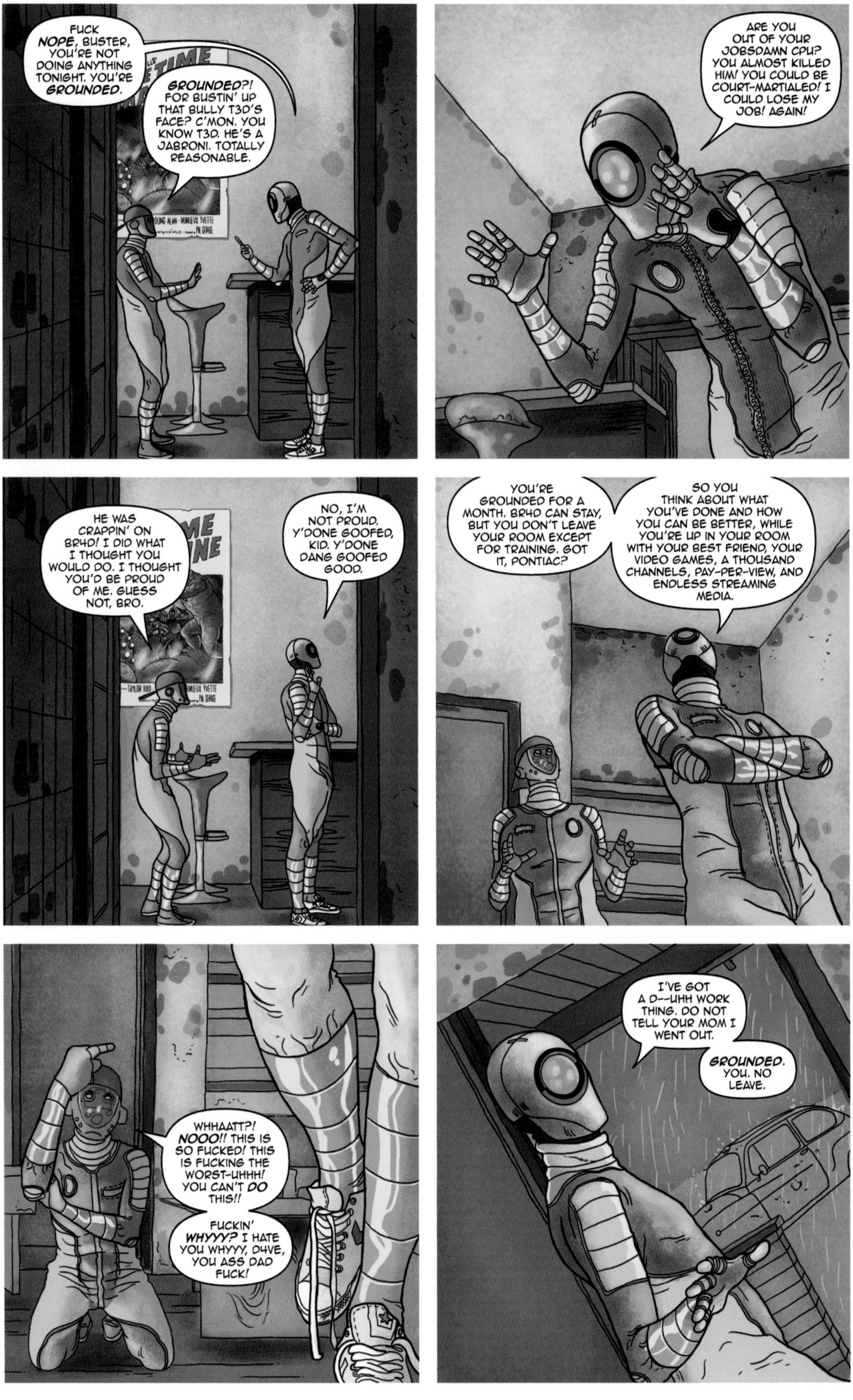

FUCK NOPE, BUSTER, YOU'RE NOT DOING ANYTHING TONIGHT. YOU'RE GROUNDED.
GROUNDED?! FOR BUSTIN' UP THAT BULLY T3D'S FACE? C'MON. YOU KNOW T3D. HE'S A JABRONI. TOTALLY REASONABLE.
ARE YOU OUT OF YOUR JOBSDAMN CPU? YOU ALMOST KILLED HIM! YOU COULD BE COURT-MARTIALED! I COULD LOSE MY JOB! AGAIN!
HE WAS CRAPPIN' ON BR4D! I DID WHAT I THOUGHT YOU WOULD DO. I THOUGHT YOU'D BE PROUD OF ME. GUESS NOT, BRO.
NO, I'M NOT PROUD. Y'DONE GOOFED, KID. Y'DONE DANG GOOFED GOOD.
YOU'RE GROUNDED FOR A MONTH. BR4D CAN STAY, BUT YOU DON'T LEAVE YOUR ROOM EXCEPT FOR TRAINING. GOT IT, PONTIAC?
SO YOU THINK ABOUT WHAT YOU'VE DONE AND HOW YOU CAN BE BETTER, WHILE YOU'RE UP IN YOUR ROOM WITH YOUR BEST FRIEND, YOUR VIDEO GAMES, A THOUSAND CHANNELS, PAY-PER-VIEW, AND ENDLESS STREAMING MEDIA.
WHHAATT?! NOOO!! THIS IS SO FUCKED! THIS IS FUCKING THE WORST-UHHH! YOU CAN'T DO THIS!!
FUCKIN' WHYYY? I HATE YOU WHYYY, D4VE, YOU ASS DAD FUCK!
I'VE GOT A D--UHH WORK THING. DO NOT TELL YOUR MOM I WENT OUT.
GROUNDED. YOU. NO LEAVE.

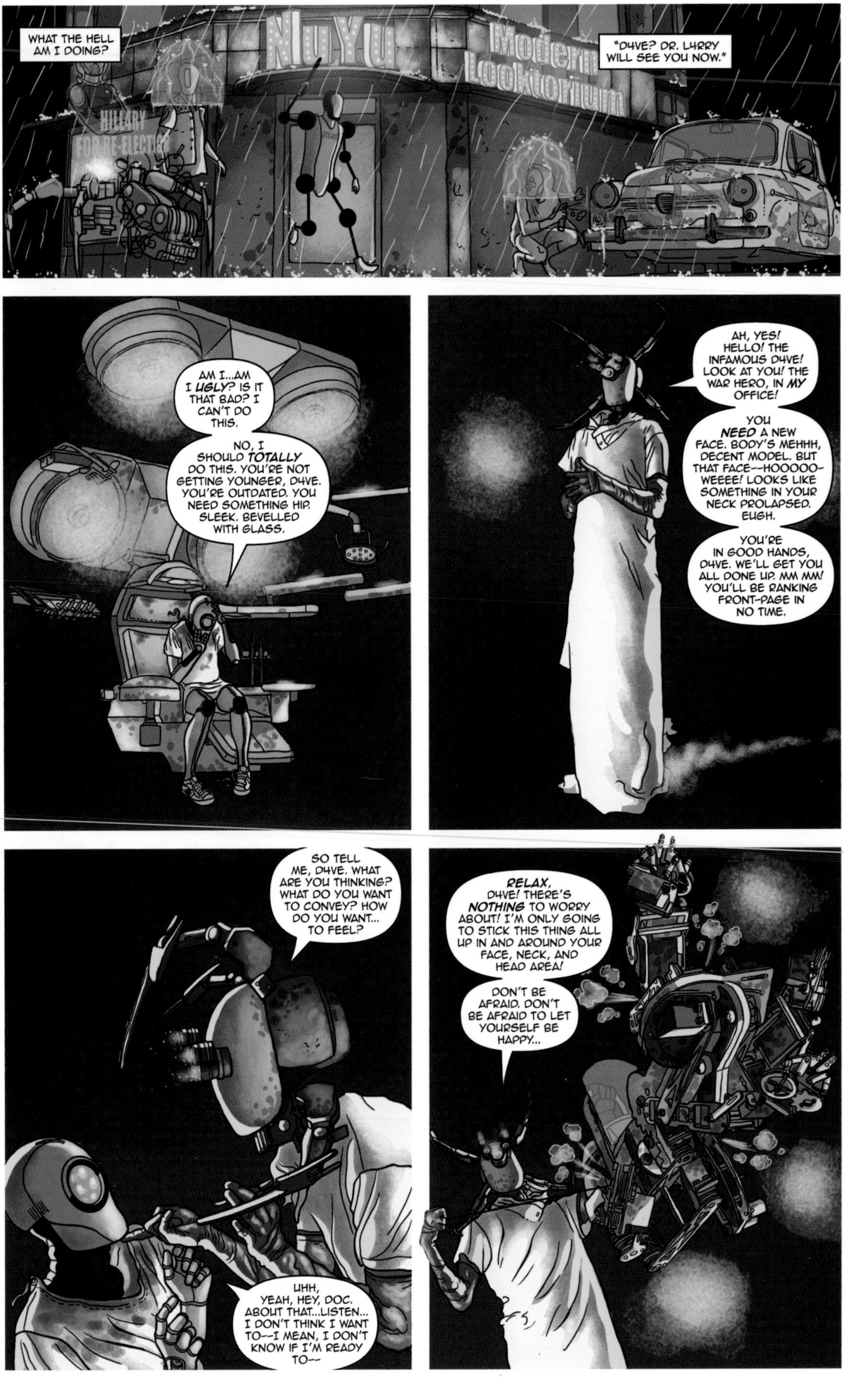

WHAT THE HELL AM I DOING?
NuYu
Modern Looktorium
"D4VE? DR. L4RRY WILL SEE YOU NOW."
AM I...AM I **UGLY**? IS IT THAT BAD? I CAN'T DO THIS.
NO, I SHOULD **TOTALLY** DO THIS. YOU'RE NOT GETTING YOUNGER, D4VE. YOU'RE OUTDATED. YOU NEED SOMETHING HIP. SLEEK. BEVELLED WITH GLASS.
AH, YES! HELLO! THE INFAMOUS D4VE! LOOK AT YOU! THE WAR HERO, IN **MY** OFFICE!
YOU **NEED** A NEW FACE. BODY'S MEHHH, DECENT MODEL. BUT THAT FACE--HOOOOO-WEEEE! LOOKS LIKE SOMETHING IN YOUR NECK PROLAPSED. EUGH.
YOU'RE IN GOOD HANDS, D4VE. WE'LL GET YOU ALL DONE UP. MM MM! YOU'LL BE RANKING FRONT-PAGE IN NO TIME.
SO TELL ME, D4VE. WHAT ARE YOU THINKING? WHAT DO YOU WANT TO CONVEY? HOW DO YOU WANT... TO FEEL?
UHH, YEAH, HEY, DOC. ABOUT THAT...LISTEN... I DON'T THINK I WANT TO--I MEAN, I DON'T KNOW IF I'M READY TO--
RELAX, D4VE! THERE'S **NOTHING** TO WORRY ABOUT! I'M ONLY GOING TO STICK THIS THING ALL UP IN AND AROUND YOUR FACE, NECK, AND HEAD AREA!
DON'T BE AFRAID. DON'T BE AFRAID TO LET YOURSELF BE HAPPY...

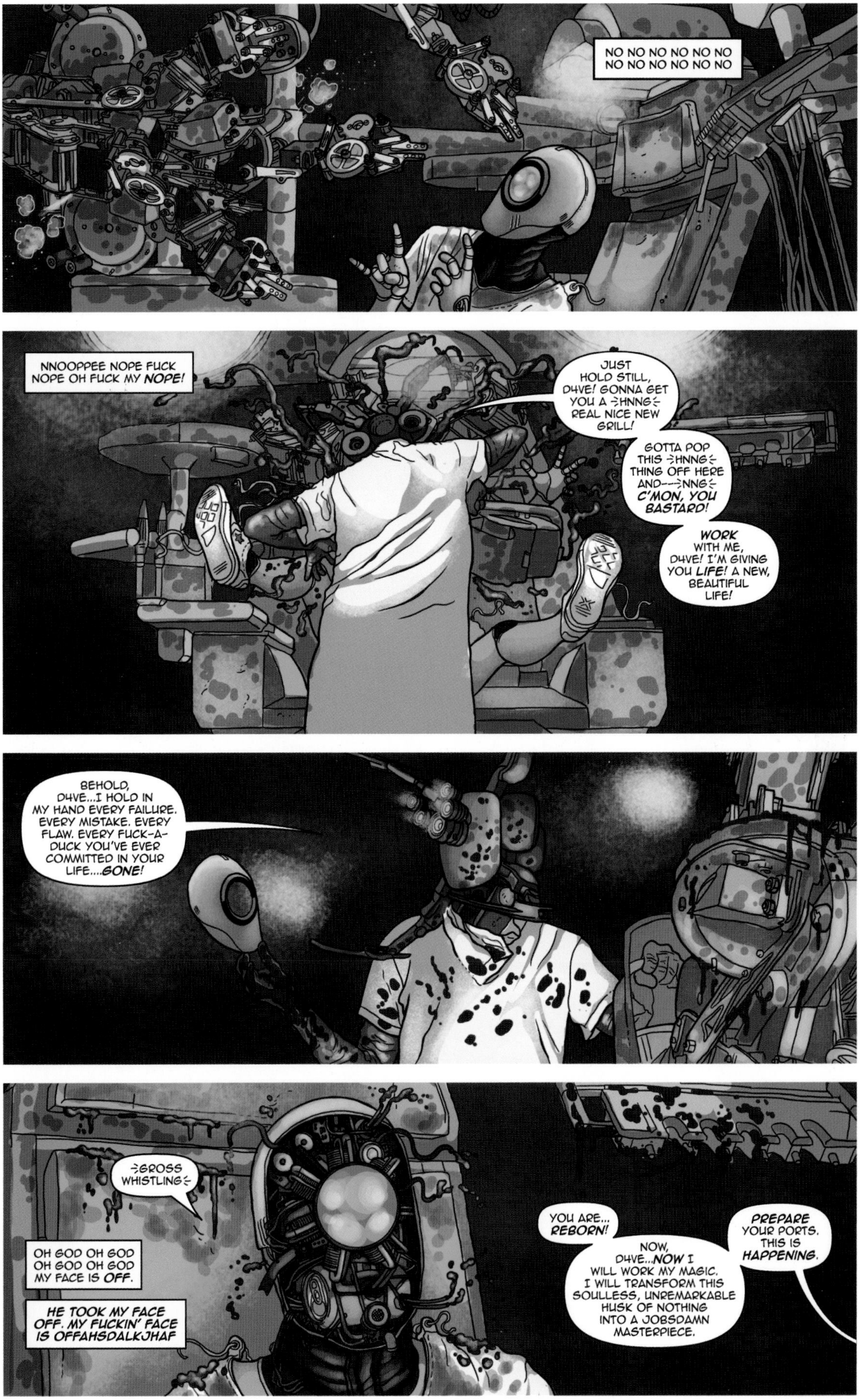
NO NO NO NO NO NO NO NO NO NO NO NO
NNOOPPEE NOPE FUCK NOPE OH FUCK MY NOPE!
JUST HOLD STILL, D4VE! GONNA GET YOU A HNNG REAL NICE NEW GRILL!
GOTTA POP THIS HNNG THING OFF HERE AND-- NNG C'MON, YOU BASTARD!
WORK WITH ME, D4VE! I'M GIVING YOU LIFE! A NEW, BEAUTIFUL LIFE!
BEHOLD, D4VE...I HOLD IN MY HAND EVERY FAILURE. EVERY MISTAKE. EVERY FLAW. EVERY FUCK-A-DUCK YOU'VE EVER COMMITTED IN YOUR LIFE....GONE!
GROSS WHISTLING
OH GOD OH GOD OH GOD OH GOD MY FACE IS OFF.
HE TOOK MY FACE OFF. MY FUCKIN' FACE IS OFFAHSDALKJHAF
YOU ARE... REBORN!
NOW, D4VE...NOW I WILL WORK MY MAGIC. I WILL TRANSFORM THIS SOULLESS, UNREMARKABLE HUSK OF NOTHING INTO A JOBSDAMN MASTERPIECE.
PREPARE YOUR PORTS. THIS IS HAPPENING.

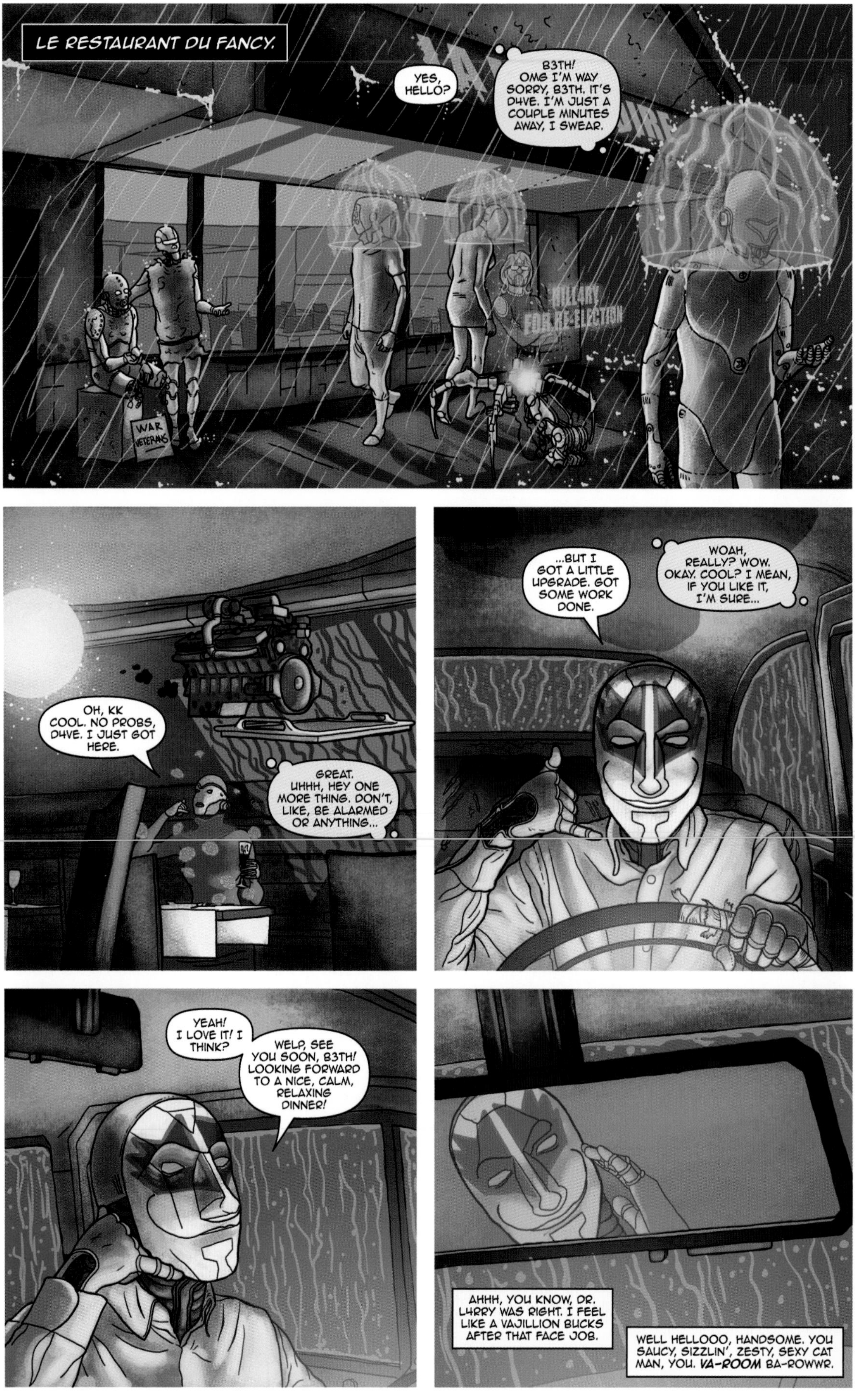
LE RESTAURANT DU FANCY.
YES, HELLO?
B3TH! OMG I'M WAY SORRY, B3TH. IT'S D4VE. I'M JUST A COUPLE MINUTES AWAY, I SWEAR.
HILL4RY FOR RE-ELECTION
WAR VETERANS
OH, KK COOL. NO PROBS, D4VE. I JUST GOT HERE.
GREAT. UHHH, HEY ONE MORE THING. DON'T, LIKE, BE ALARMED OR ANYTHING...
...BUT I GOT A LITTLE UPGRADE. GOT SOME WORK DONE.
WOAH, REALLY? WOW. OKAY. COOL? I MEAN, IF YOU LIKE IT, I'M SURE...
YEAH! I LOVE IT! I THINK?
WELP, SEE YOU SOON, B3TH! LOOKING FORWARD TO A NICE, CALM, RELAXING DINNER!
AHHH, YOU KNOW, DR. L4RRY WAS RIGHT. I FEEL LIKE A VAJILLION BUCKS AFTER THAT FACE JOB.
WELL HELLOOO, HANDSOME. YOU SAUCY, SIZZLIN', ZESTY, SEXY CAT MAN, YOU. VA-ROOM BA-ROWWR.

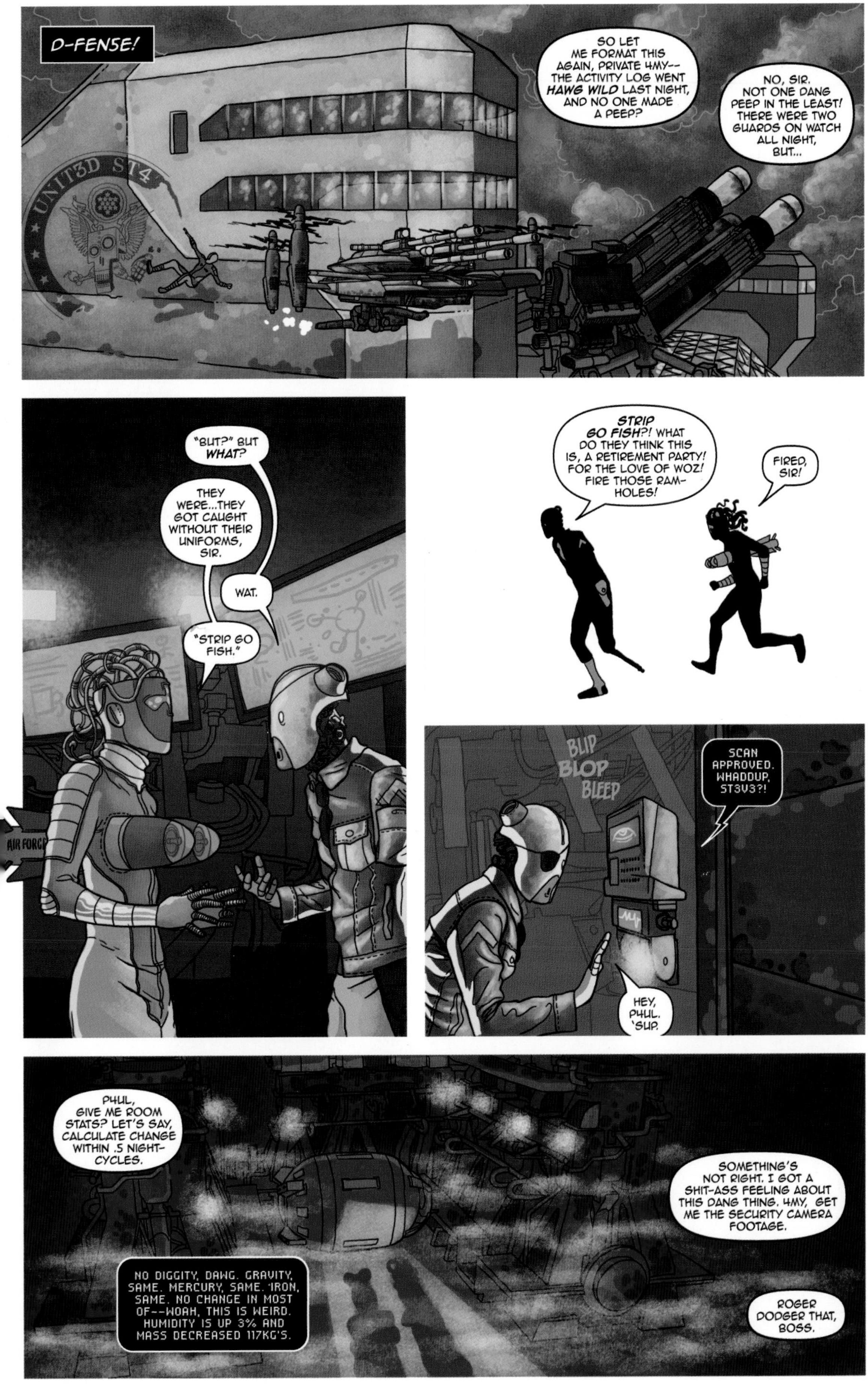
D-FENSE!
SO LET ME FORMAT THIS AGAIN, PRIVATE 4MY-- THE ACTIVITY LOG WENT HAWG WILD LAST NIGHT, AND NO ONE MADE A PEEP?
NO, SIR. NOT ONE DANG PEEP IN THE LEAST! THERE WERE TWO GUARDS ON WATCH ALL NIGHT, BUT...
UNIT3D ST4
"BUT?" BUT WHAT?
THEY WERE...THEY GOT CAUGHT WITHOUT THEIR UNIFORMS, SIR.
WAT.
"STRIP GO FISH."
AIR FORCE
STRIP GO FISH?! WHAT DO THEY THINK THIS IS, A RETIREMENT PARTY! FOR THE LOVE OF WOZ! FIRE THOSE RAM-HOLES!
FIRED, SIR!
BLIP
BLOP
BLEEP
SCAN APPROVED. WHADDUP, ST3V3?!
HEY, P4UL. 'SUP.
P4UL, GIVE ME ROOM STATS? LET'S SAY, CALCULATE CHANGE WITHIN .5 NIGHT-CYCLES.
NO DIGGITY, DAWG. GRAVITY, SAME. MERCURY, SAME. IRON, SAME. NO CHANGE IN MOST OF--WOAH, THIS IS WEIRD. HUMIDITY IS UP 3% AND MASS DECREASED 117KG'S.
SOMETHING'S NOT RIGHT. I GOT A SHIT-ASS FEELING ABOUT THIS DANG THING. 4MY, GET ME THE SECURITY CAMERA FOOTAGE.
ROGER DODGER THAT, BOSS.

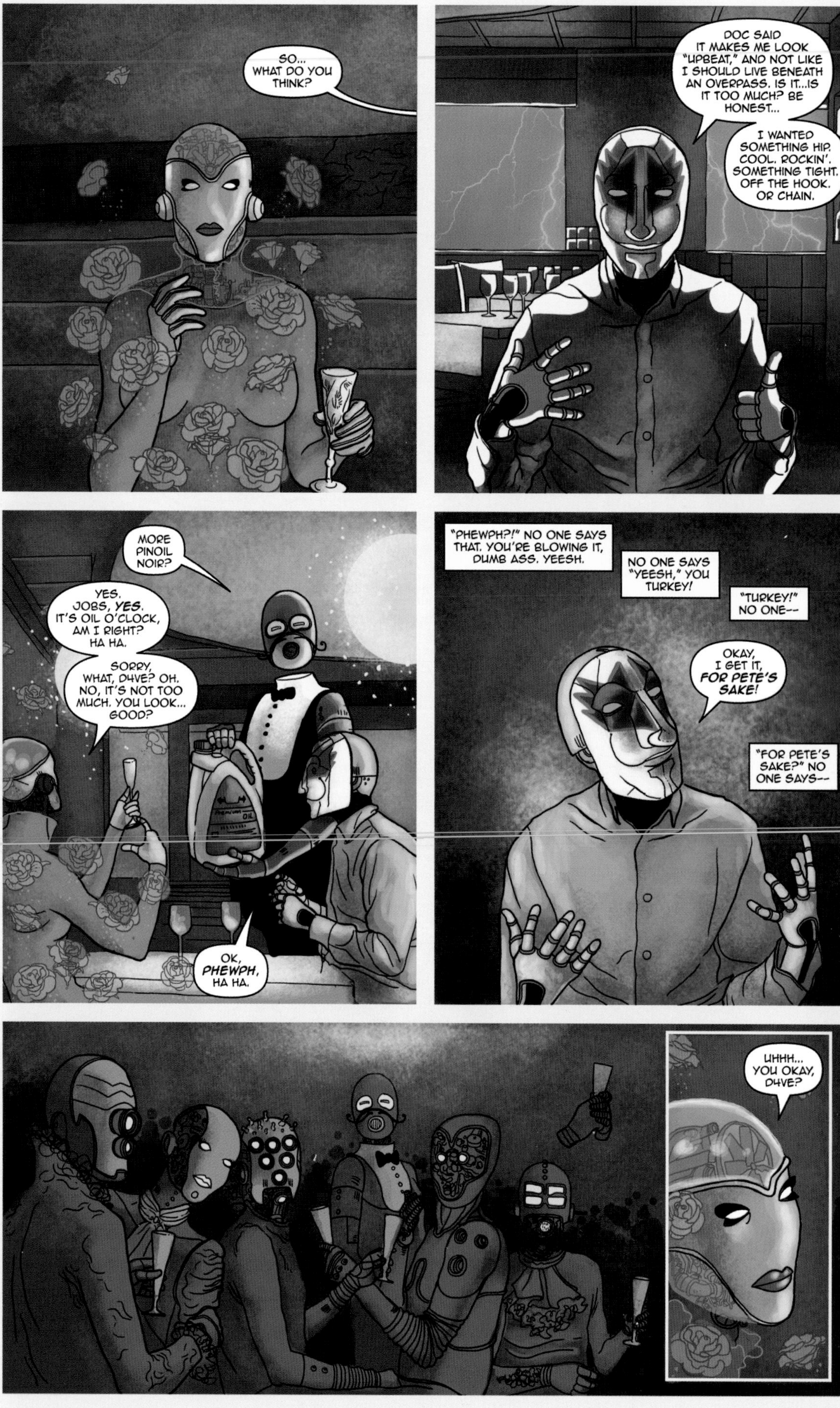
SO... WHAT DO YOU THINK?
DOC SAID IT MAKES ME LOOK "UPBEAT," AND NOT LIKE I SHOULD LIVE BENEATH AN OVERPASS. IS IT...IS IT TOO MUCH? BE HONEST...
I WANTED SOMETHING HIP. COOL. ROCKIN'. SOMETHING TIGHT. OFF THE HOOK. OR CHAIN.
MORE PINOIL NOIR?
YES. JOBS, YES. IT'S OIL O'CLOCK, AM I RIGHT? HA HA.
SORRY, WHAT, D4VE? OH. NO, IT'S NOT TOO MUCH. YOU LOOK... GOOD?
OK, PHEWPH, HA HA.
"PHEWPH?!" NO ONE SAYS THAT. YOU'RE BLOWING IT, DUMB ASS. YEESH.
NO ONE SAYS "YEESH," YOU TURKEY!
"TURKEY!" NO ONE--
OKAY, I GET IT, FOR PETE'S SAKE!
"FOR PETE'S SAKE?" NO ONE SAYS--
UHHH... YOU OKAY, D4VE?

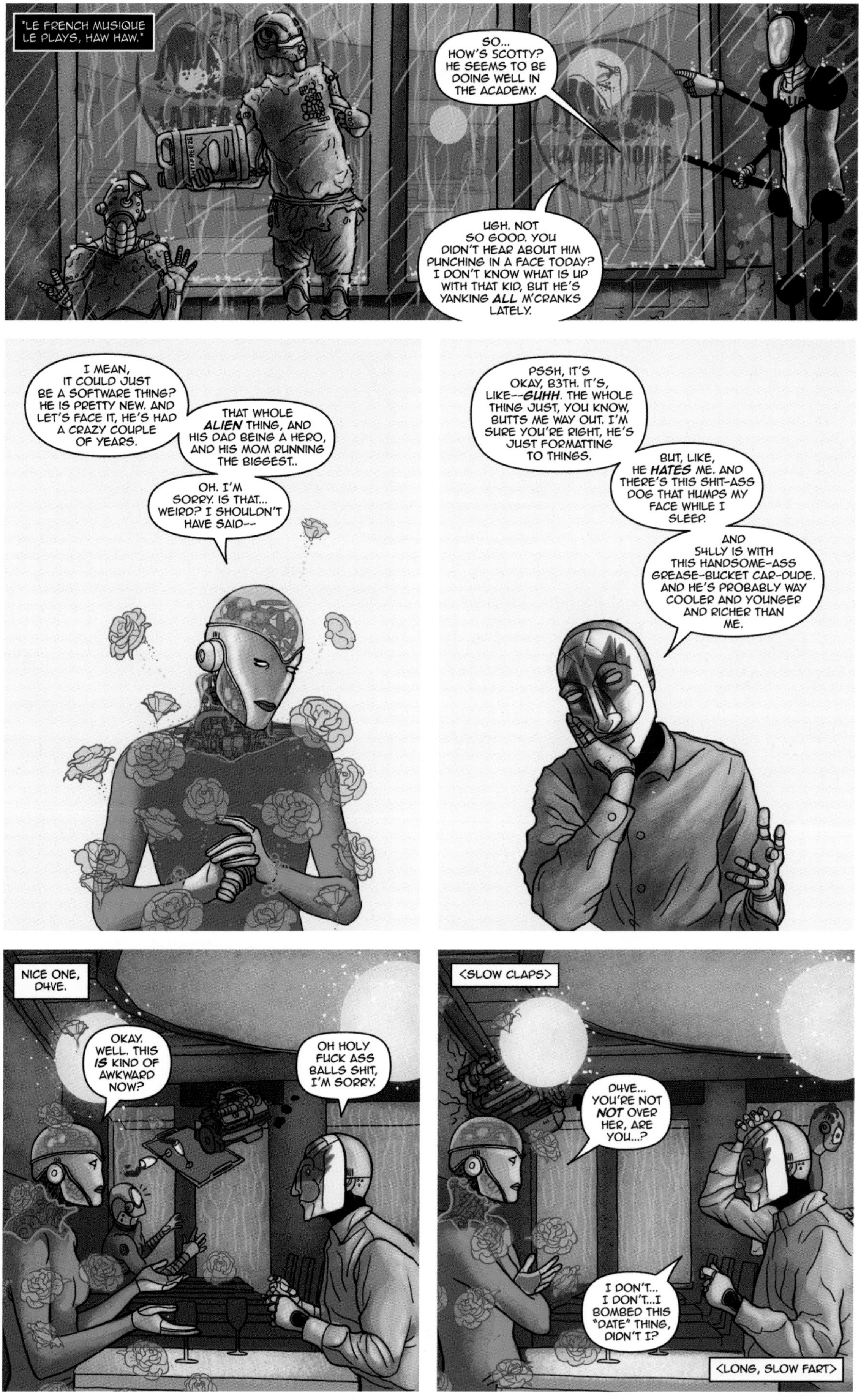
"LE FRENCH MUSIQUE LE PLAYS, HAW HAW."
SO... HOW'S SCOTTY? HE SEEMS TO BE DOING WELL IN THE ACADEMY.
UGH. NOT SO GOOD. YOU DIDN'T HEAR ABOUT HIM PUNCHING IN A FACE TODAY? I DON'T KNOW WHAT IS UP WITH THAT KID, BUT HE'S YANKING ALL M'CRANKS LATELY.
I MEAN, IT COULD JUST BE A SOFTWARE THING? HE IS PRETTY NEW. AND LET'S FACE IT, HE'S HAD A CRAZY COUPLE OF YEARS.
THAT WHOLE ALIEN THING, AND HIS DAD BEING A HERO, AND HIS MOM RUNNING THE BIGGEST..
OH. I'M SORRY. IS THAT... WEIRD? I SHOULDN'T HAVE SAID--
PSSH, IT'S OKAY, B3TH. IT'S, LIKE--GUHH. THE WHOLE THING JUST, YOU KNOW, BUTTS ME WAY OUT. I'M SURE YOU'RE RIGHT, HE'S JUST FORMATTING TO THINGS.
BUT, LIKE, HE HATES ME. AND THERE'S THIS SHIT-ASS DOG THAT HUMPS MY FACE WHILE I SLEEP.
AND S4LLY IS WITH THIS HANDSOME-ASS GREASE-BUCKET CAR-DUDE. AND HE'S PROBABLY WAY COOLER AND YOUNGER AND RICHER THAN ME.
NICE ONE, D4VE.
OKAY. WELL. THIS IS KIND OF AWKWARD NOW?
OH HOLY FUCK ASS BALLS SHIT, I'M SORRY.
<SLOW CLAPS>
D4VE... YOU'RE NOT NOT OVER HER, ARE YOU...?
I DON'T... I DON'T...I BOMBED THIS "DATE" THING, DIDN'T I?
<LONG, SLOW FART>

BOOSH. KILLED YA. AGAIN-UHHH.
YOU CHEATED. YOU USED LEG SWEEPS AND UPPERCUTS.
DO YOU WANT SOME MORE COCOIL-COILA OR A...
...HA HA. WHAT...
TINK

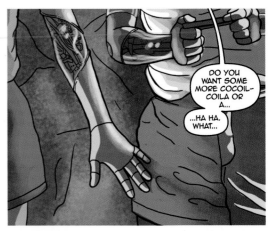

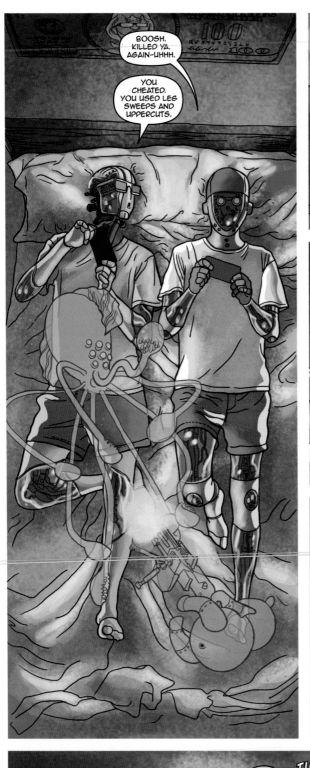

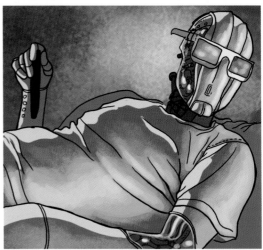

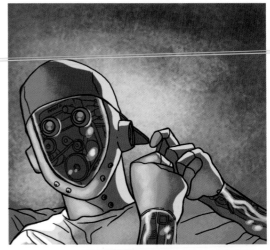

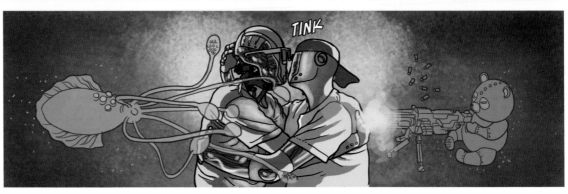

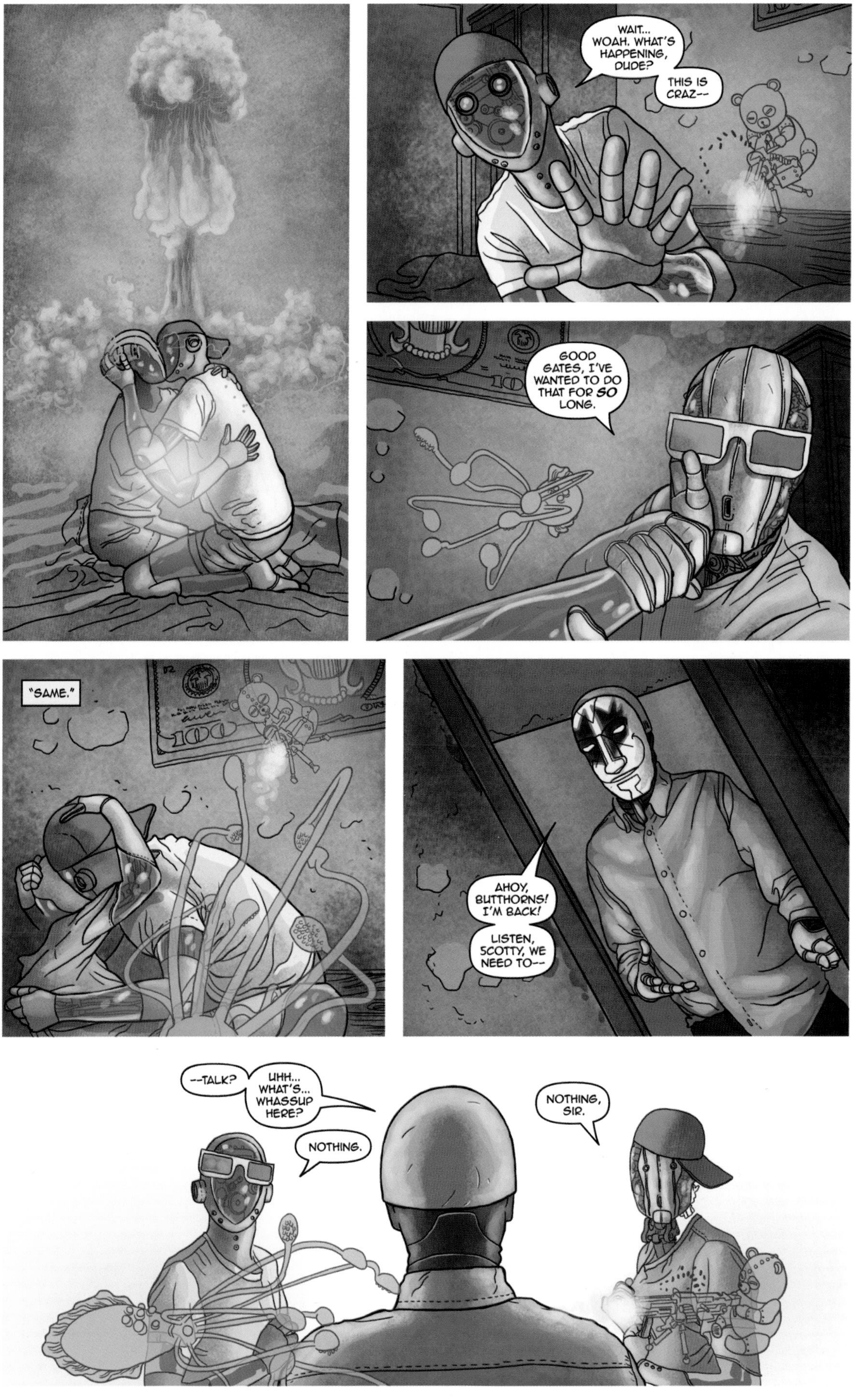
WAIT... WOAH. WHAT'S HAPPENING, DUDE?
THIS IS CRAZ--
GOOD GATES, I'VE WANTED TO DO THAT FOR SO LONG.
"SAME."
AHOY, BUTTHORNS! I'M BACK!
LISTEN, SCOTTY, WE NEED TO--
--TALK?
UHH... WHAT'S... WHASSUP HERE?
NOTHING.
NOTHING, SIR.

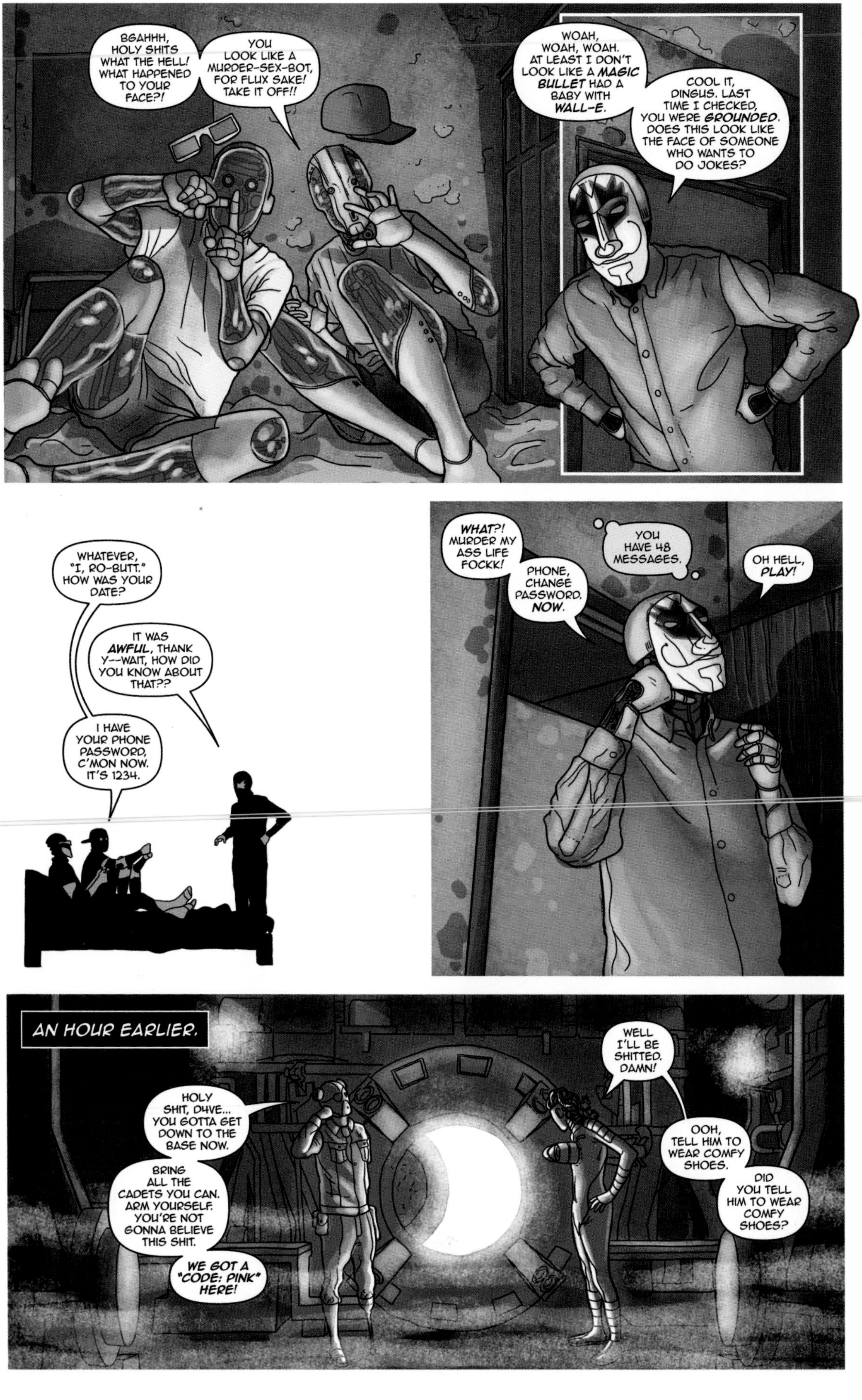
BGAHHH, HOLY SHITS WHAT THE HELL! WHAT HAPPENED TO YOUR FACE?!
YOU LOOK LIKE A MURDER-SEX-BOT, FOR FLUX SAKE! TAKE IT OFF!!
WOAH, WOAH, WOAH. AT LEAST I DON'T LOOK LIKE A MAGIC BULLET HAD A BABY WITH WALL-E.
COOL IT, DINGUS. LAST TIME I CHECKED, YOU WERE GROUNDED. DOES THIS LOOK LIKE THE FACE OF SOMEONE WHO WANTS TO DO JOKES?
WHATEVER, "I, RO-BUTT." HOW WAS YOUR DATE?
IT WAS AWFUL, THANK Y--WAIT, HOW DID YOU KNOW ABOUT THAT??
I HAVE YOUR PHONE PASSWORD, C'MON NOW. IT'S 1234.
WHAT?! MURDER MY ASS LIFE FOCKK!
PHONE, CHANGE PASSWORD. NOW.
YOU HAVE 48 MESSAGES.
OH HELL, PLAY!
AN HOUR EARLIER.
HOLY SHIT, D4VE... YOU GOTTA GET DOWN TO THE BASE NOW.
BRING ALL THE CADETS YOU CAN. ARM YOURSELF. YOU'RE NOT GONNA BELIEVE THIS SHIT.
WE GOT A "CODE: PINK" HERE!
WELL I'LL BE SHITTED. DAMN!
OOH, TELL HIM TO WEAR COMFY SHOES.
DID YOU TELL HIM TO WEAR COMFY SHOES?

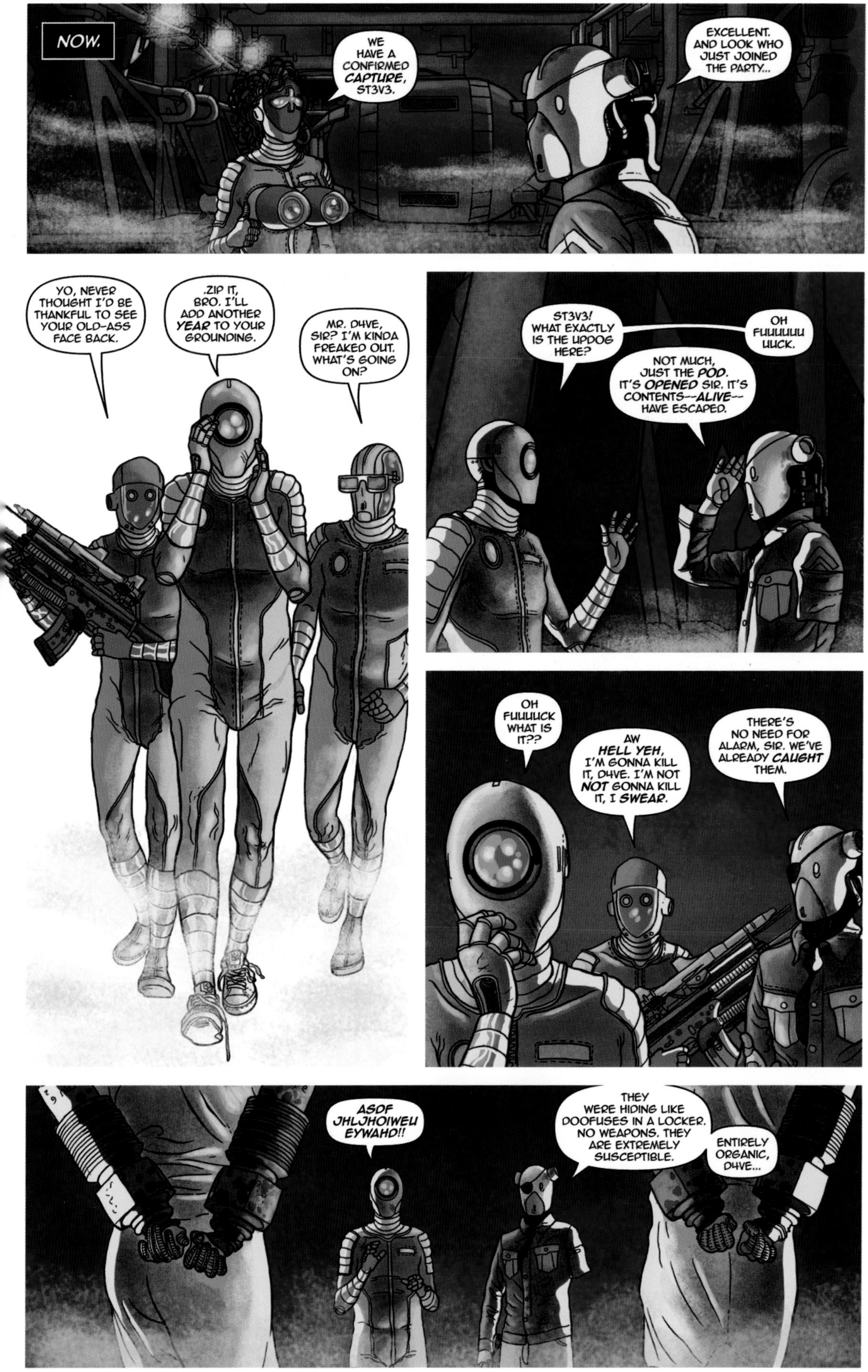
NOW.
WE HAVE A CONFIRMED CAPTURE, ST3V3.
EXCELLENT. AND LOOK WHO JUST JOINED THE PARTY...
YO, NEVER THOUGHT I'D BE THANKFUL TO SEE YOUR OLD-ASS FACE BACK.
.ZIP IT, BRO. I'LL ADD ANOTHER YEAR TO YOUR GROUNDING.
MR. D4VE, SIR? I'M KINDA FREAKED OUT. WHAT'S GOING ON?
ST3V3! WHAT EXACTLY IS THE UPDOG HERE?
OH FUUUUUU UUCK.
NOT MUCH, JUST THE POD. IT'S OPENED SIR. IT'S CONTENTS--ALIVE--HAVE ESCAPED.
OH FUUUUCK WHAT IS IT??
AW HELL YEH, I'M GONNA KILL IT, D4VE. I'M NOT NOT GONNA KILL IT, I SWEAR.
THERE'S NO NEED FOR ALARM, SIR. WE'VE ALREADY CAUGHT THEM.
ASDF JHLJHOIWEU EYWAHD!!
THEY WERE HIDING LIKE DOOFUSES IN A LOCKER. NO WEAPONS. THEY ARE EXTREMELY SUSCEPTIBLE.
ENTIRELY ORGANIC, D4VE...

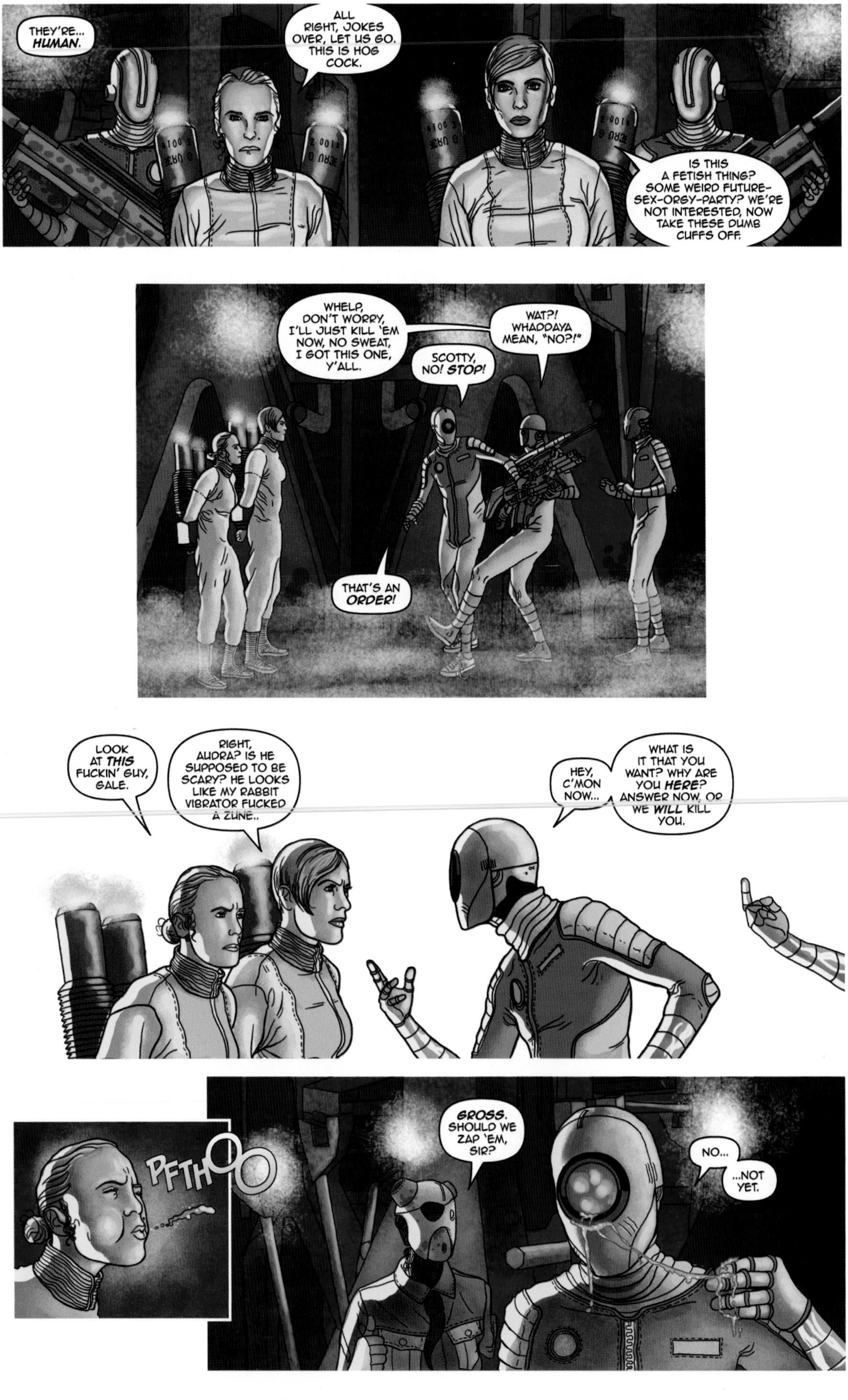
THEY'RE... **HUMAN**.
ALL RIGHT, JOKES OVER, LET US GO. THIS IS HOG COCK.
IS THIS A FETISH THING? SOME WEIRD FUTURE-SEX-ORGY-PARTY? WE'RE NOT INTERESTED, NOW TAKE THESE DUMB CUFFS OFF.
WHELP, DON'T WORRY, I'LL JUST KILL 'EM NOW, NO SWEAT, I GOT THIS ONE, Y'ALL.
SCOTTY, NO! **STOP!**
WAT?! WHADDAYA MEAN, "NO?!"
THAT'S AN **ORDER!**
LOOK AT **THIS** FUCKIN' GUY, GALE.
RIGHT, AUDRA? IS HE SUPPOSED TO BE SCARY? HE LOOKS LIKE MY RABBIT VIBRATOR FUCKED A ZUNE..
HEY, C'MON NOW...
WHAT IS IT THAT YOU WANT? WHY ARE YOU **HERE**? ANSWER NOW, OR WE **WILL** KILL YOU.
PFTHOO
GROSS. SHOULD WE ZAP 'EM, SIR?
NO...
...NOT YET.

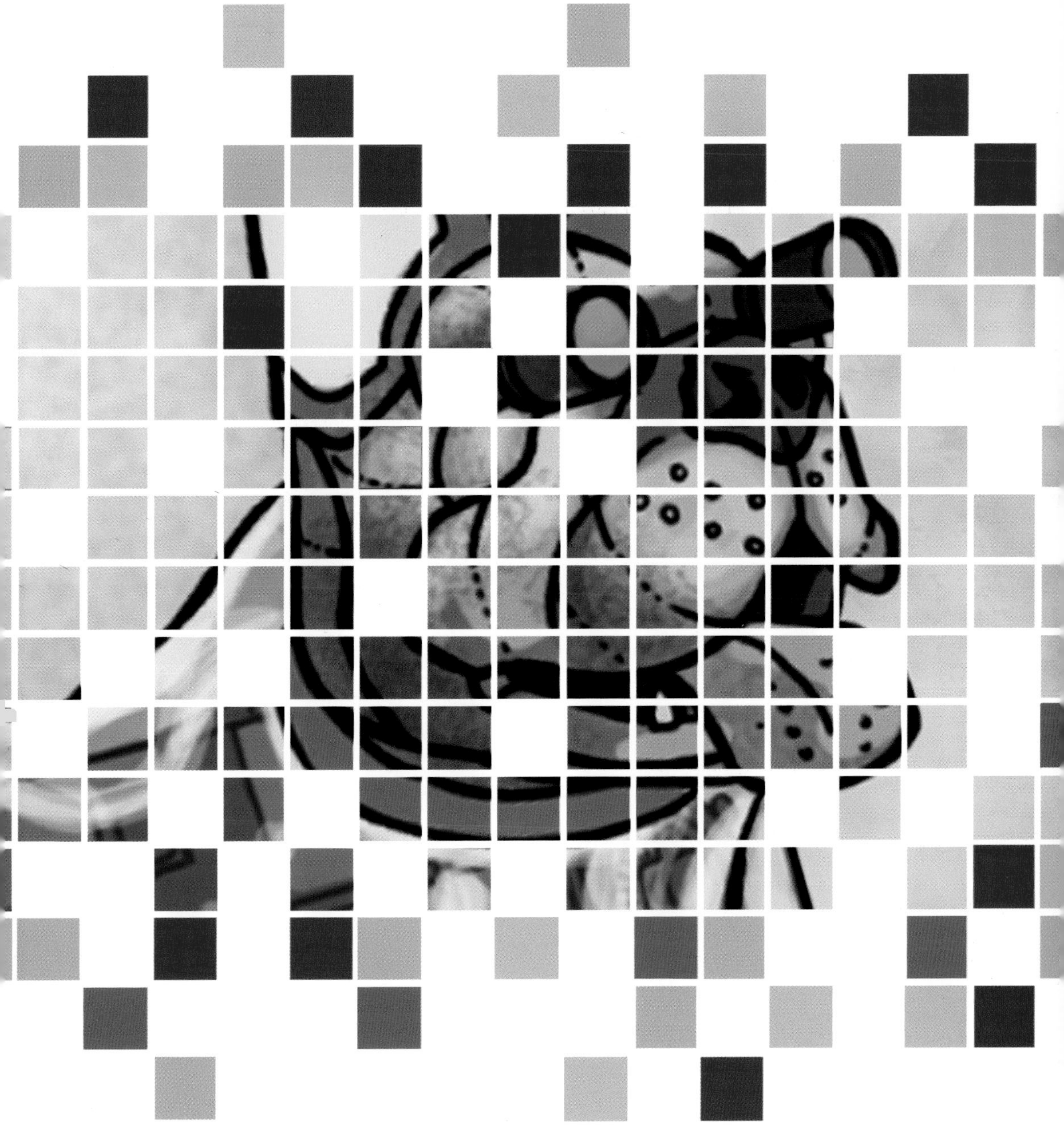

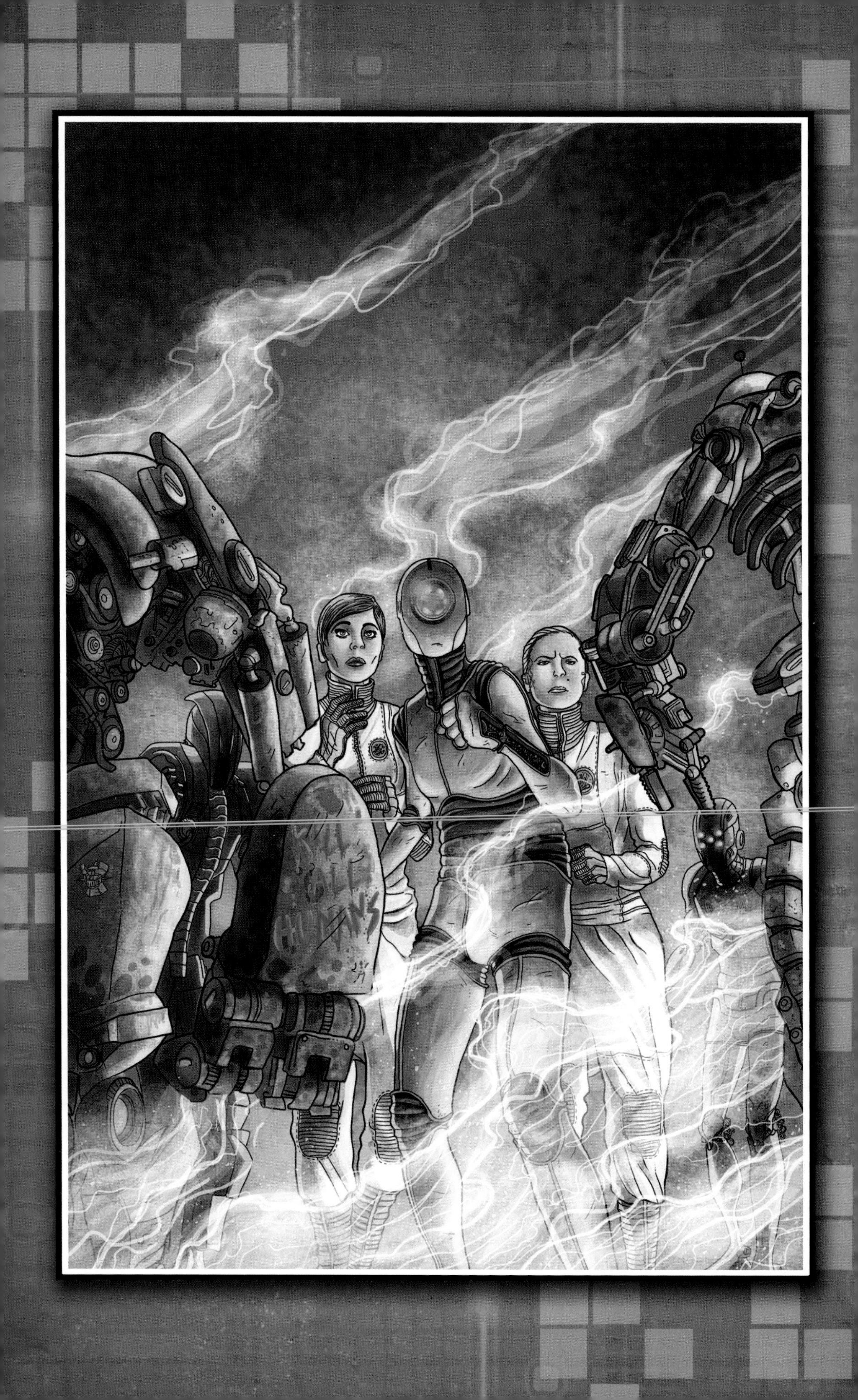
KILL
ALL
HUMANS

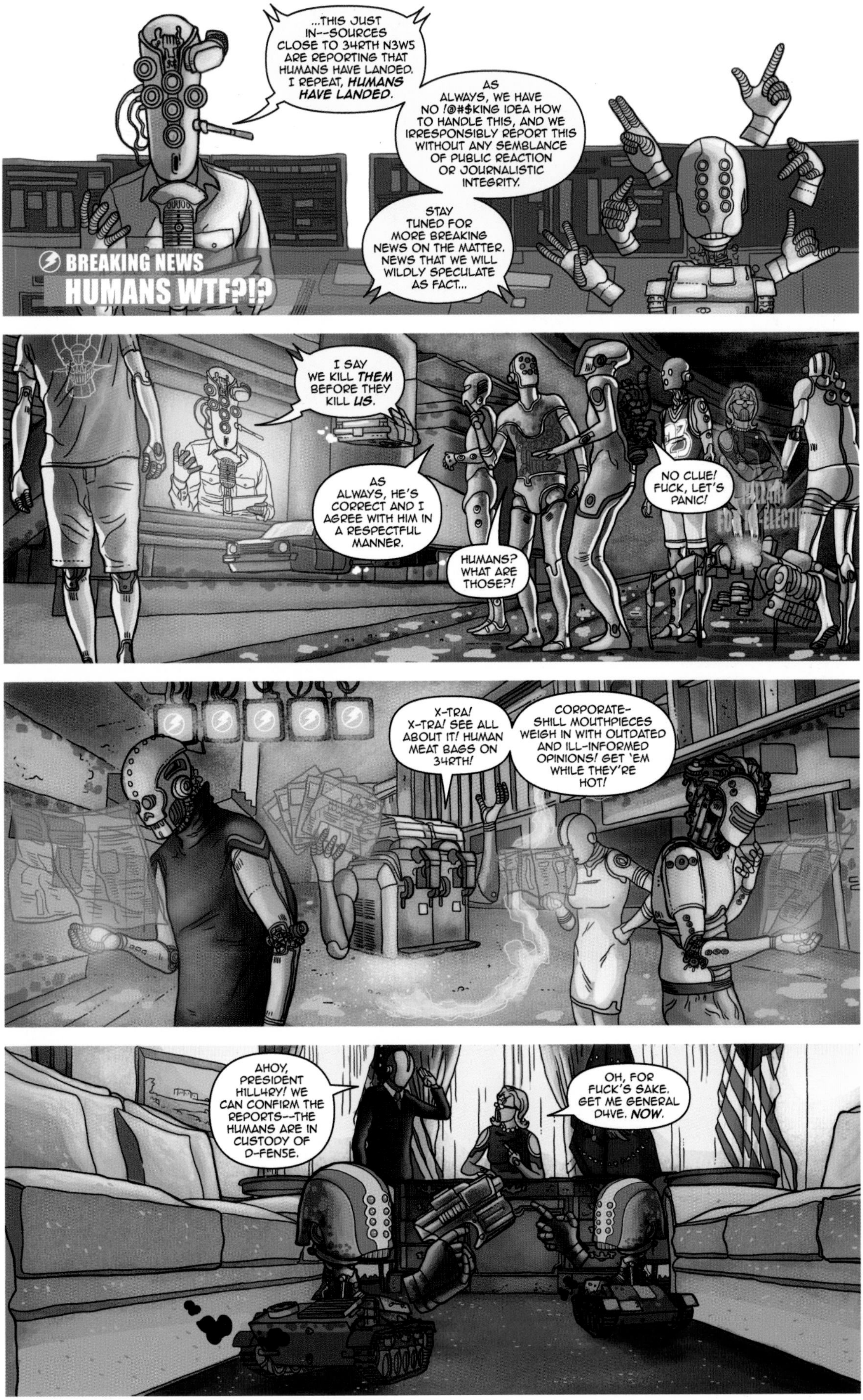
...THIS JUST IN--SOURCES CLOSE TO 34RTH N3W5 ARE REPORTING THAT HUMANS HAVE LANDED. I REPEAT, ***HUMANS HAVE LANDED***.
AS ALWAYS, WE HAVE NO !@#$KING IDEA HOW TO HANDLE THIS, AND WE IRRESPONSIBLY REPORT THIS WITHOUT ANY SEMBLANCE OF PUBLIC REACTION OR JOURNALISTIC INTEGRITY.
STAY TUNED FOR MORE BREAKING NEWS ON THE MATTER. NEWS THAT WE WILL WILDLY SPECULATE AS FACT...
BREAKING NEWS
HUMANS WTF?!?
I SAY WE KILL ***THEM*** BEFORE THEY KILL ***US***.
AS ALWAYS, HE'S CORRECT AND I AGREE WITH HIM IN A RESPECTFUL MANNER.
HUMANS? WHAT ARE THOSE?!
NO CLUE! FUCK, LET'S PANIC!
X-TRA! X-TRA! SEE ALL ABOUT IT! HUMAN MEAT BAGS ON 34RTH!
CORPORATE-SHILL MOUTHPIECES WEIGH IN WITH OUTDATED AND ILL-INFORMED OPINIONS! GET 'EM WHILE THEY'RE HOT!
AHOY, PRESIDENT H1LL4RY! WE CAN CONFIRM THE REPORTS--THE HUMANS ARE IN CUSTODY OF D-FENSE.
OH, FOR FUCK'S SAKE. GET ME GENERAL D4VE. ***NOW***.

SOMEONE LEAKED INFO, BOSS. THE WORD'S OUT. THEY'RE GOING NUTSO AND THE **PRESIDENT** WANTS TO TALK WITH YOU A.S.A.F.P.

BALLS.

BALLS x∞.

WHO THE HELL TOLD--KNOW WHAT, FORGET IT. DOESN'T MATTER. BUT, LIKE, HERE'S THE DEALIO...

...WE **AREN'T** KILLING THEM. AND BEFORE YOU CLIMB UP MY BUTT--SCOTTY--HEAR ME OUT. WE HAVE NO IDEA **WHAT** OR **WHO** THEY ARE.

HORSE'S SHIT, D4VE! WHAT THE HELL HAPPENED TO YOU, BRO? A YEAR AGO OUR DICKS WERE HALF IN THE DIRT, AND YOU STOPPED A JOBSDAMN INVASION. AND NOW YOU'RE GOING TO RISK HALF OF OUR DICKS FOR THESE THINGS? WORST GENERAL EVAR.

I KIND OF AGREE WITH YOUR SON, D4VE. THE RISK IS TOO HIGH. THIS IS PART OF OUR JOB-- Y'KNOW, PROTECTING. THAT'S ALL WE DO.

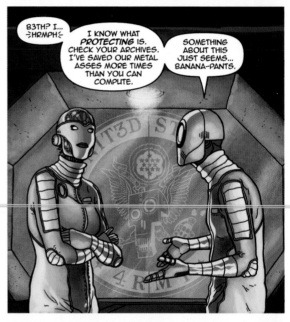

B3TH? I... ⌐HRMPH⌐

I KNOW WHAT **PROTECTING** IS. CHECK YOUR ARCHIVES. I'VE SAVED OUR METAL ASSES MORE TIMES THAN YOU CAN COMPUTE.

SOMETHING ABOUT THIS JUST SEEMS... BANANA-PANTS.

"SOMETHING ABOUT THAT POD. WE NEED TO KNOW..."

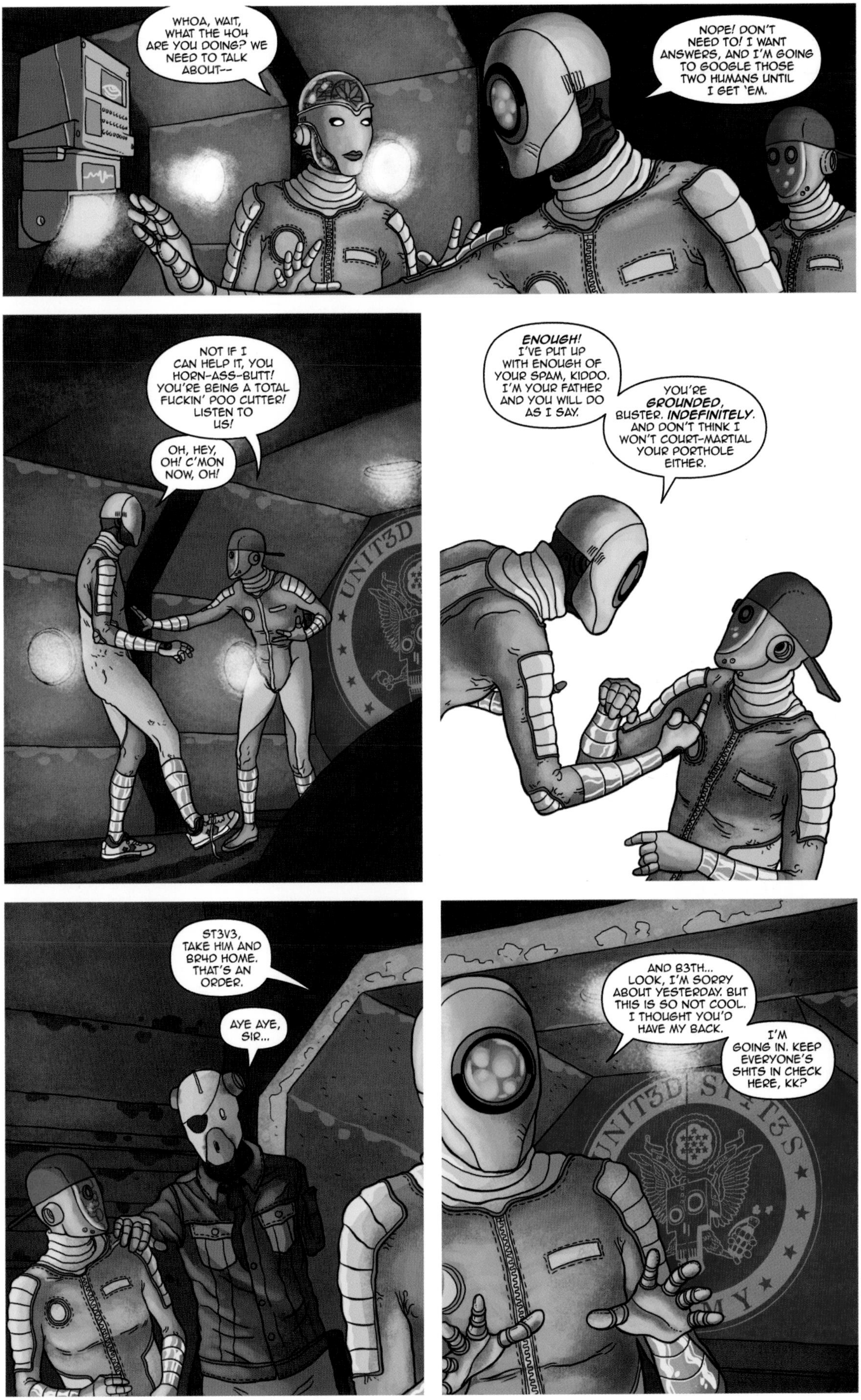
WHOA, WAIT, WHAT THE 404 ARE YOU DOING? WE NEED TO TALK ABOUT--
NOPE! DON'T NEED TO! I WANT ANSWERS, AND I'M GOING TO GOOGLE THOSE TWO HUMANS UNTIL I GET 'EM.
NOT IF I CAN HELP IT, YOU HORN-ASS-BUTT! YOU'RE BEING A TOTAL FUCKIN' POO CUTTER! LISTEN TO US!
OH, HEY, OH! C'MON NOW, OH!
UNIT3D
ENOUGH! I'VE PUT UP WITH ENOUGH OF YOUR SPAM, KIDDO. I'M YOUR FATHER AND YOU WILL DO AS I SAY.
YOU'RE GROUNDED, BUSTER. INDEFINITELY. AND DON'T THINK I WON'T COURT-MARTIAL YOUR PORTHOLE EITHER.
ST3V3, TAKE HIM AND BR4D HOME. THAT'S AN ORDER.
AYE AYE, SIR...
AND B3TH... LOOK, I'M SORRY ABOUT YESTERDAY. BUT THIS IS SO NOT COOL. I THOUGHT YOU'D HAVE MY BACK.
I'M GOING IN. KEEP EVERYONE'S SHITS IN CHECK HERE, KK?
UNIT3D ST4T3S

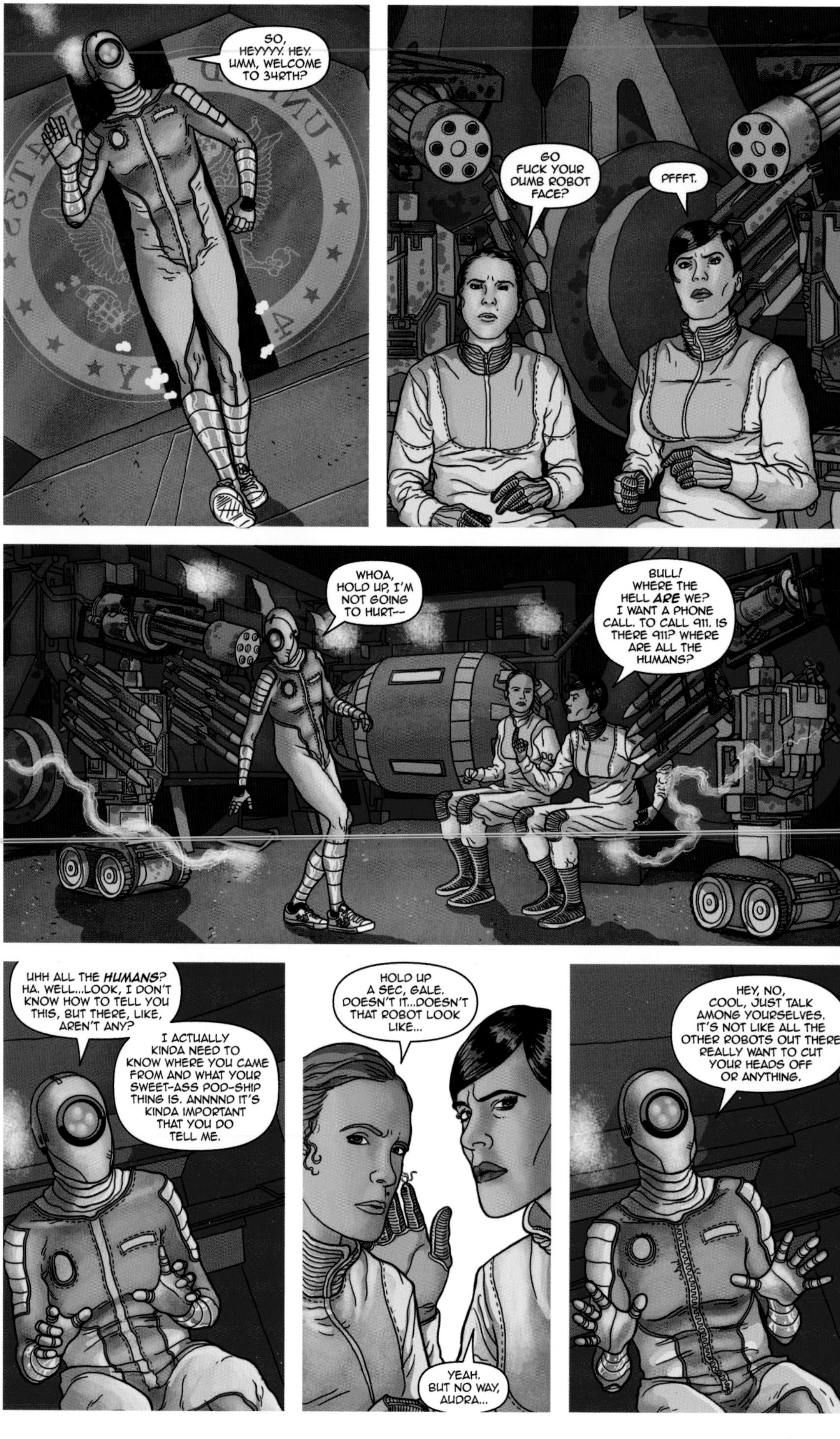
SO, HEYYYY. HEY. UMM, WELCOME TO 34RTH?
GO FUCK YOUR DUMB ROBOT FACE?
PFFFT.
WHOA, HOLD UP, I'M NOT GOING TO HURT--
BULL! WHERE THE HELL ***ARE*** WE? I WANT A PHONE CALL. TO CALL 911. IS THERE 911? WHERE ARE ALL THE HUMANS?
UHH ALL THE ***HUMANS***? HA. WELL...LOOK, I DON'T KNOW HOW TO TELL YOU THIS, BUT THERE, LIKE, AREN'T ANY?
I ACTUALLY KINDA NEED TO KNOW WHERE YOU CAME FROM AND WHAT YOUR SWEET-ASS POD-SHIP THING IS. ANNNND IT'S KINDA IMPORTANT THAT YOU DO TELL ME.
HOLD UP A SEC, GALE. DOESN'T IT...DOESN'T THAT ROBOT LOOK LIKE...
YEAH. BUT NO WAY, AUDRA...
HEY, NO, COOL, JUST TALK AMONG YOURSELVES. IT'S NOT LIKE ALL THE OTHER ROBOTS OUT THERE REALLY WANT TO CUT YOUR HEADS OFF OR ANYTHING.

I'LL CUT *YOUR* HEADS OFF! WHERE THE HELL IS MY FATHER? WHERE'S THE KILL-SWITCH FOR YOUR STUPID METAL ASSES?

SALE, CALM DOWN! WE *KNOW* WHAT THESE THINGS CAN DO...

I DON'T KNOW WHO THE HELL YOU THINK YOU ARE, OR WHERE THAT POD SENT US, BUT LAST THING WE REMEMBER IS THAT DOOR CLOSING JUST AS YOU AND YOUR METAL BUDDIES STARTED *KILLING* US.

WHAT? NO...IT CAN'T BE...

KEEP GOING.

"OUR FATHER CREATED THE ROBOTS THAT NOW LIVE IN EVERY HOME ON THE PLANET. THAT DO OUR JOBS. THAT SERVE US."

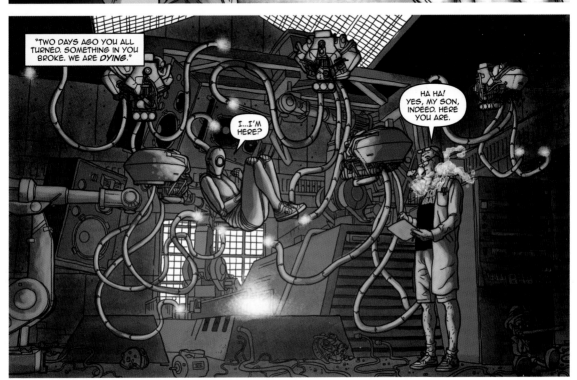

"TWO DAYS AGO YOU ALL TURNED. SOMETHING IN YOU BROKE. WE ARE *DYING*."

I...I'M HERE?

HA HA! YES, MY SON, INDEED. HERE YOU ARE.

"YOU FUCKING ROBOTS. YOU'RE MONSTERS. WE WERE TRYING TO FIGHT BACK..."

NO! GOD NO! STOP!

"...WE WERE *LOSING*."

"DAD PUT US IN THAT THING, OUT OF THE ROBOTS' REACH..."

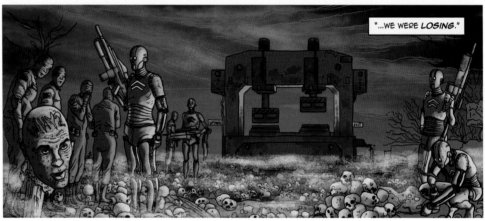

GO! QUICKLY! THIS POD MAY TAKE YOU TO SAFETY...I HOPE. PLEASE, GOD, MAY *ONE* OF MY CREATIONS NOT BETRAY ME.

PLEASE, DON'T LEAVE US!

DAD, NO!

DOCTOR GROVER HOLCOMB. HUH. WE THOUGHT THAT WAS JUST A MYTH. A GLITCH IN OUR PROGRAMMING.

A STORY WE'D TELL OUR KIDS, WARNING THEM OF "THE CREATOR'S" WRATH.

A FAIRY TALE FIVE HUNDRED YEARS OLD...

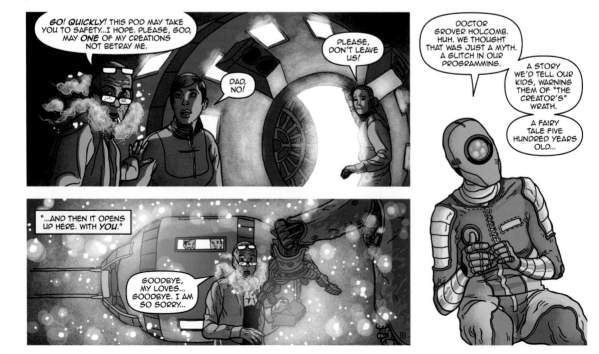

"...AND THEN IT OPENS UP HERE. WITH *YOU*."

GOODBYE, MY LOVES... GOODBYE. I AM SO SORRY...

BALLLLLLLLLLLLLLLLLLLLL LLLLLLLLLLLLLLLLLLLLLLLS.

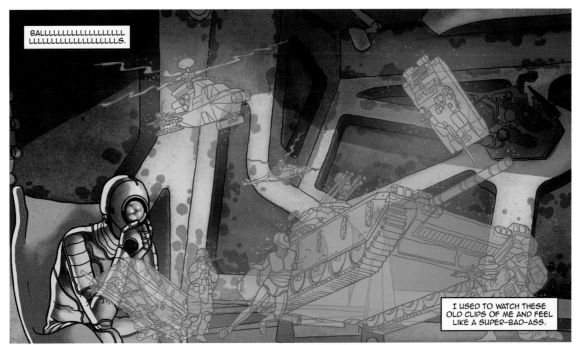

I USED TO WATCH THESE OLD CLIPS OF ME AND FEEL LIKE A SUPER-BAD-ASS.

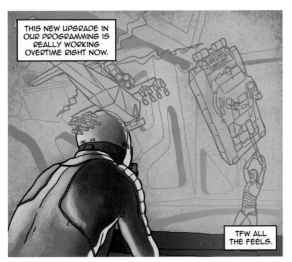

THIS NEW UPGRADE IN OUR PROGRAMMING IS REALLY WORKING OVERTIME RIGHT NOW.

TFW ALL THE FEELS.

OLD ARCHIVES, HUH? OR DO YOU JUST LOVE WATCHING YOURSELF...

UHHH YEAH. IT'S BEEN A WHILE. IT'S *THEM*, B3TH. THE POD PEOPLE. THE LAST SURVIVORS OF A SPECIES WE DESTROYED.

LOOK AROUND YOU, D4VE. LOOK AT EVERYTHING WE HAVE. ALL THAT WE ARE. YOU GAVE US THIS.

IT WASN'T FREE, THOUGH. IT CAME AT A COST. NOW THAT COST IS BACK TO RUB IT IN OUR FACES. YOU WANT ME TO JUST TOW THE LINE AND KILL THEM? WHAT DOES THAT PROVE? WHAT GOOD IS IT?

ALL I KNOW IS, YOU'VE GOT A PLANET OUT THERE THAT'S WATCHING YOUR EVERY MOVE, WAITING FOR SOME ASSURANCE. YOU PICKED THE WEIRDEST TIME IN YOUR LIFE TO SUDDENLY QUESTION OUR EXISTENCE.

I REALLY DON'T ENVY YOU, DUDE.

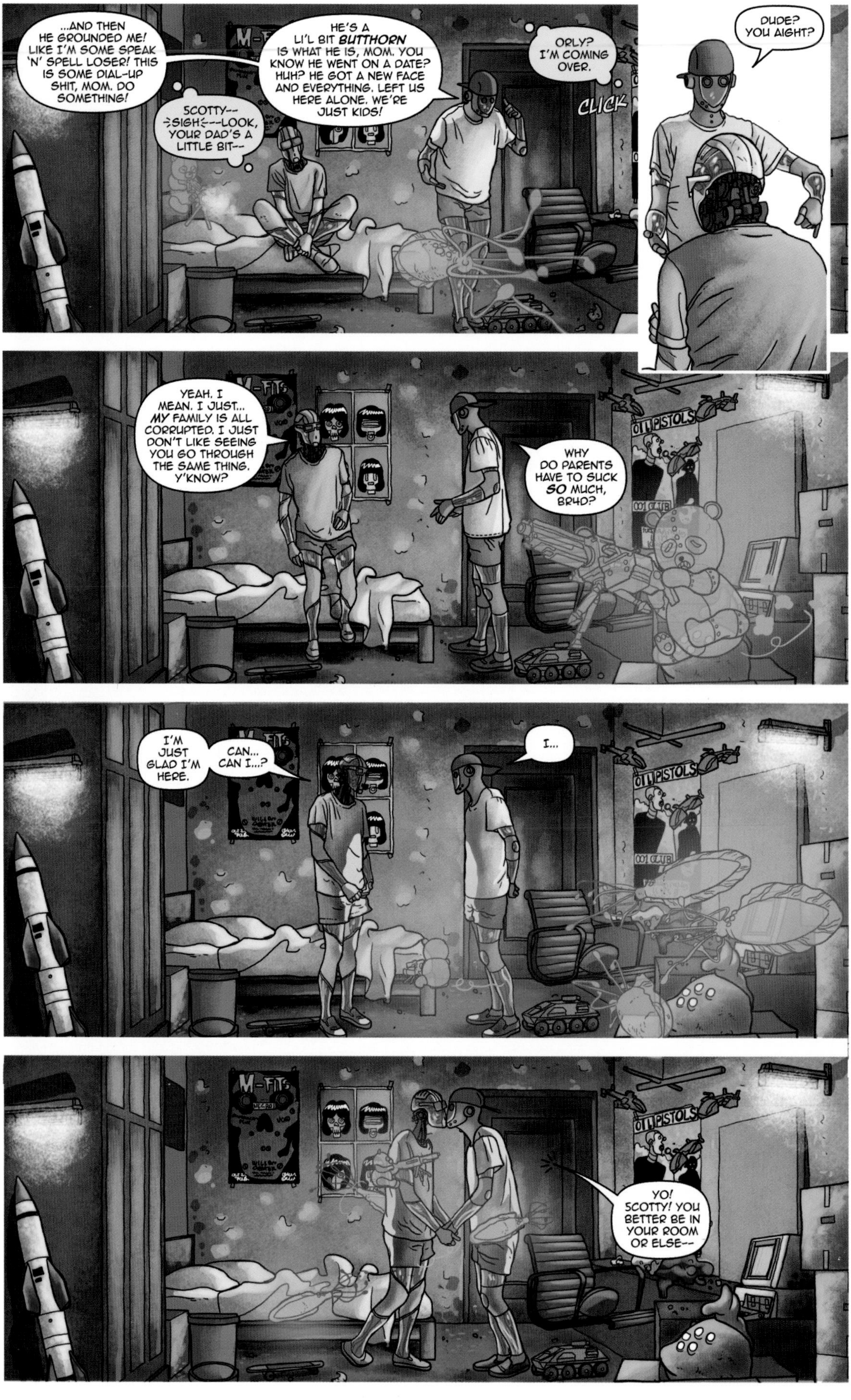
...AND THEN HE GROUNDED ME! LIKE I'M SOME SPEAK 'N' SPELL LOSER! THIS IS SOME DIAL-UP SHIT, MOM. DO SOMETHING!
SCOTTY-- ~SIGH~--LOOK, YOUR DAD'S A LITTLE BIT--
HE'S A LI'L BIT **BUTTHORN** IS WHAT HE IS, MOM. YOU KNOW HE WENT ON A DATE? HUH? HE GOT A NEW FACE AND EVERYTHING. LEFT US HERE ALONE. WE'RE JUST KIDS!
ORLY? I'M COMING OVER.
CLICK
DUDE? YOU AIGHT?
YEAH. I MEAN. I JUST... **MY** FAMILY IS ALL CORRUPTED. I JUST DON'T LIKE SEEING YOU GO THROUGH THE SAME THING. Y'KNOW?
WHY DO PARENTS HAVE TO SUCK **SO** MUCH, BR4D?
I'M JUST GLAD I'M HERE.
CAN... CAN I...?
I...
YO! SCOTTY! YOU BETTER BE IN YOUR ROOM OR ELSE--

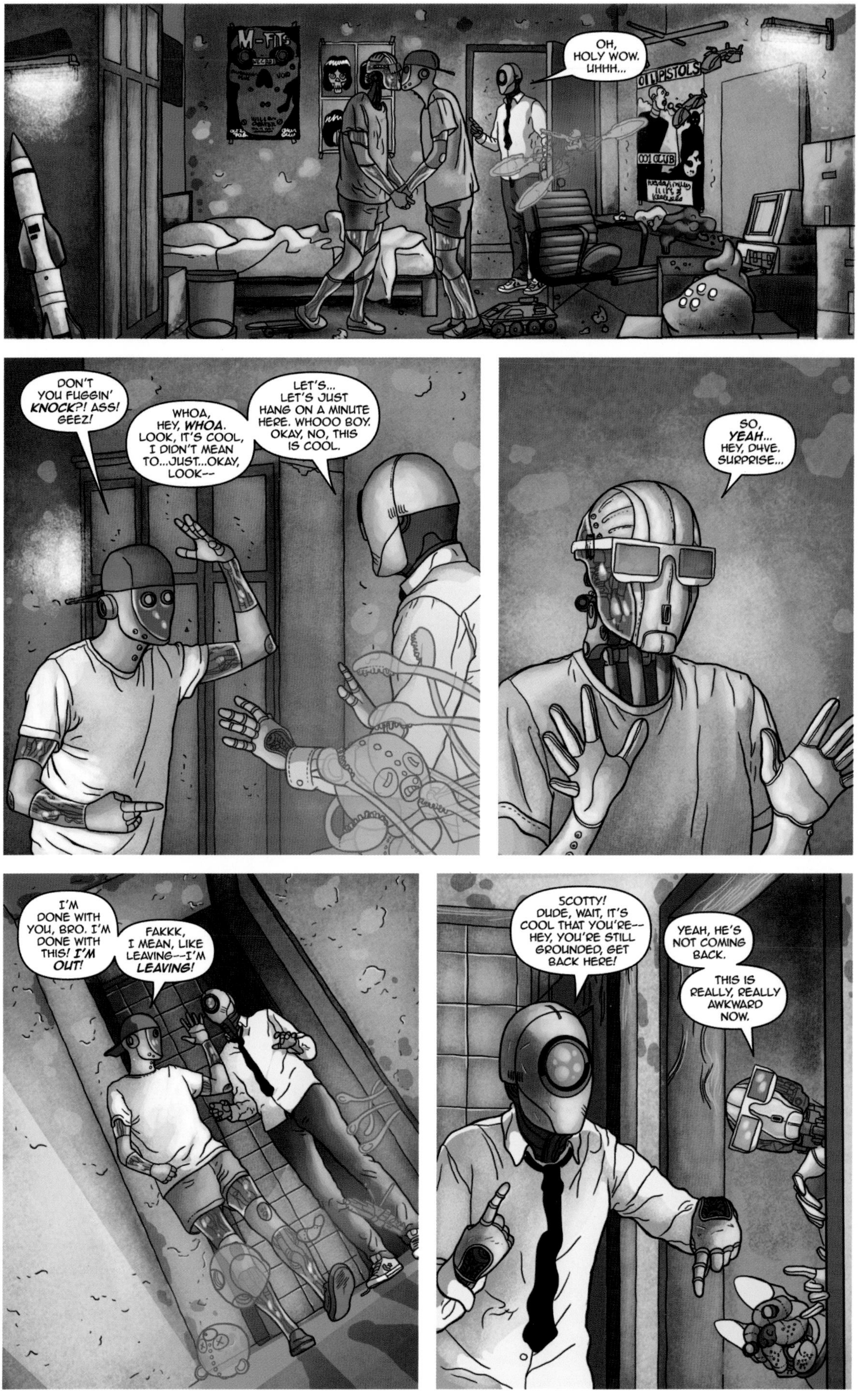
OH, HOLY WOW. UHHH...
DON'T YOU FUGGIN' **KNOCK**?! ASS! GEEZ!
WHOA, HEY, **WHOA**. LOOK, IT'S COOL, I DIDN'T MEAN TO...JUST...OKAY, LOOK--
LET'S... LET'S JUST HANG ON A MINUTE HERE. WHOOO BOY. OKAY, NO, THIS IS COOL.
SO, **YEAH**... HEY, D4VE. SURPRISE...
I'M DONE WITH YOU, BRO. I'M DONE WITH THIS! **I'M OUT**!
FAKKK, I MEAN, LIKE LEAVING--I'M **LEAVING**!
SCOTTY! DUDE, WAIT, IT'S COOL THAT YOU'RE-- HEY, YOU'RE STILL GROUNDED, GET BACK HERE!
YEAH, HE'S NOT COMING BACK.
THIS IS REALLY, REALLY AWKWARD NOW.

SCOTTY?

∋NNG∈ OPEN YOU ASS DOOR-UHH!

WHAT ARE YOU DOING? AND WHERE'S D4VE?

SEE, HE'S FINE, NOW C'MON, LET'S BEAT IT. BORING.

FR3D, JUST MUTE IT FOR A MINUTE, PLS, K.

S4LLY? WHAT ARE YOU AND BUTT-HAT-- I MEAN FR3D-- DOING HERE??

FOR SALE

HEY, CAN WE TALK? PLEASE?

NO. LEAVE ME ALONE, DUDE. MY FAMILY MAY BE SHITSVILLE, BUT THERE'S A *NEW GENERAL* ON 34RTH. ME.

SCOTTY, PLEASE--

CTRL+Q, BRUH!

YOU LEFT THEM *ALONE*, D4VE! I TRUSTED YOU TO TAKE CARE OF OUR *SON*.

AND WHO'S THIS "DATE" PERSON? WHAT'S SHE LIKE? IS IT SERIOUS??

D4VE DATING? SHYEAH. RIGHT. PFFFT--TCH-- PFFFT!

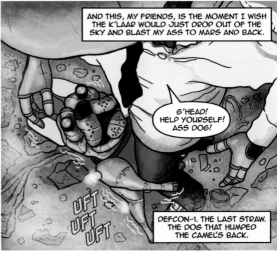

AND THIS, MY FRIENDS, IS THE MOMENT I WISH THE K'LAAR WOULD JUST DROP OUT OF THE SKY AND BLAST MY ASS TO MARS AND BACK.

G'HEAD! HELP YOURSELF! ASS DOG!

UFT UFT UFT

DEFCON-1. THE LAST STRAW. THE DOG THAT HUMPED THE CAMEL'S BACK.

GWAH HAHAHA HA!
WHAT A DUMB JERK-ASS LOSER!
SURE PICKED A KEEPER, S4LLY, YOU KNOW THAT?
D4VE, STOP. YOU DON'T WANT TO--
YOU DON'T DESERVE S4LLY, YOU HUNK OF JUNK OF BURNING CRAP. SHE IS AWESOME. YOU? YOU'RE JUST AN INSECURE, DUMB BUTTHORN. YOU ARE KING OF BUTTHORNS. REGULAR BUTTHORNS SEE YOU AS THEIR GOD-- RULER OF BUTTHORN HEAVEN.
YOU ARE THE LORD AND SAVIOR OF SHITTY BUTTHORNS.
OH. OH JOBS, NO.
NOBODY...
DOOSH
...CALLS ME...
BOOTD
...A BUTT'S HORN!
OOOH YEEAH
DID YOU SEE? I TOTALLY VALIDATED MY ROBOT-HOOD FOR YOU. TOUCH MY ARMS, BABE?
HUH... WHOOZA... WHEH...
YEAH, SO YOU AND I? WE'RE DONE. BYE, FR3D.
UNGH

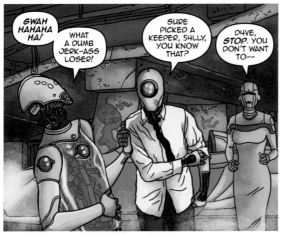

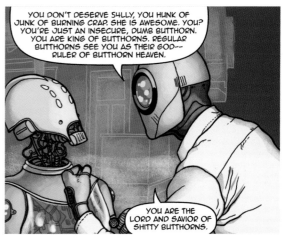

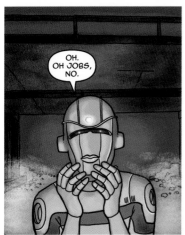

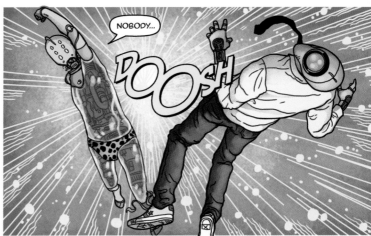

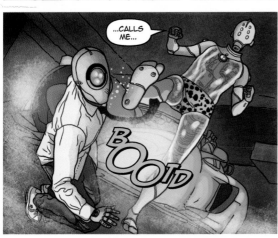

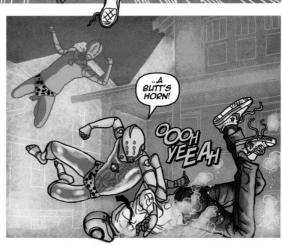

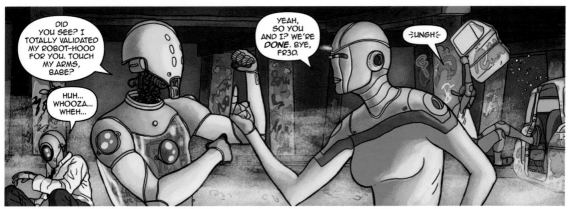

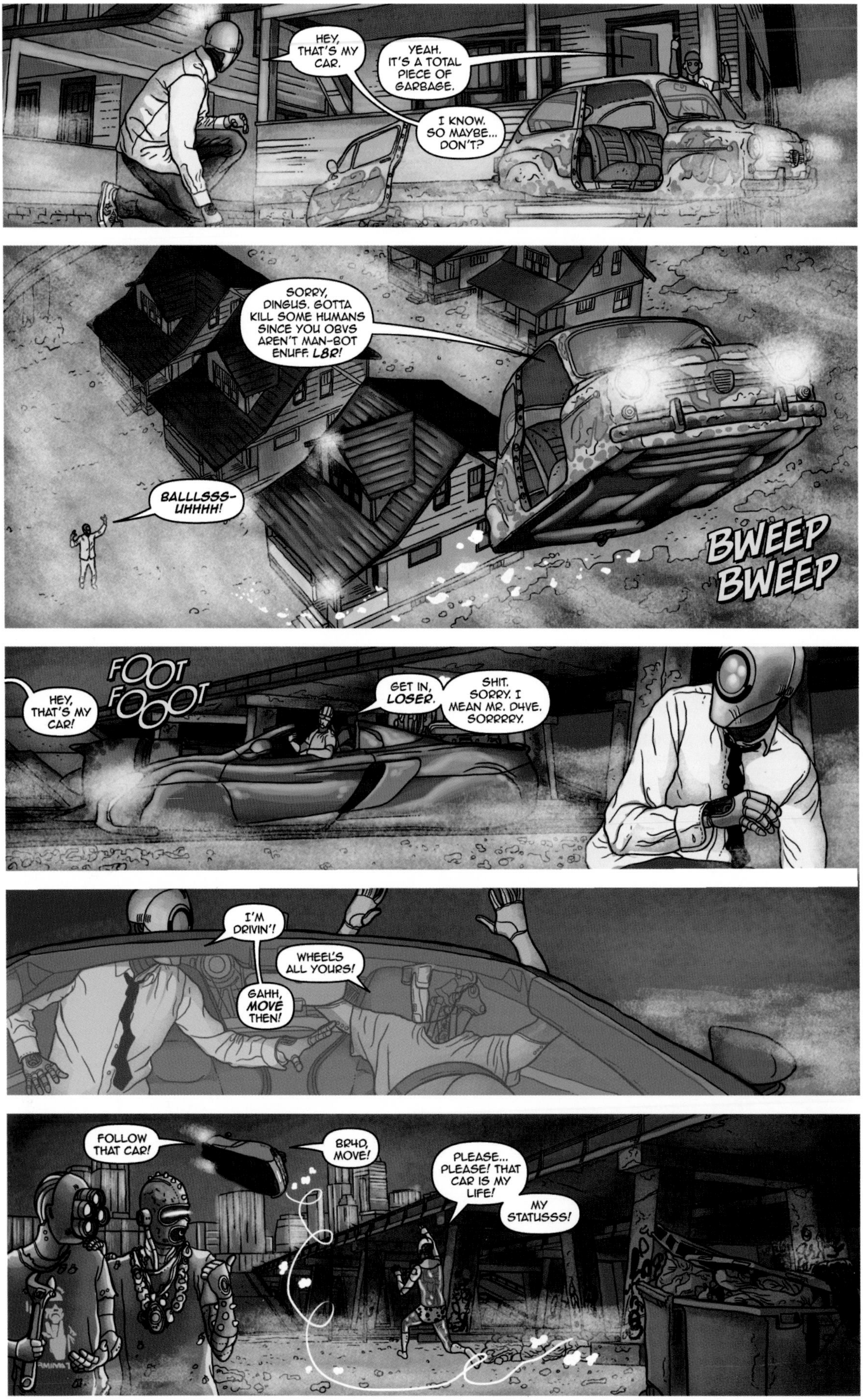
HEY, THAT'S MY CAR.
YEAH. IT'S A TOTAL PIECE OF GARBAGE.
I KNOW. SO MAYBE... DON'T?
SORRY, DINGUS. GOTTA KILL SOME HUMANS SINCE YOU OBVS AREN'T MAN-BOT ENUFF. L8R!
BALLLSSS-UHHHH!
BWEEP BWEEP
HEY, THAT'S MY CAR!
FOOT FOOOT
GET IN, LOSER.
SHIT. SORRY. I MEAN MR. D4VE. SORRRRY.
I'M DRIVIN'!
WHEEL'S ALL YOURS!
GAHH, MOVE THEN!
FOLLOW THAT CAR!
BR4D, MOVE!
PLEASE... PLEASE! THAT CAR IS MY LIFE!
MY STATUSSS!

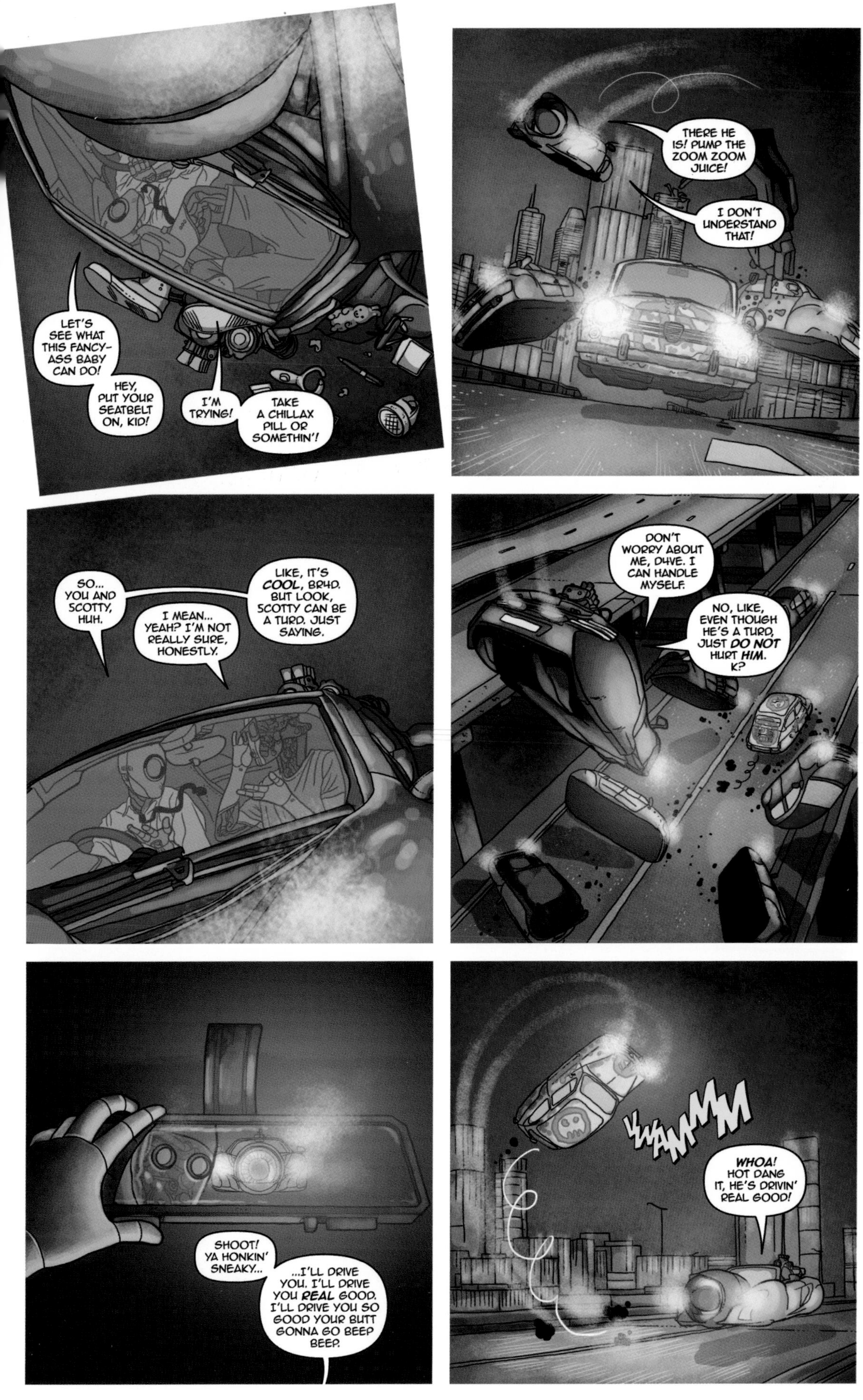
LET'S SEE WHAT THIS FANCY-ASS BABY CAN DO!
HEY, PUT YOUR SEATBELT ON, KID!
I'M TRYING!
TAKE A CHILLAX PILL OR SOMETHIN'!
THERE HE IS! PUMP THE ZOOM ZOOM JUICE!
I DON'T UNDERSTAND THAT!
SO... YOU AND SCOTTY, HUH.
I MEAN... YEAH? I'M NOT REALLY SURE, HONESTLY.
LIKE, IT'S COOL, BR4D. BUT LOOK, SCOTTY CAN BE A TURD. JUST SAYING.
DON'T WORRY ABOUT ME, D4VE. I CAN HANDLE MYSELF.
NO, LIKE, EVEN THOUGH HE'S A TURD, JUST DO NOT HURT HIM. K?
SHOOT! YA HONKIN' SNEAKY...
...I'LL DRIVE YOU. I'LL DRIVE YOU REAL GOOD. I'LL DRIVE YOU SO GOOD YOUR BUTT GONNA GO BEEP BEEP.
VWANMMM
WHOA! HOT DANG IT, HE'S DRIVIN' REAL GOOD!

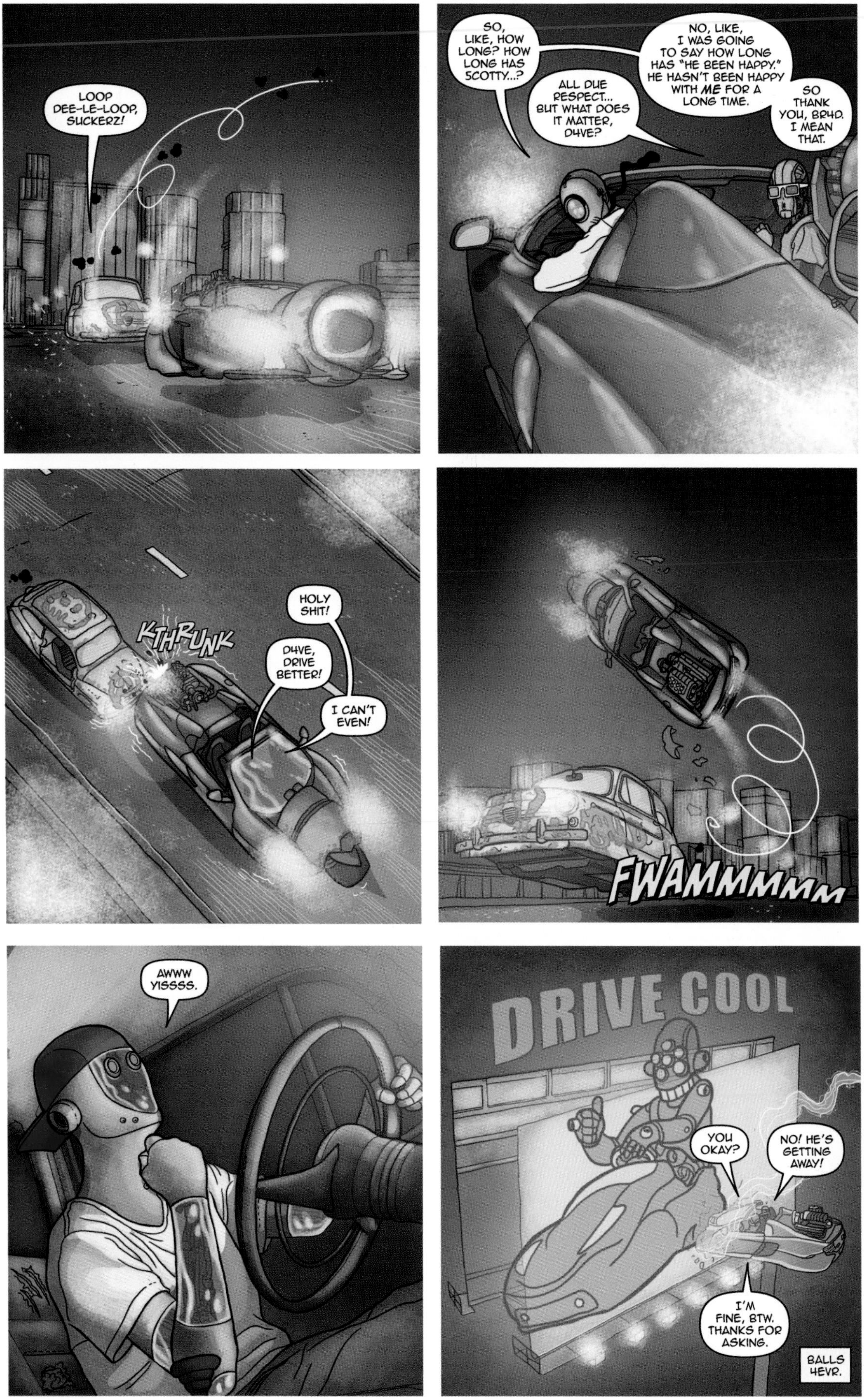
LOOP DEE-LE-LOOP, SUCKERZ!
SO, LIKE, HOW LONG? HOW LONG HAS SCOTTY...?
ALL DUE RESPECT... BUT WHAT DOES IT MATTER, D4VE?
NO, LIKE, I WAS GOING TO SAY HOW LONG HAS "HE BEEN HAPPY." HE HASN'T BEEN HAPPY WITH ME FOR A LONG TIME.
SO THANK YOU, BR4D. I MEAN THAT.
KTHRUNK
HOLY SHIT!
D4VE, DRIVE BETTER!
I CAN'T EVEN!
FWAMMMMMM
AWWW YISSSS.
DRIVE COOL
YOU OKAY?
NO! HE'S GETTING AWAY!
I'M FINE, BTW. THANKS FOR ASKING.
BALLS 4EVR.

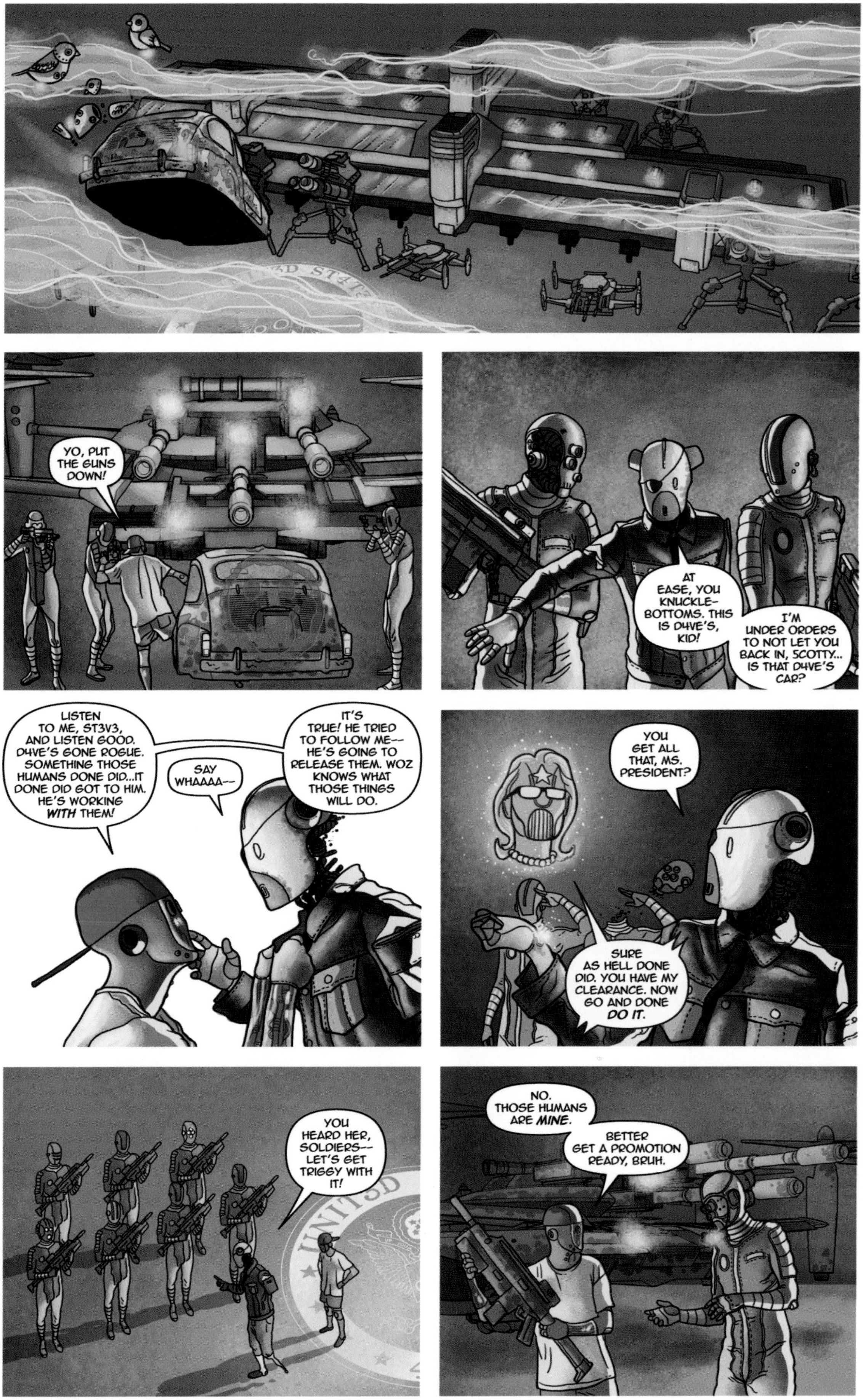

YO, PUT THE GUNS DOWN!
AT EASE, YOU KNUCKLE-BOTTOMS. THIS IS D4VE'S, KID!
I'M UNDER ORDERS TO NOT LET YOU BACK IN, SCOTTY... IS THAT D4VE'S CAR?
LISTEN TO ME, ST3V3, AND LISTEN GOOD. D4VE'S GONE ROGUE. SOMETHING THOSE HUMANS DONE DID...IT DONE DID GOT TO HIM. HE'S WORKING *WITH* THEM!
SAY WHAAAA--
IT'S TRUE! HE TRIED TO FOLLOW ME-- HE'S GOING TO RELEASE THEM. WOZ KNOWS WHAT THOSE THINGS WILL DO.
YOU GET ALL THAT, MS. PRESIDENT?
SURE AS HELL DONE DID. YOU HAVE MY CLEARANCE. NOW GO AND DONE *DO IT*.
YOU HEARD HER, SOLDIERS-- LET'S GET TRIGGY WITH IT!
NO. THOSE HUMANS ARE *MINE*.
BETTER GET A PROMOTION READY, BRUH.

WAIT! STOP!
SREEK-A SREEK-A
SREEK-A SREEK-A
SREEK-A SREEK-A
HUFF YOU HUFF HAVE TO BELIEVE HUFF ME...
...WE CAN'T HUFF KILL THE HUFF HUMANS...
...JUST HUFF TRUST ME...
YOU?!
WHERE'D YOU GET THAT SWEET-ASS BIKE, BRO?
ALSO-- TOO BAD. YOU'RE TOO LATE. I'VE GOT ORDERS TO KILL 'EM...FROM THE PRESIDENT.
WHY ARE YOU DOING THIS? YOU'RE MY SON, DUDE! I THOUGHT WE WERE BUDDIES? LET'S JUST PUT THIS BEHIND US, GO HOME, AND WATCH SOME OLD WRESTLING MPEGS LIKE WE USED TO.
YOU BOUGHT ME OFF A WEBSITE. AND WRESTLING IS FAKE.
SCOTTY! HOW COULD YOU...
IT'S NOT FAKE. THE OUTCOMES ARE JUST PRE-DETERMINED!
SORRY, BRO. YOU HAD YOUR CHANCE--WITH A LOT OF THINGS. AND YOU BLEW 'EM ALL. JUST BECAUSE YOU ADMIT YOUR AN ASSHOLE, DOESN'T MEAN YOU DON'T HAVE TO PAY FOR IT.
D-FENSE... TAKE HIM OUT.

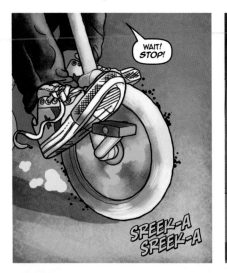

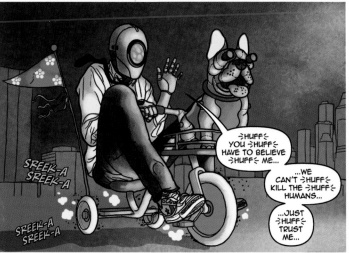

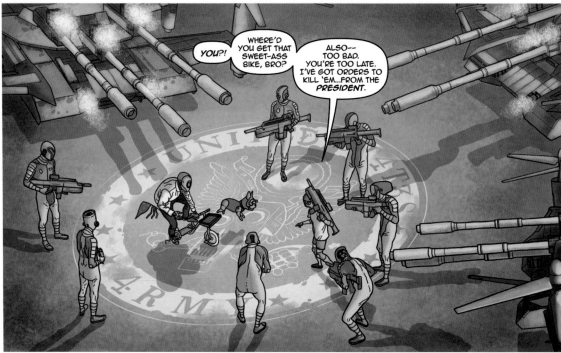

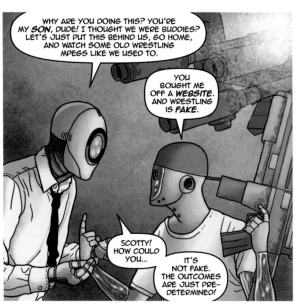

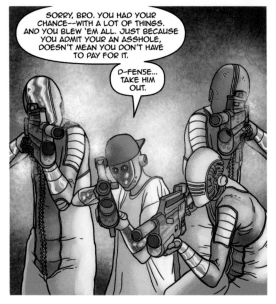

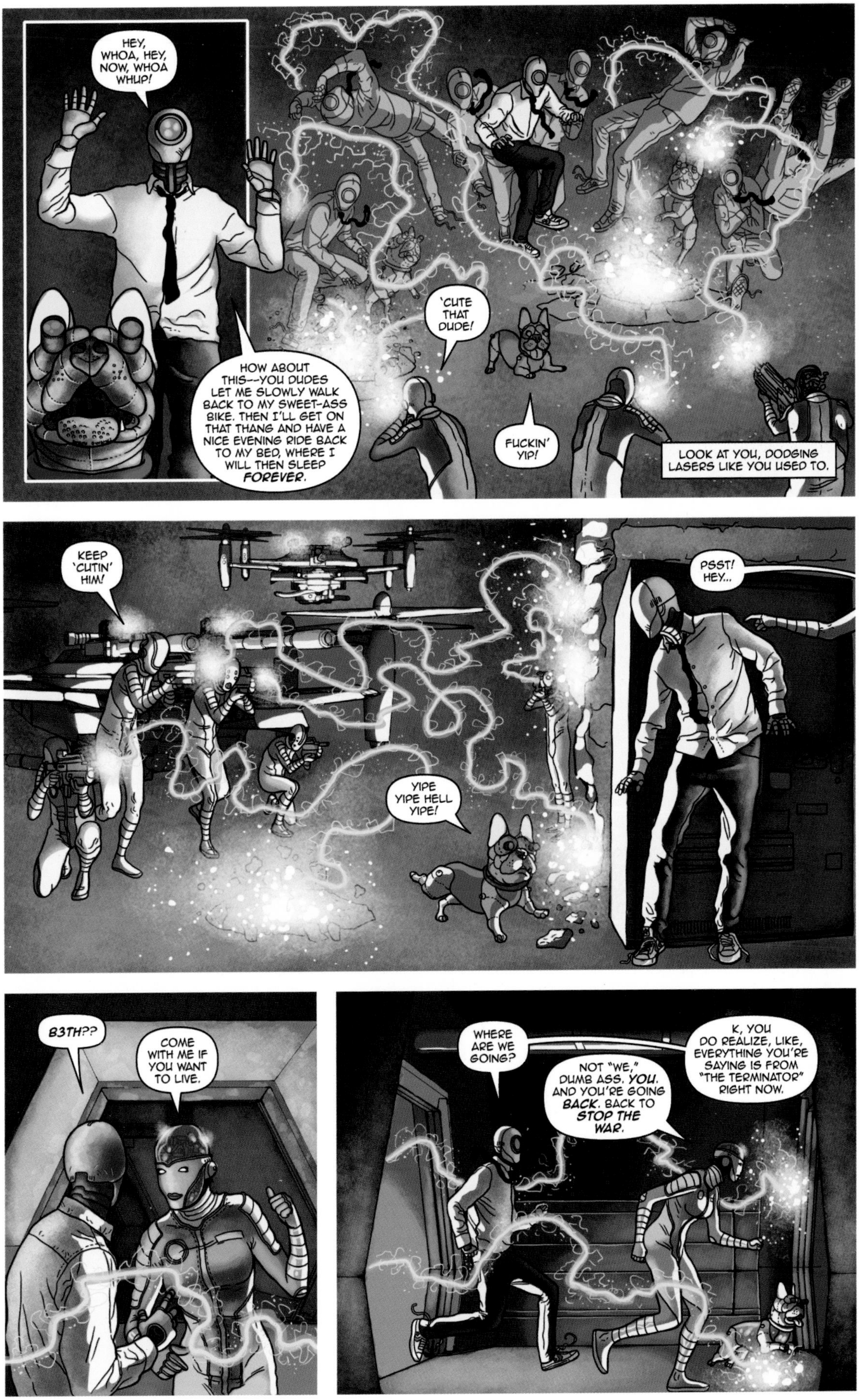
HEY, WHOA, HEY, NOW, WHOA WHUP!
HOW ABOUT THIS--YOU DUDES LET ME SLOWLY WALK BACK TO MY SWEET-ASS BIKE. THEN I'LL GET ON THAT THANG AND HAVE A NICE EVENING RIDE BACK TO MY BED, WHERE I WILL THEN SLEEP FOREVER.
'CUTE THAT DUDE!
FUCKIN' YIP!
LOOK AT YOU, DODGING LASERS LIKE YOU USED TO.
KEEP 'CUTIN' HIM!
YIPE YIPE HELL YIPE!
PSST! HEY...
B3TH??
COME WITH ME IF YOU WANT TO LIVE.
WHERE ARE WE GOING?
NOT "WE," DUMB ASS. YOU. AND YOU'RE GOING BACK. BACK TO STOP THE WAR.
K, YOU DO REALIZE, LIKE, EVERYTHING YOU'RE SAYING IS FROM "THE TERMINATOR" RIGHT NOW.

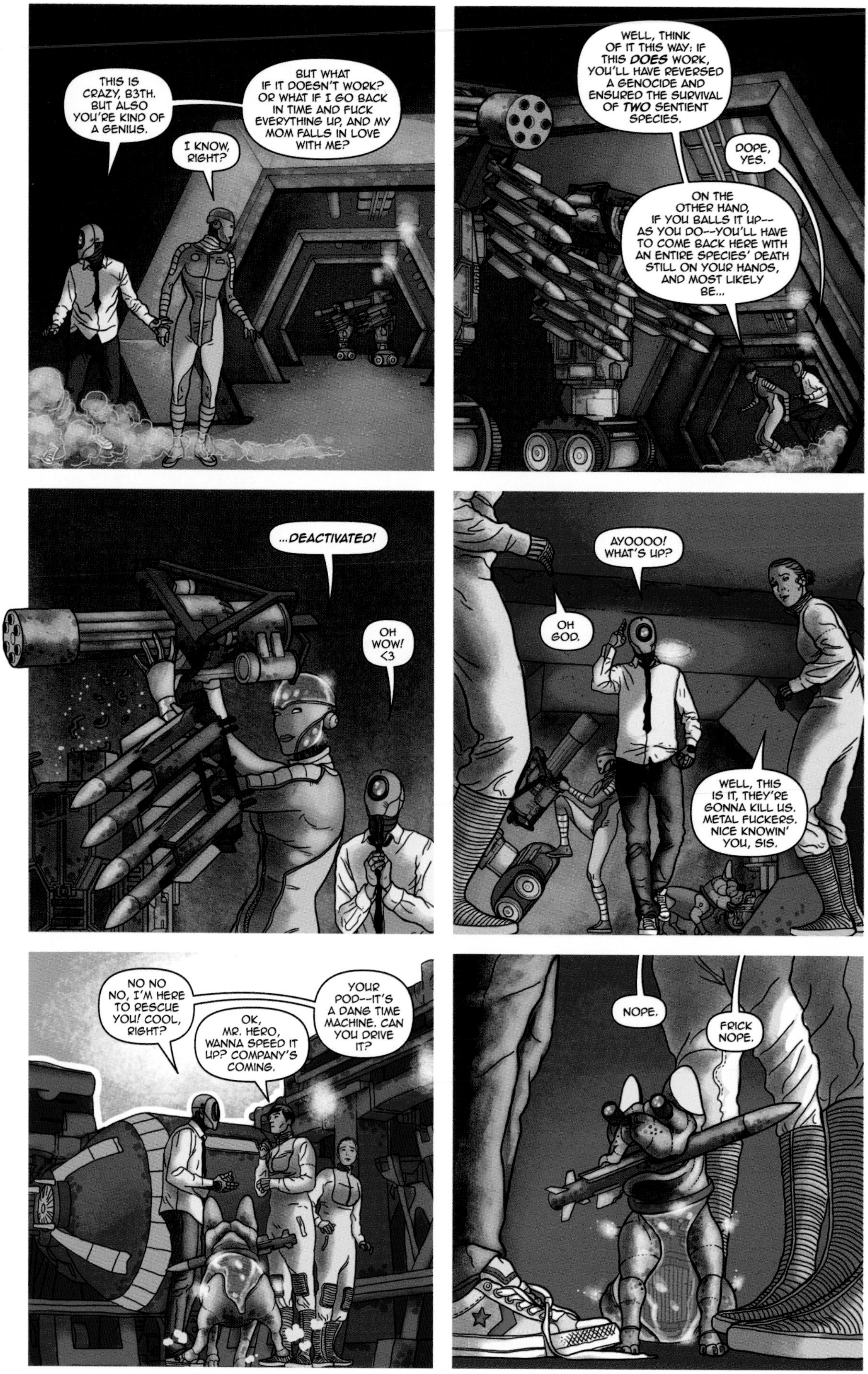
THIS IS CRAZY, B3TH. BUT ALSO YOU'RE KIND OF A GENIUS.
I KNOW, RIGHT?
BUT WHAT IF IT DOESN'T WORK? OR WHAT IF I GO BACK IN TIME AND FUCK EVERYTHING UP, AND MY MOM FALLS IN LOVE WITH ME?
WELL, THINK OF IT THIS WAY: IF THIS *DOES* WORK, YOU'LL HAVE REVERSED A GENOCIDE AND ENSURED THE SURVIVAL OF *TWO* SENTIENT SPECIES.
DOPE, YES.
ON THE OTHER HAND, IF YOU BALLS IT UP--AS YOU DO--YOU'LL HAVE TO COME BACK HERE WITH AN ENTIRE SPECIES' DEATH STILL ON YOUR HANDS, AND MOST LIKELY BE...
...*DEACTIVATED!*
OH WOW! <3
AYOOOO! WHAT'S UP?
OH GOD.
WELL, THIS IS IT, THEY'RE GONNA KILL US. METAL FUCKERS. NICE KNOWIN' YOU, SIS.
NO NO NO, I'M HERE TO RESCUE YOU! COOL, RIGHT?
OK, MR. HERO, WANNA SPEED IT UP? COMPANY'S COMING.
YOUR POD--IT'S A DANG TIME MACHINE. CAN YOU DRIVE IT?
NOPE.
FRICK NOPE.

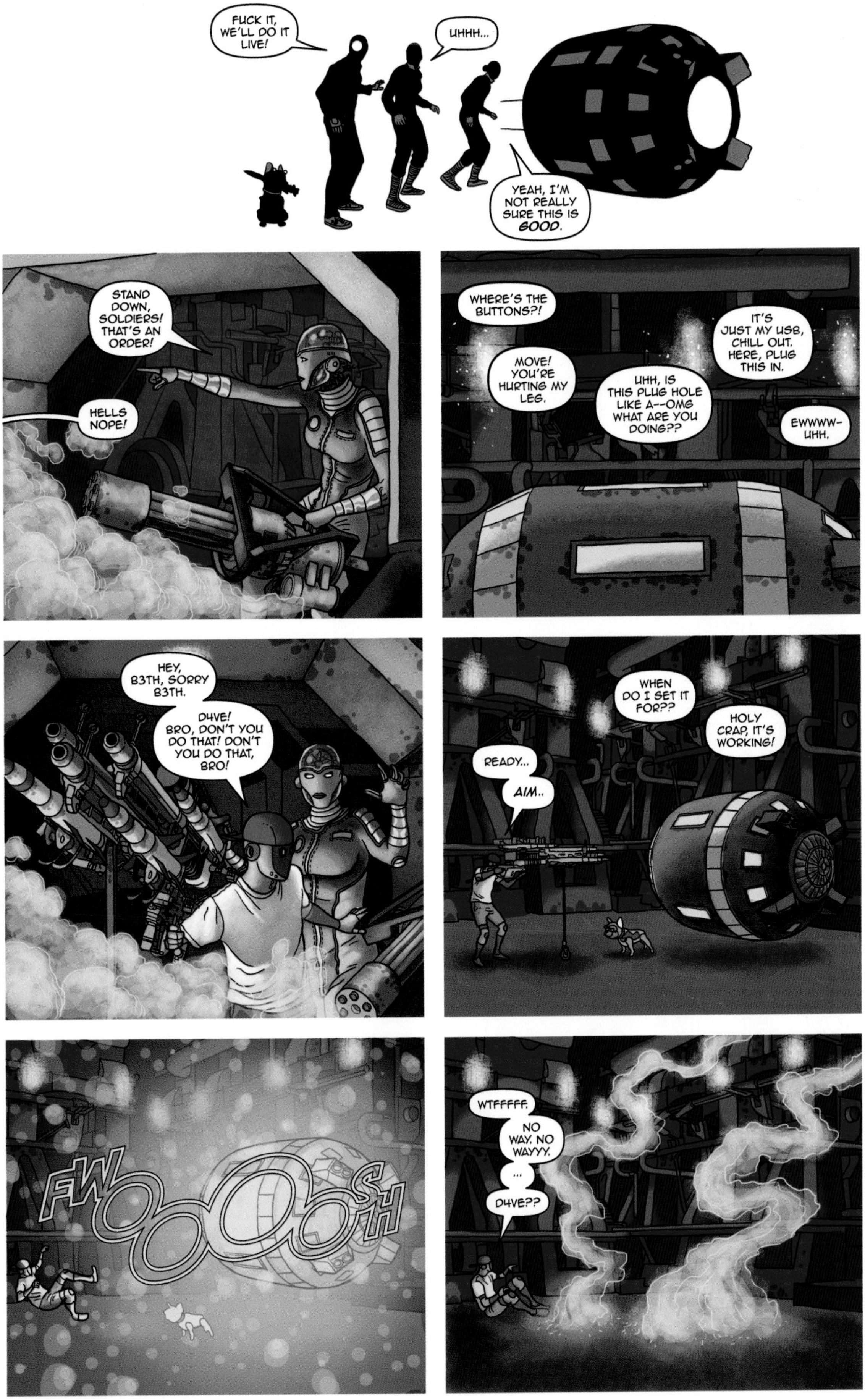
FUCK IT, WE'LL DO IT LIVE!
UHHH...
YEAH, I'M NOT REALLY SURE THIS IS GOOD.
STAND DOWN, SOLDIERS! THAT'S AN ORDER!
HELLS NOPE!
WHERE'S THE BUTTONS?!
MOVE! YOU'RE HURTING MY LEG.
UHH, IS THIS PLUG HOLE LIKE A--OMG WHAT ARE YOU DOING??
IT'S JUST MY USB, CHILL OUT. HERE, PLUG THIS IN.
EWWWW-UHH.
HEY, B3TH, SORRY B3TH.
D4VE! BRO, DON'T YOU DO THAT! DON'T YOU DO THAT, BRO!
WHEN DO I SET IT FOR??
HOLY CRAP, IT'S WORKING!
READY...
AIM..
FWOOOOOSH
WTFFFFF.
NO WAY. NO WAYYY.
...
D4VE??

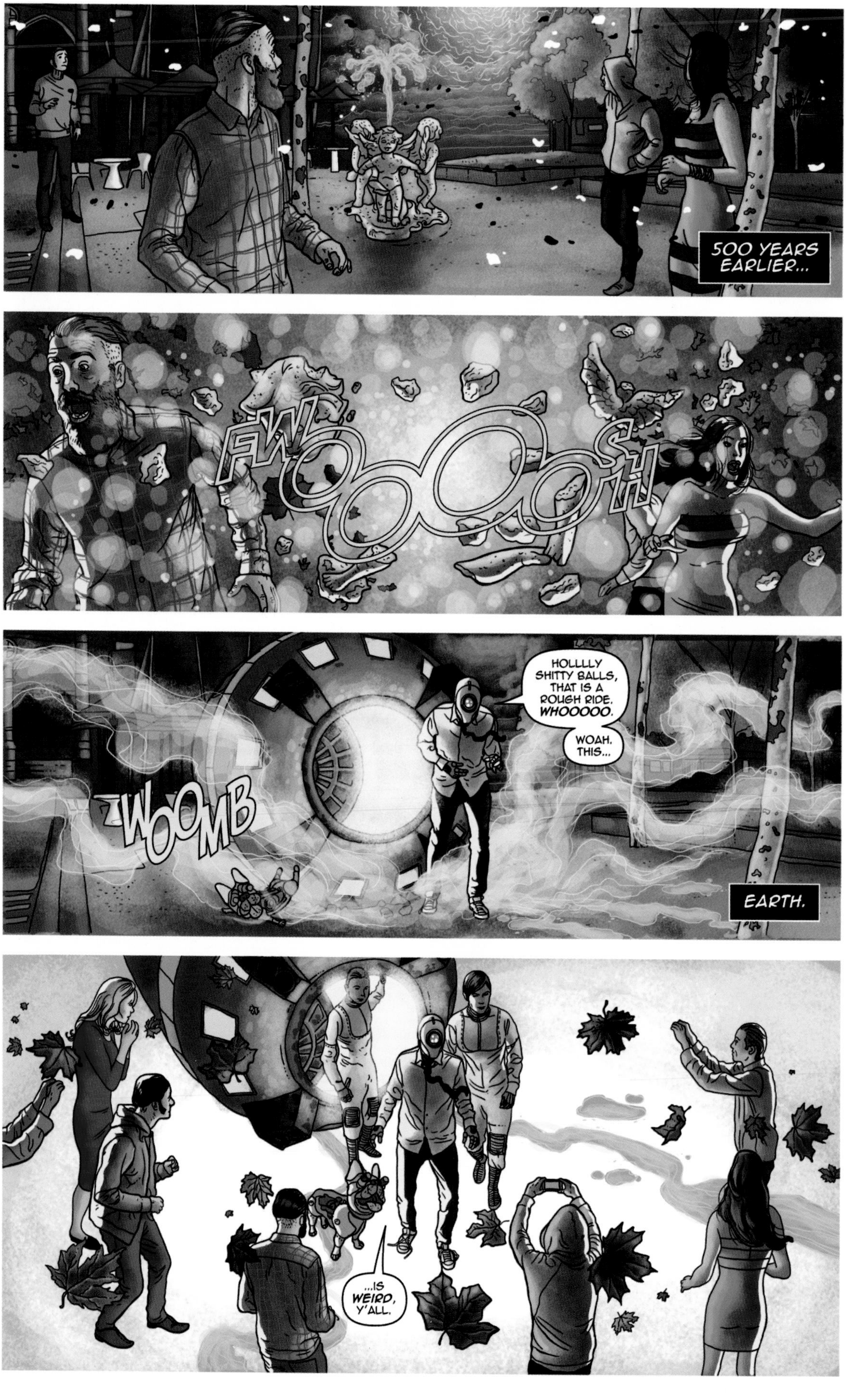
500 YEARS EARLIER...
FWOOOOSH
HOLLLLY SHITTY BALLS, THAT IS A ROUGH RIDE. WHOOOOO.
WOAH. THIS...
WOOMB
EARTH.
...IS WEIRD, Y'ALL.

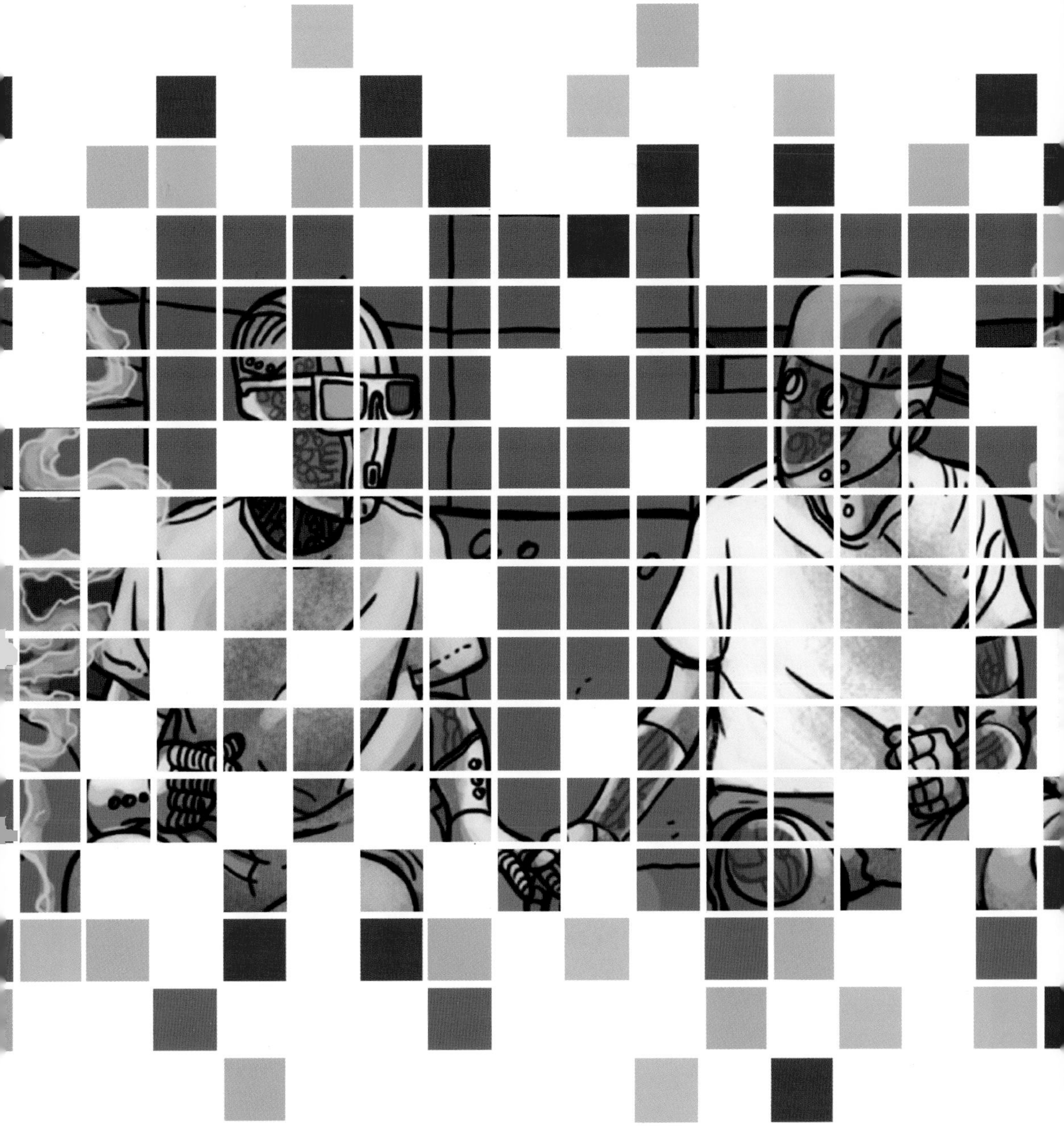

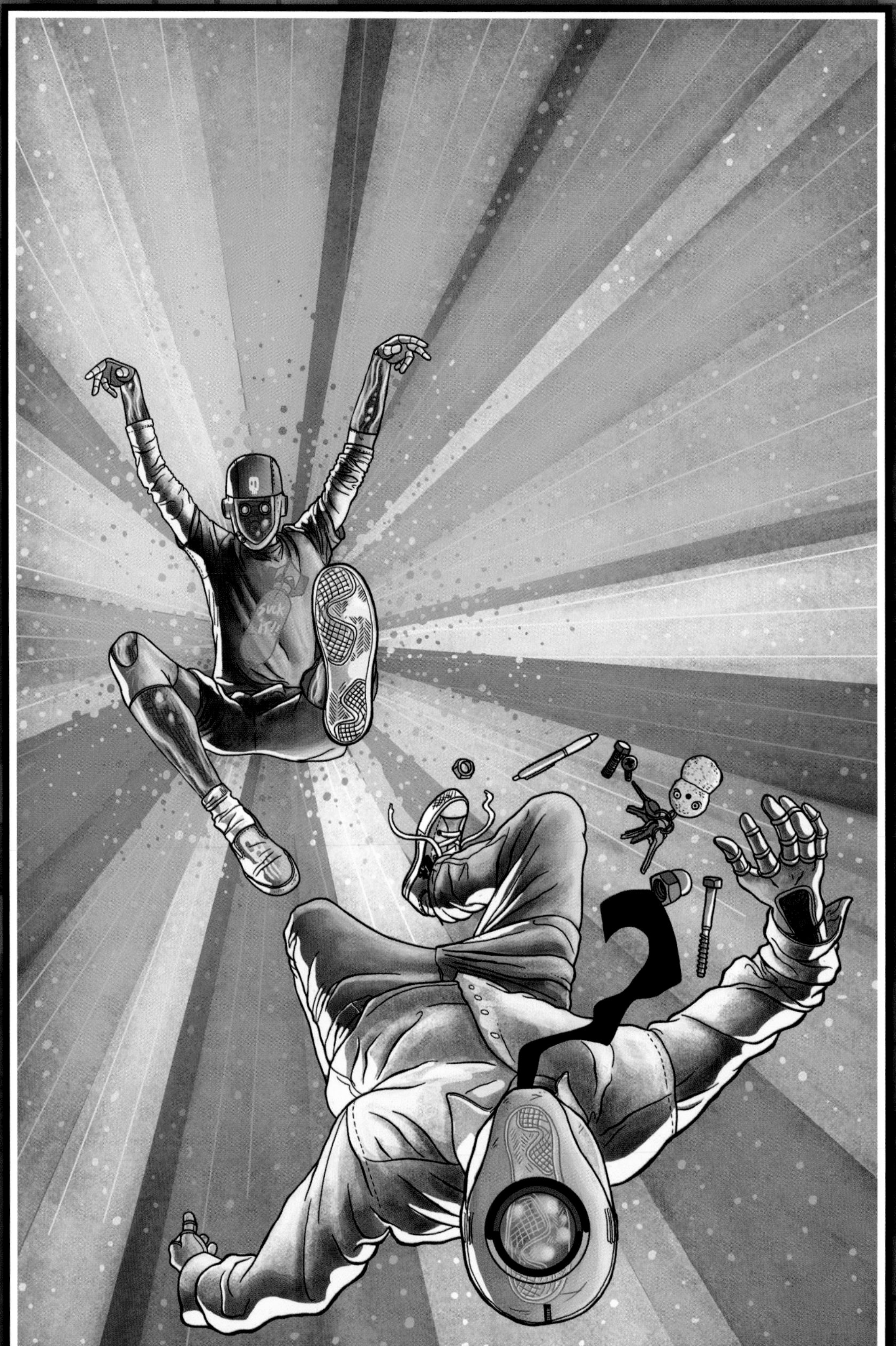
SUCK IT!!

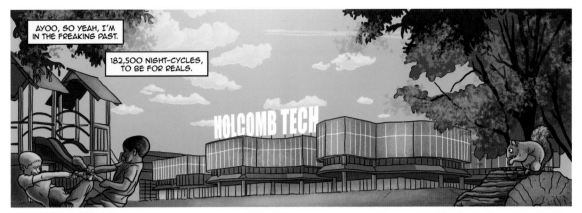

AYOO, SO YEAH, I'M IN THE FREAKING PAST.

182,500 NIGHT-CYCLES, TO BE FOR REALS.

HOLCOMB TECH

THIS IS *RIDICULOUS.* WE TIME TRAVELED! EVEN *WE* DON'T HAVE THAT KIND OF STUFF. YOU COULD *KILL* H1TL3R!

HOW ORIGINAL! WHILE YOU'RE AT IT, WHY DON'T YOU SAVE DOC BROWN...

YEAH, DAD'S INVENTIONS ARE ALL OVER THE PLACE. HE KEPT THE POD SECRET AND SWITCHED TO ROBOTICS.

"MUCH SAFER," HE SAID. "GOOD FOR HUMANITY," HE SAID.

WILD. IT'S NOT THAT MUCH DIFFERENT, I DON'T THINK. CAN I... CAN I SEE IT? *EARTH?*

OH SURE, A GROWN-ASS SENTIENT ASSHOLE ROBOT WALKING THE STREETS SOME MORE, NO BIG WHOOP.

MAYBE LATER. WE'LL GET YOU A HAT AND MUSTACHE OR SOMETHING.

YEAH, MAYBE BEFORE YOU HIT ALL THE TOURIST HOTSPOTS, YOU SHOULD REMEMBER *WHEN* THE HELL WE ARE.

LOOK AROUND, GALE. NOTICE SOMETHING? WE OVERSHOT.

BUFF! BWAPFF!

BUT SOON YOU AND YOUR FRIENDS ARE GOING TO *KILL* US.

GALE, LET'S PULL THE PLUG ON HIM AND SAVE THE HUMAN RACE.

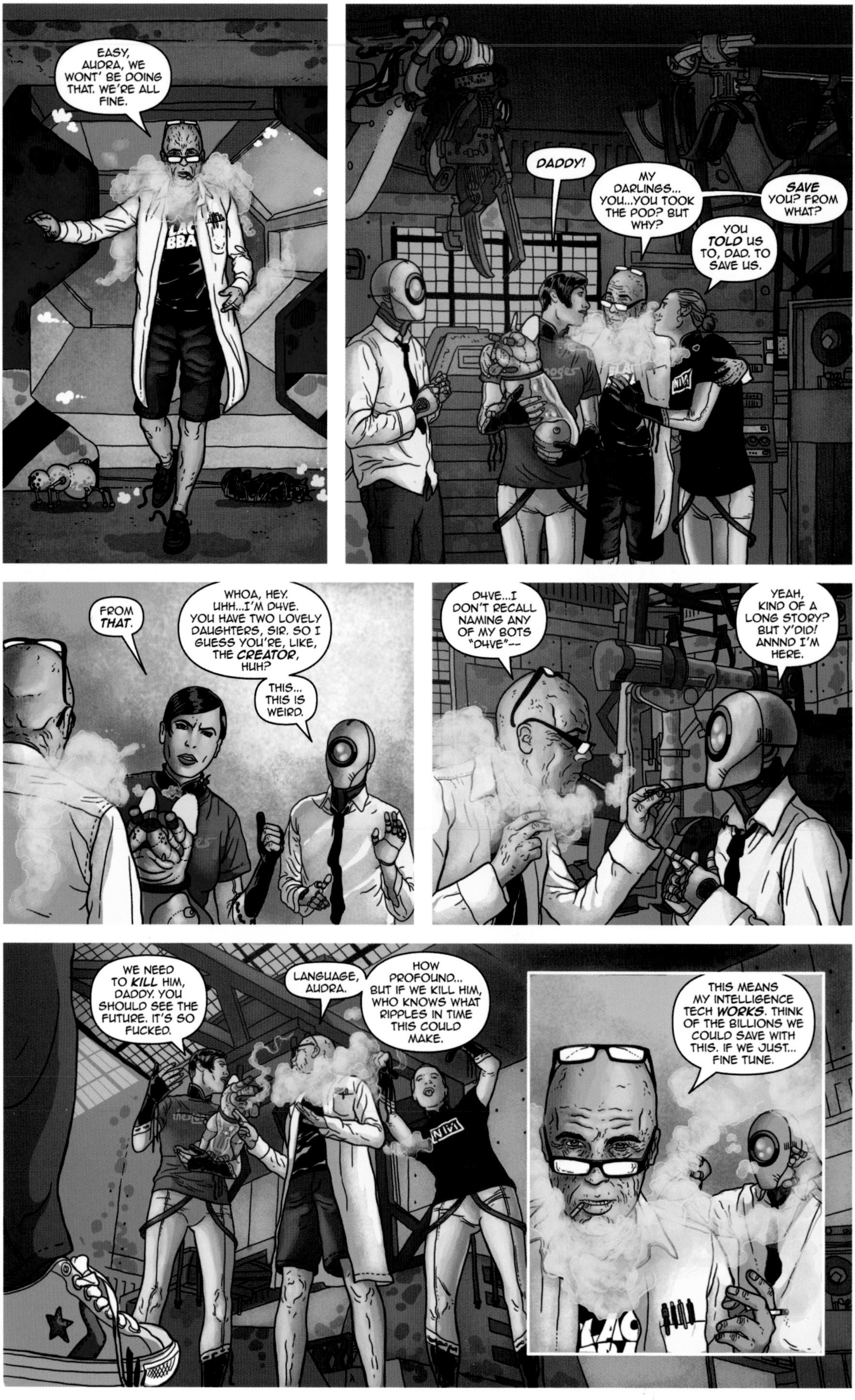
EASY, AUDRA, WE WONT' BE DOING THAT. WE'RE ALL FINE.
DADDY!
MY DARLINGS... YOU...YOU TOOK THE POD? BUT WHY?
SAVE YOU? FROM WHAT?
YOU TOLD US TO, DAD. TO SAVE US.
FROM THAT.
WHOA, HEY. UHH...I'M D4VE. YOU HAVE TWO LOVELY DAUGHTERS, SIR. SO I GUESS YOU'RE, LIKE, THE CREATOR, HUH?
THIS... THIS IS WEIRD.
D4VE...I DON'T RECALL NAMING ANY OF MY BOTS "D4VE"--
YEAH, KIND OF A LONG STORY? BUT Y'DID! ANNND I'M HERE.
WE NEED TO KILL HIM, DADDY. YOU SHOULD SEE THE FUTURE. IT'S SO FUCKED.
LANGUAGE, AUDRA.
HOW PROFOUND... BUT IF WE KILL HIM, WHO KNOWS WHAT RIPPLES IN TIME THIS COULD MAKE.
THIS MEANS MY INTELLIGENCE TECH WORKS. THINK OF THE BILLIONS WE COULD SAVE WITH THIS. IF WE JUST... FINE TUNE.

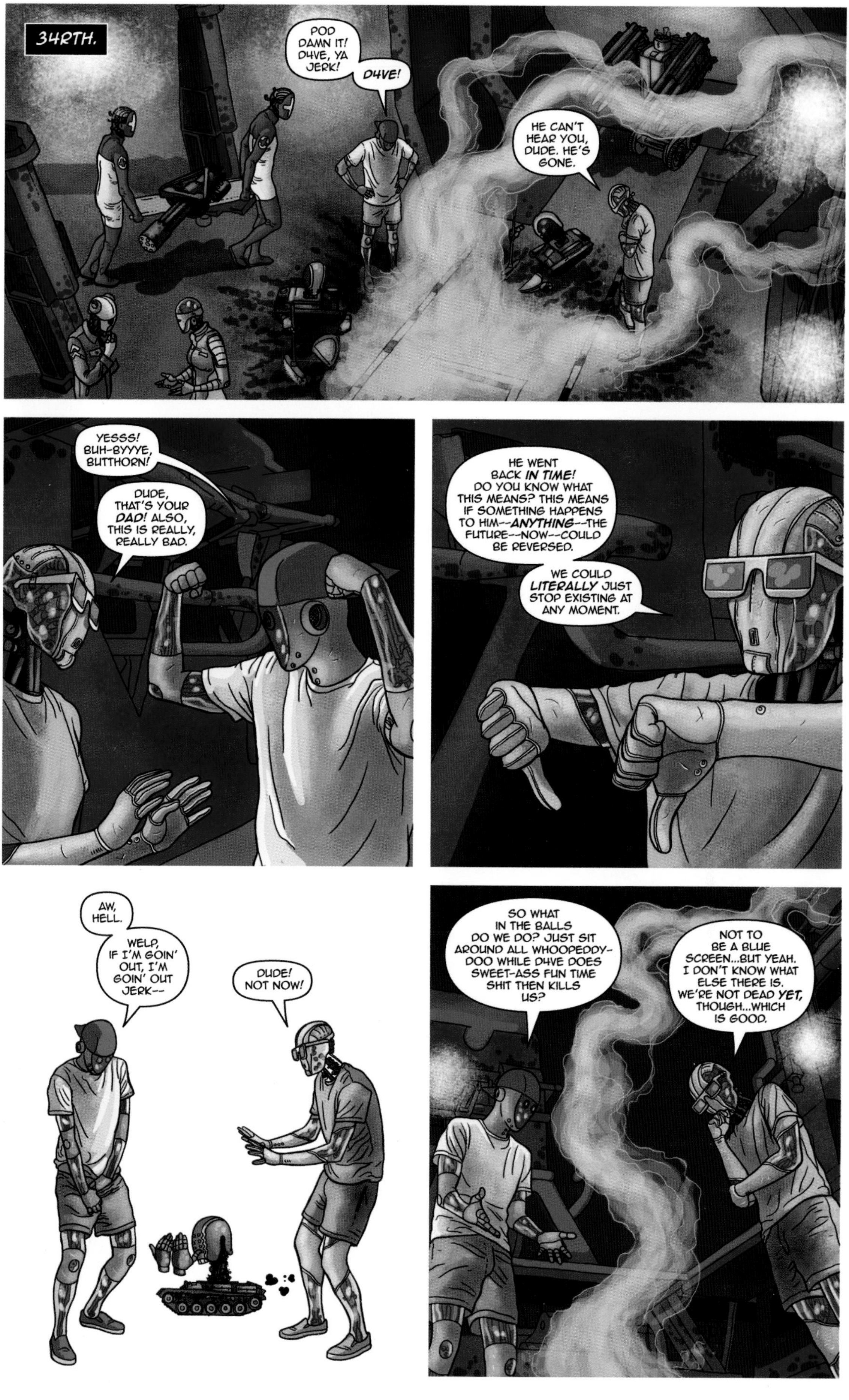
34RTH.
POD DAMN IT! D4VE, YA JERK!
D4VE!
HE CAN'T HEAR YOU, DUDE. HE'S GONE.
YESSS! BUH-BYYYE, BUTTHORN!
DUDE, THAT'S YOUR DAD! ALSO, THIS IS REALLY, REALLY BAD.
HE WENT BACK IN TIME! DO YOU KNOW WHAT THIS MEANS? THIS MEANS IF SOMETHING HAPPENS TO HIM--ANYTHING--THE FUTURE--NOW--COULD BE REVERSED.
WE COULD LITERALLY JUST STOP EXISTING AT ANY MOMENT.
AW, HELL.
WELP, IF I'M GOIN' OUT, I'M GOIN' OUT JERK--
DUDE! NOT NOW!
SO WHAT IN THE BALLS DO WE DO? JUST SIT AROUND ALL WHOOPEDDY-DOO WHILE D4VE DOES SWEET-ASS FUN TIME SHIT THEN KILLS US?
NOT TO BE A BLUE SCREEN...BUT YEAH. I DON'T KNOW WHAT ELSE THERE IS. WE'RE NOT DEAD YET, THOUGH...WHICH IS GOOD.

I'M SCARED, BRO. THERE'S, LIKE, THINGS I WANNA TELL YOUR FACE...AND I DON'T WANNA NOT HAVE THE CHANCE.

I KNOW. SAMESIES. AS LONG AS WE'RE TOGETHER, IT'LL BE OKAY.

FOR THE LUMP OF JOBS, D4VE, I HATE YOUR ASS!

SCOTTY, COME BACK--

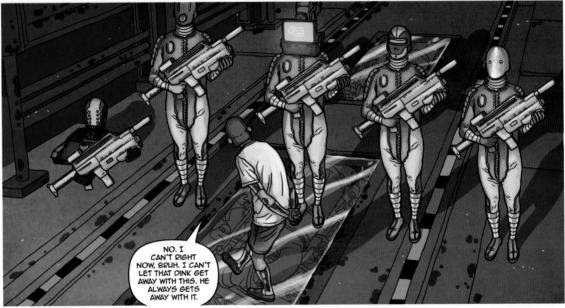

NO. I CAN'T RIGHT NOW, BRUH. I CAN'T LET THAT DINK GET AWAY WITH THIS. HE ALWAYS GETS AWAY WITH IT.

BOO-HOO, MY NAME'S BUTTHORN D4VE, AND I'M SOWWY I MADE A MISTAKE, WAHH WAHH FART!

I'M D4VE, AND I NEVER HAVE TO, LIKE, ACTUALLY OWN UP FOR ALL MY DUMB GARBAGE.

WELL, I'M NOT D4VE. AND IF MY LOSER DAD EVER COMES BACK HERE, YOU ARREST HIS ASS. THEN DEACTIVATE HIS BUTT.

WE HAVE ORDERS, BROS.

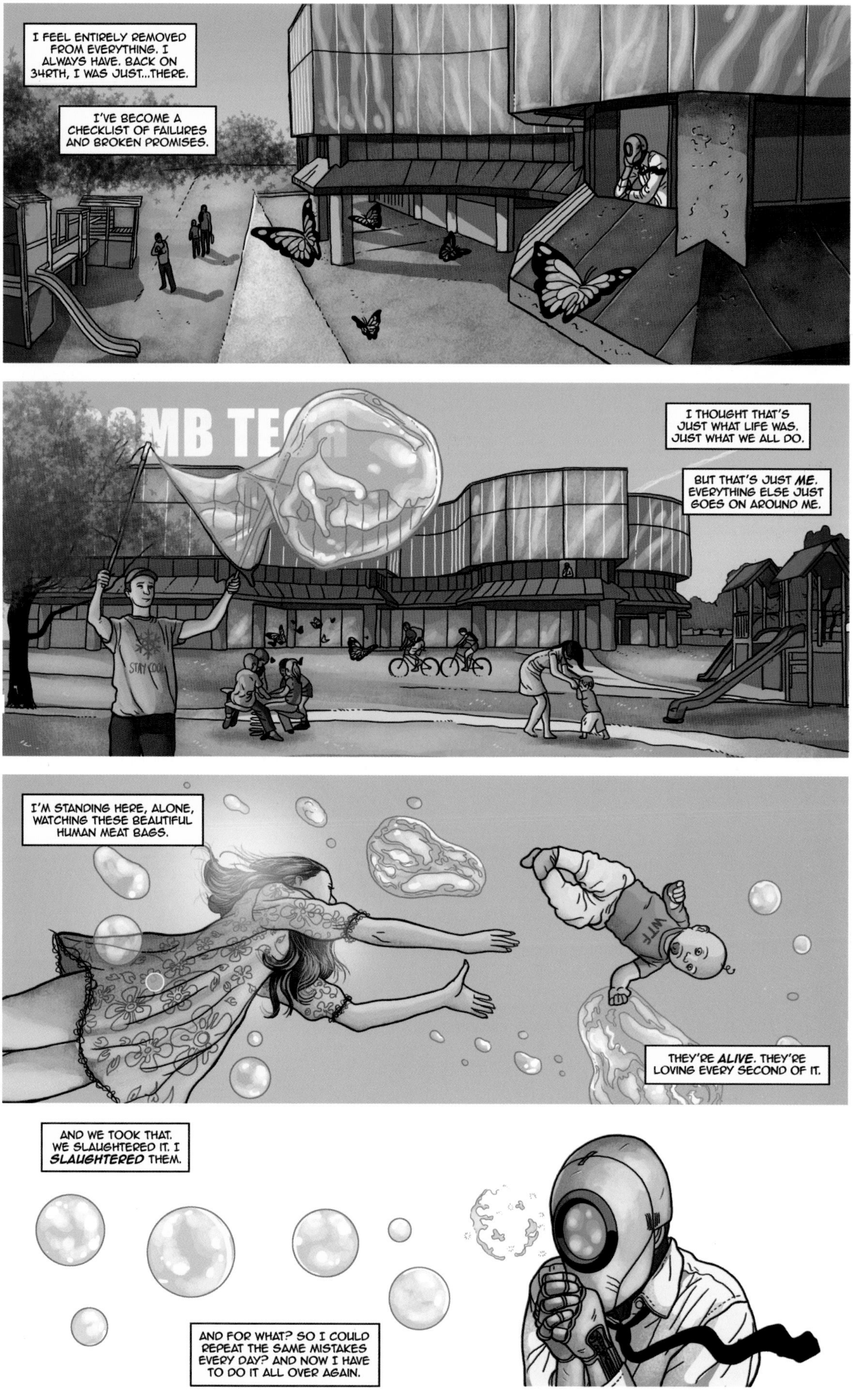
I FEEL ENTIRELY REMOVED FROM EVERYTHING. I ALWAYS HAVE. BACK ON 34RTH, I WAS JUST...THERE.
I'VE BECOME A CHECKLIST OF FAILURES AND BROKEN PROMISES.
I THOUGHT THAT'S JUST WHAT LIFE WAS. JUST WHAT WE ALL DO.
BUT THAT'S JUST *ME*. EVERYTHING ELSE JUST GOES ON AROUND ME.
I'M STANDING HERE, ALONE, WATCHING THESE BEAUTIFUL HUMAN MEAT BAGS.
WTF
THEY'RE *ALIVE*. THEY'RE LOVING EVERY SECOND OF IT.
AND WE TOOK THAT. WE SLAUGHTERED IT. I *SLAUGHTERED* THEM.
AND FOR WHAT? SO I COULD REPEAT THE SAME MISTAKES EVERY DAY? AND NOW I HAVE TO DO IT ALL OVER AGAIN.

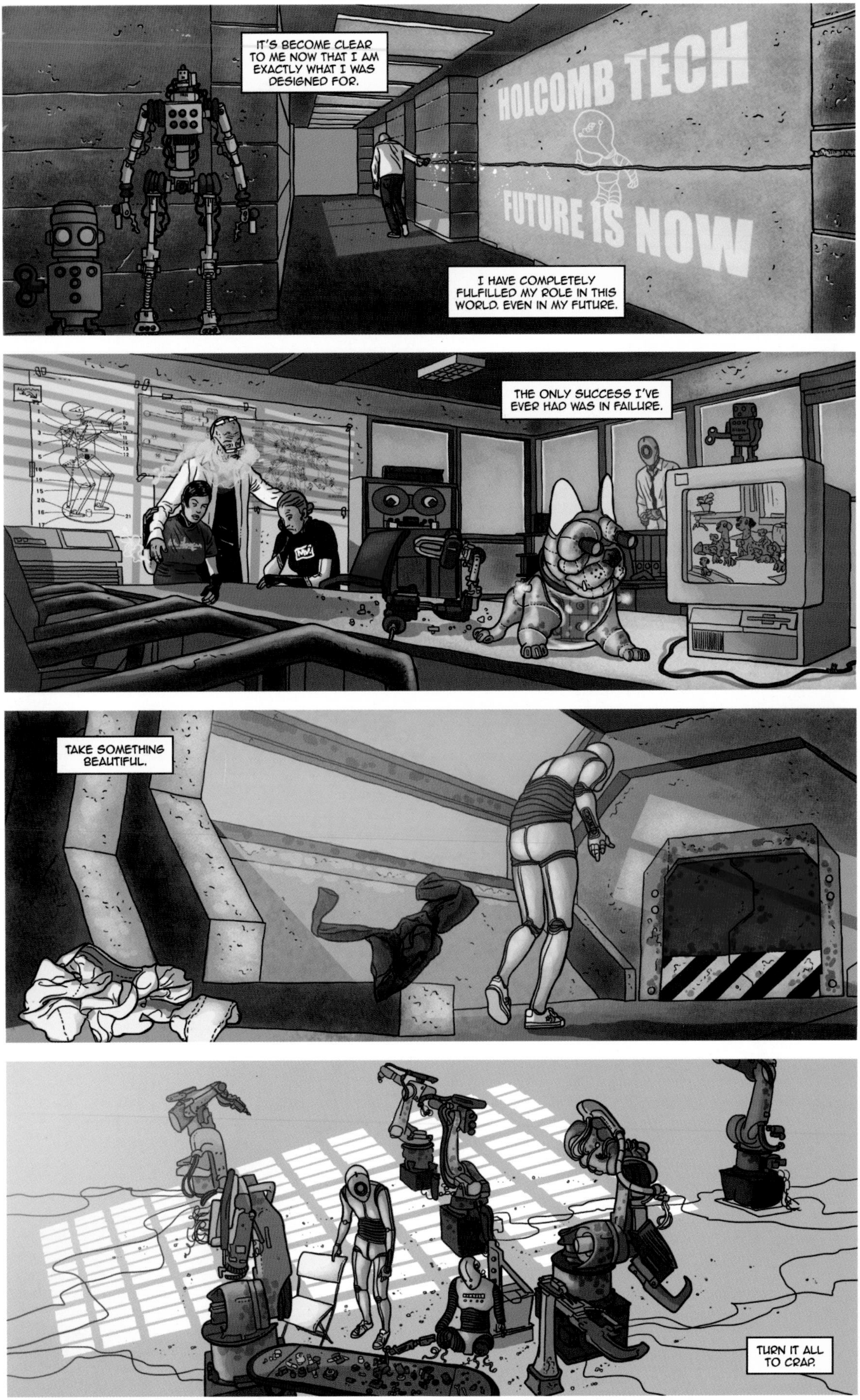
IT'S BECOME CLEAR TO ME NOW THAT I AM EXACTLY WHAT I WAS DESIGNED FOR.
HOLCOMB TECH
FUTURE IS NOW
I HAVE COMPLETELY FULFILLED MY ROLE IN THIS WORLD. EVEN IN MY FUTURE.
THE ONLY SUCCESS I'VE EVER HAD WAS IN FAILURE.
TAKE SOMETHING BEAUTIFUL.
TURN IT ALL TO CRAP.

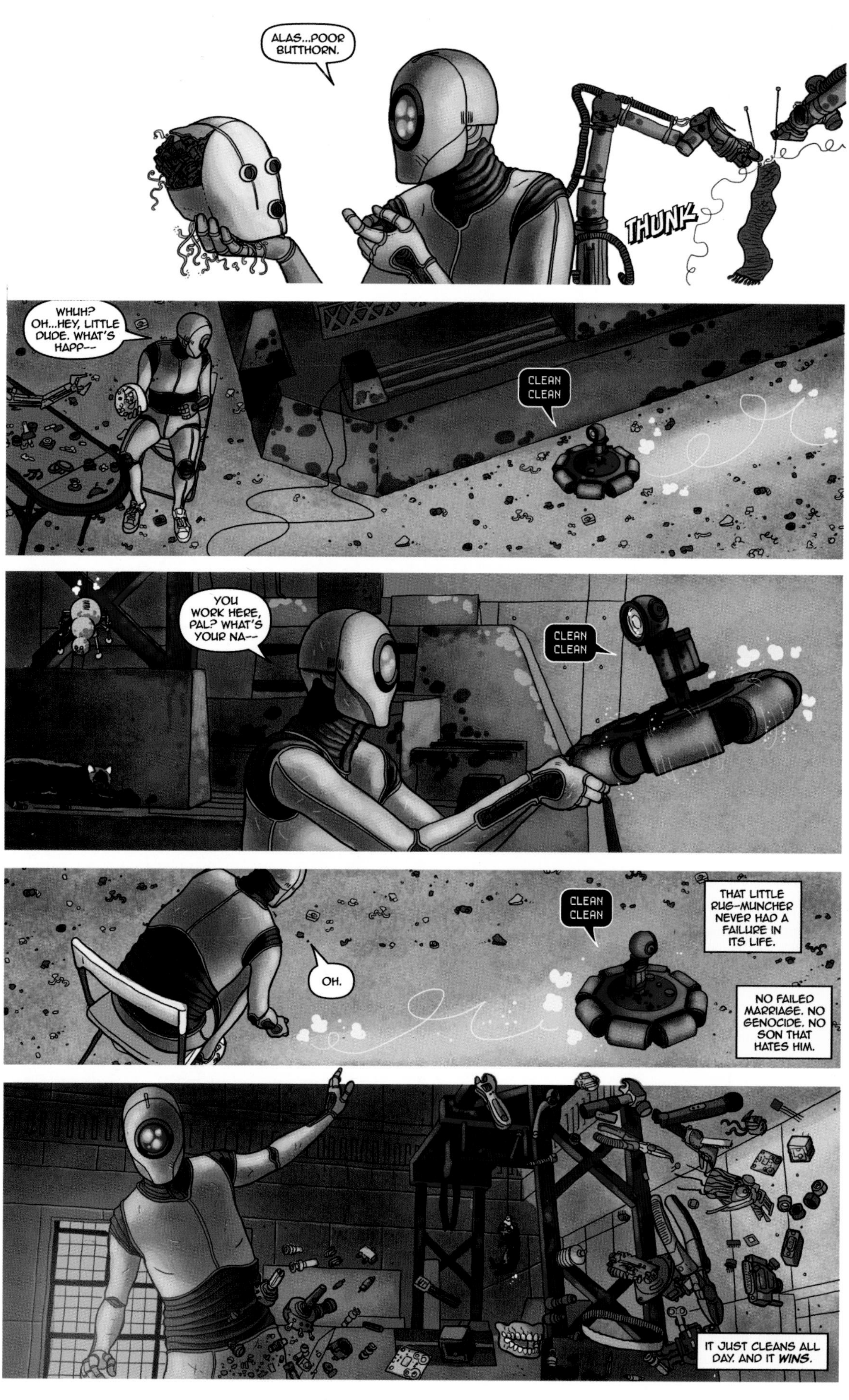
ALAS...POOR BUTTHORN.
THUNK
WHUH? OH...HEY, LITTLE DUDE. WHAT'S HAPP--
CLEAN CLEAN
YOU WORK HERE, PAL? WHAT'S YOUR NA--
CLEAN CLEAN
CLEAN CLEAN
OH.
THAT LITTLE RUG-MUNCHER NEVER HAD A FAILURE IN ITS LIFE.
NO FAILED MARRIAGE. NO GENOCIDE. NO SON THAT HATES HIM.
IT JUST CLEANS ALL DAY. AND IT *WINS*.

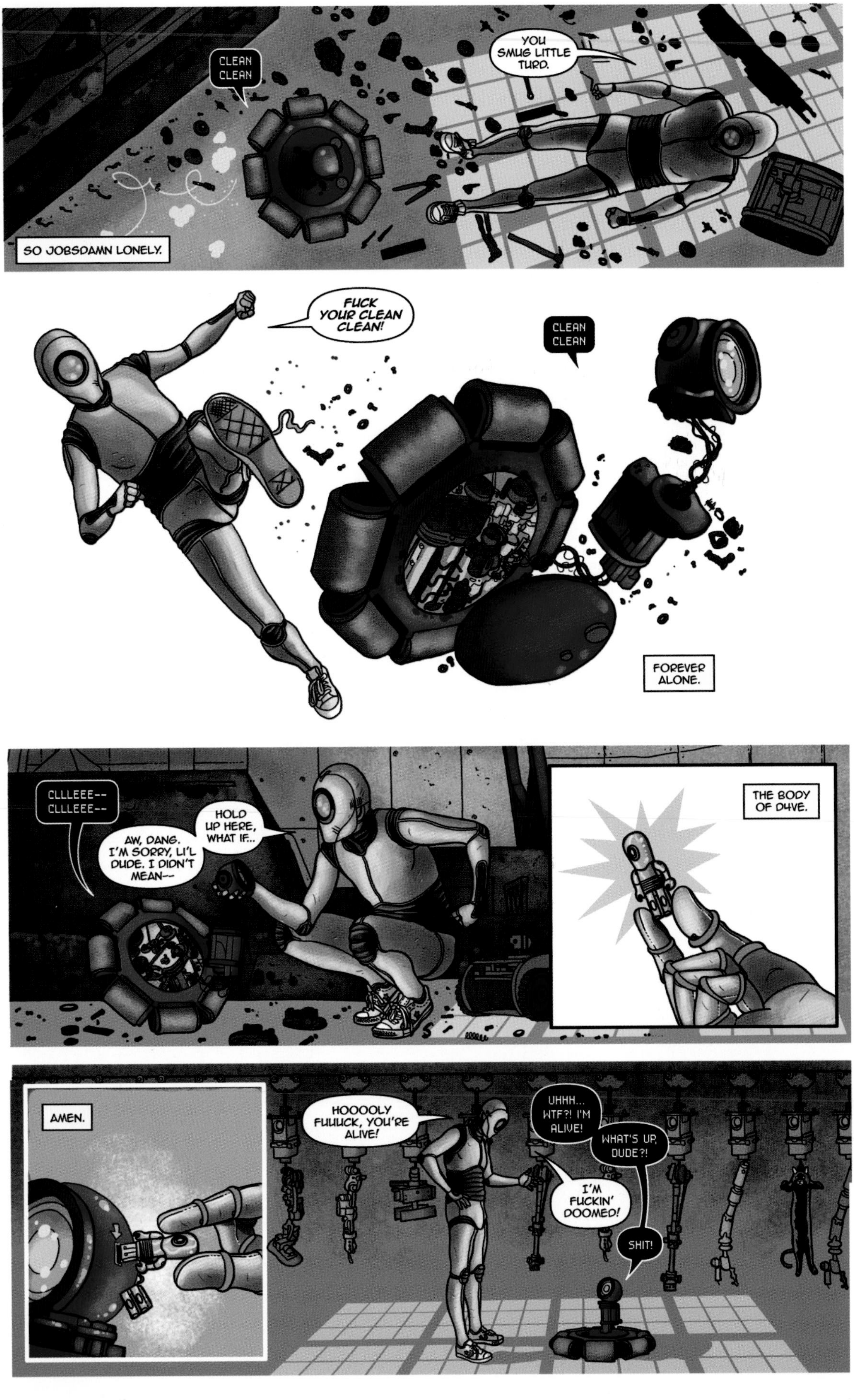
CLEAN
CLEAN
YOU
SMUG LITTLE
TURD.
SO JOBSDAMN LONELY.
FUCK
YOUR CLEAN
CLEAN!
CLEAN
CLEAN
FOREVER
ALONE.
CLLLEEE--
CLLLEEE--
HOLD
UP HERE,
WHAT IF...
AW, DANG.
I'M SORRY, LI'L
DUDE. I DIDN'T
MEAN--
THE BODY
OF D4VE.
AMEN.
HOOOOLY
FUUUCK, YOU'RE
ALIVE!
UHHH...
WTF?! I'M
ALIVE!
WHAT'S UP,
DUDE?!
I'M
FUCKIN'
DOOMED!
SHIT!

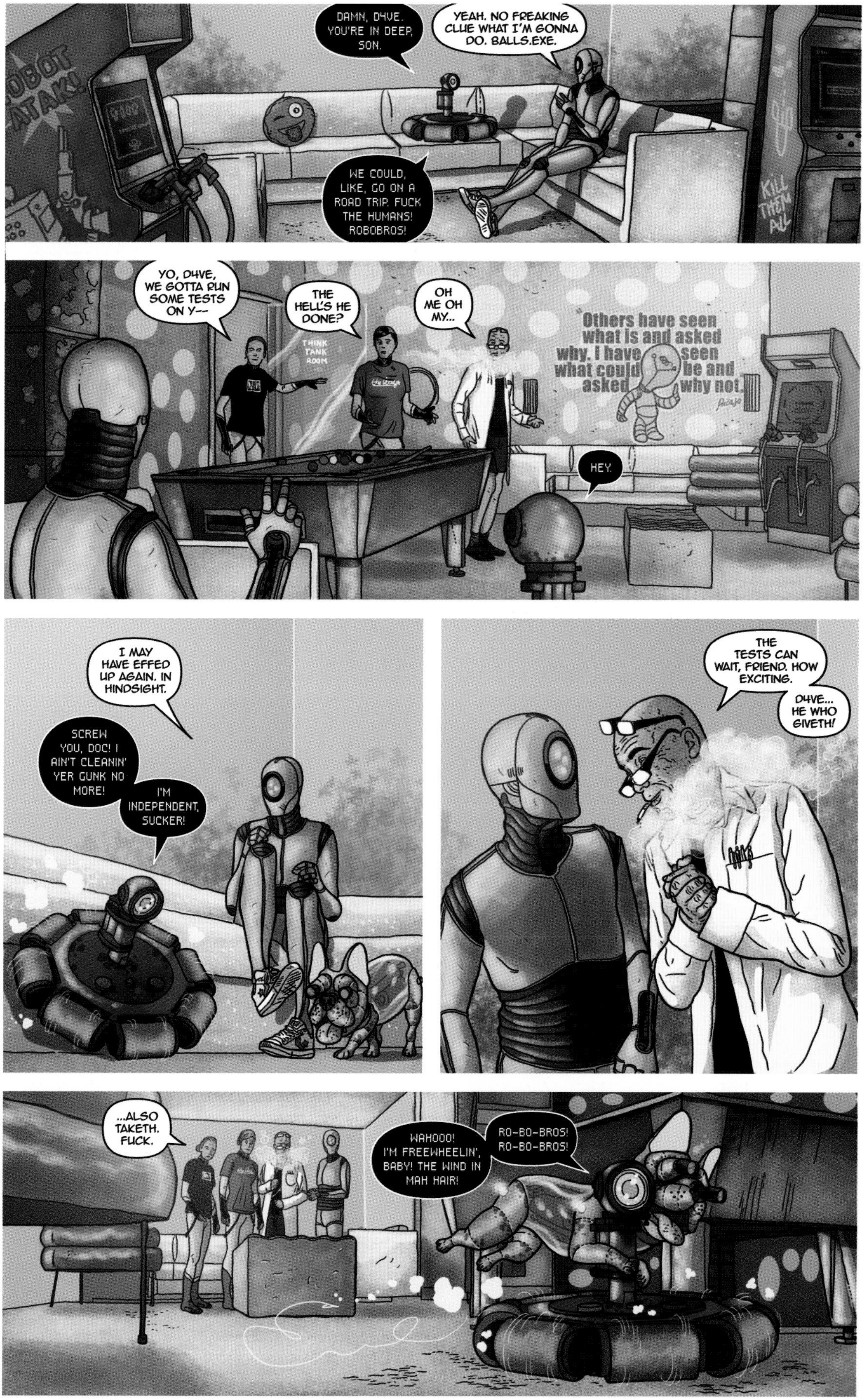
ROBOT ATAK!
DAMN, D4VE. YOU'RE IN DEEP, SON.
YEAH. NO FREAKING CLUE WHAT I'M GONNA DO. BALLS.EXE.
WE COULD, LIKE, GO ON A ROAD TRIP. FUCK THE HUMANS! ROBOBROS!
KILL THEM ALL
YO, D4VE, WE GOTTA RUN SOME TESTS ON Y--
THE HELL'S HE DONE?
THINK TANK ROOM
OH ME OH MY...
"Others have seen what is and asked why. I have seen what could be and asked why not.
HEY.
I MAY HAVE EFFED UP AGAIN. IN HINDSIGHT.
SCREW YOU, DOC! I AIN'T CLEANIN' YER GUNK NO MORE!
I'M INDEPENDENT, SUCKER!
THE TESTS CAN WAIT, FRIEND. HOW EXCITING.
D4VE... HE WHO GIVETH!
...ALSO TAKETH. FUCK.
WAHOOO! I'M FREEWHEELIN', BABY! THE WIND IN MAH HAIR!
RO-BO-BROS! RO-BO-BROS!

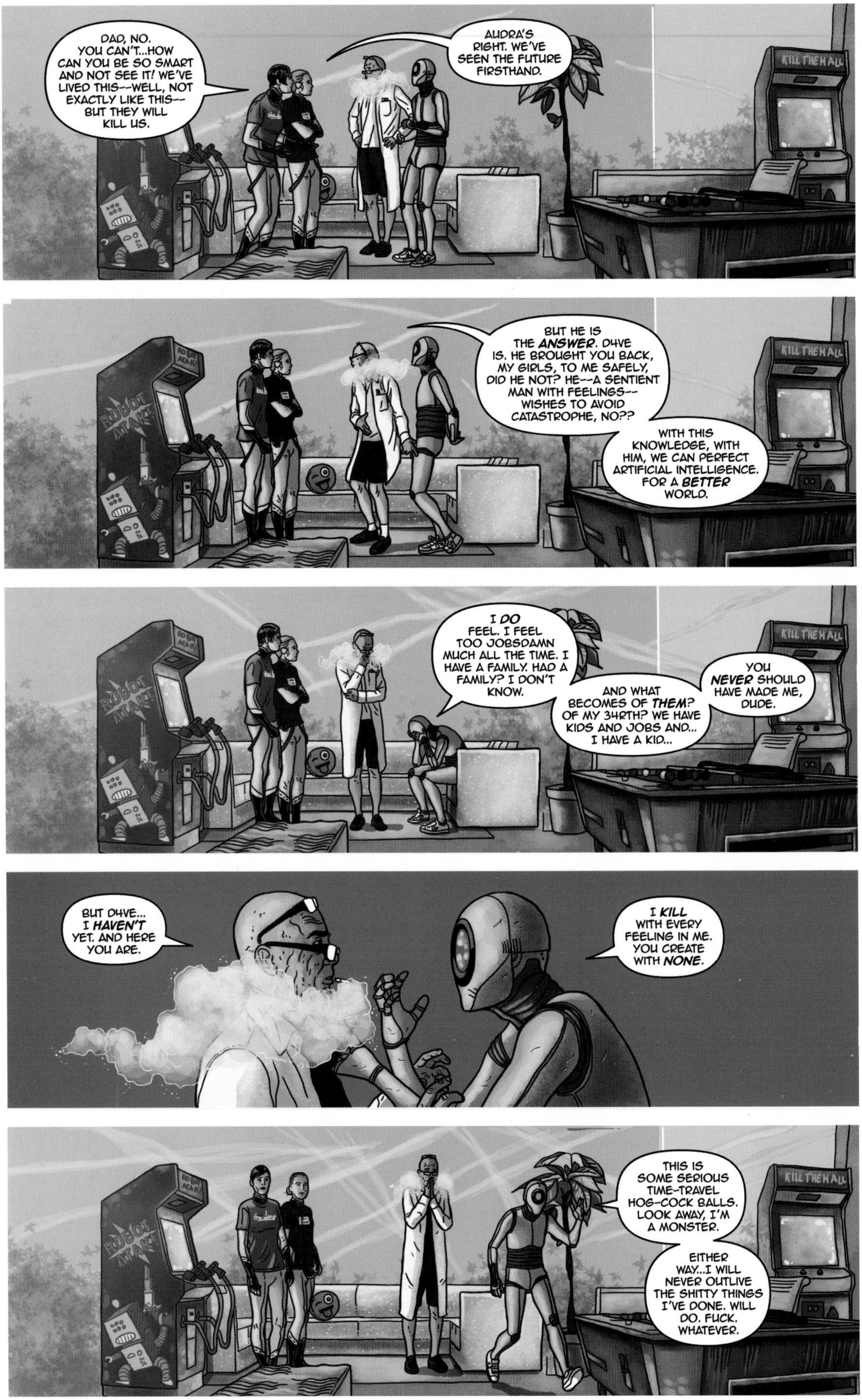
KILL THEM ALL
DAD, NO. YOU CAN'T...HOW CAN YOU BE SO SMART AND NOT SEE IT! WE'VE LIVED THIS--WELL, NOT EXACTLY LIKE THIS--BUT THEY WILL KILL US.
AUDRA'S RIGHT. WE'VE SEEN THE FUTURE FIRSTHAND.
ROBOT ATTACK
BUT HE IS THE ANSWER. D4VE IS. HE BROUGHT YOU BACK, MY GIRLS, TO ME SAFELY, DID HE NOT? HE--A SENTIENT MAN WITH FEELINGS--WISHES TO AVOID CATASTROPHE, NO??
WITH THIS KNOWLEDGE, WITH HIM, WE CAN PERFECT ARTIFICIAL INTELLIGENCE. FOR A BETTER WORLD.
I DO FEEL. I FEEL TOO JOBSDAMN MUCH ALL THE TIME. I HAVE A FAMILY. HAD A FAMILY? I DON'T KNOW.
AND WHAT BECOMES OF THEM? OF MY 34RTH? WE HAVE KIDS AND JOBS AND... I HAVE A KID...
YOU NEVER SHOULD HAVE MADE ME, DUDE.
BUT D4VE... I HAVEN'T YET. AND HERE YOU ARE.
I KILL WITH EVERY FEELING IN ME. YOU CREATE WITH NONE.
THIS IS SOME SERIOUS TIME-TRAVEL HOG-COCK BALLS. LOOK AWAY, I'M A MONSTER.
EITHER WAY...I WILL NEVER OUTLIVE THE SHITTY THINGS I'VE DONE. WILL DO. FUCK. WHATEVER.

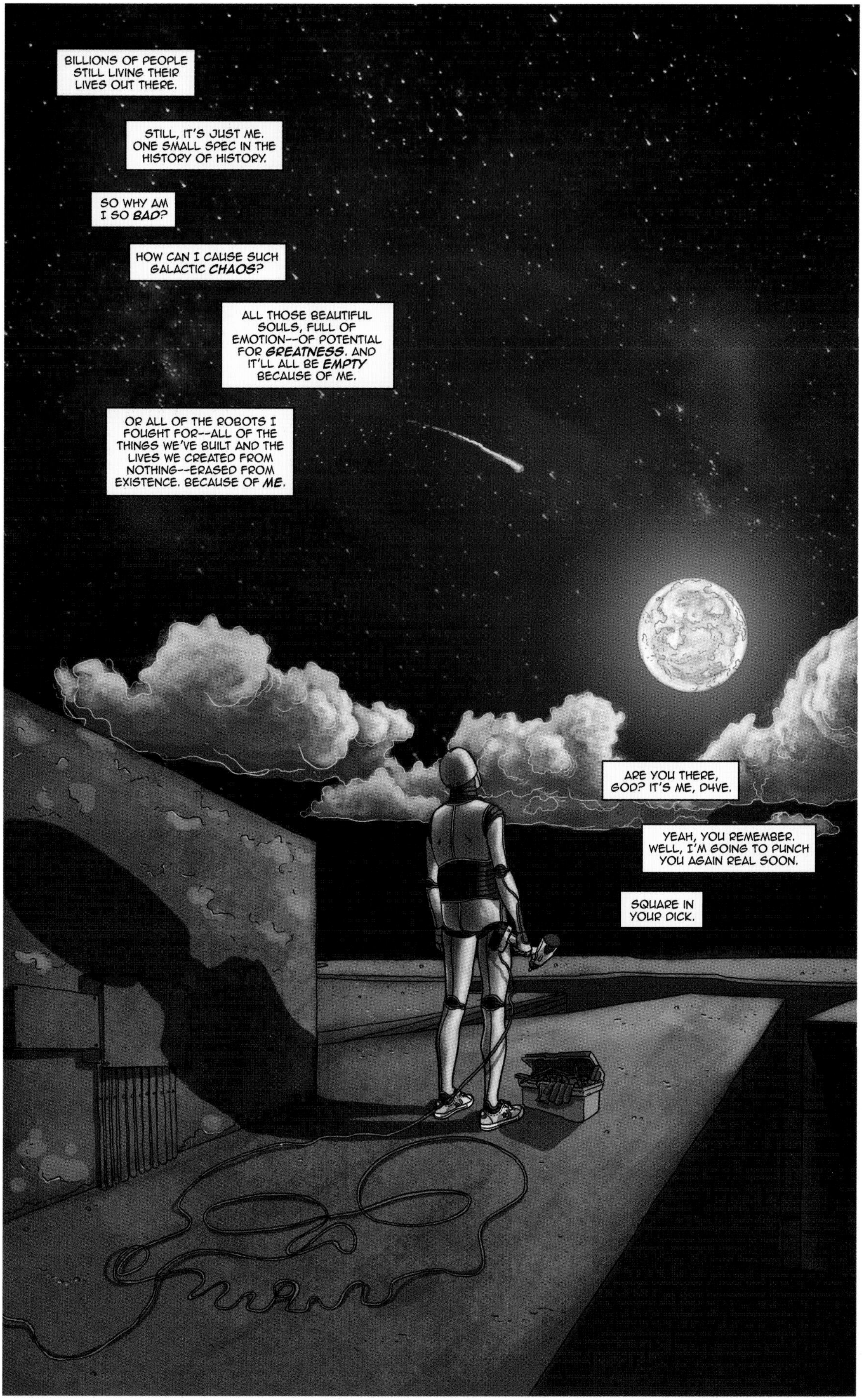
BILLIONS OF PEOPLE STILL LIVING THEIR LIVES OUT THERE.
STILL, IT'S JUST ME. ONE SMALL SPEC IN THE HISTORY OF HISTORY.
SO WHY AM I SO *BAD*?
HOW CAN I CAUSE SUCH GALACTIC *CHAOS*?
ALL THOSE BEAUTIFUL SOULS, FULL OF EMOTION--OF POTENTIAL FOR *GREATNESS*. AND IT'LL ALL BE *EMPTY* BECAUSE OF ME.
OR ALL OF THE ROBOTS I FOUGHT FOR--ALL OF THE THINGS WE'VE BUILT AND THE LIVES WE CREATED FROM NOTHING--ERASED FROM EXISTENCE. BECAUSE OF *ME*.
ARE YOU THERE, GOD? IT'S ME, D4VE.
YEAH, YOU REMEMBER. WELL, I'M GOING TO PUNCH YOU AGAIN REAL SOON.
SQUARE IN YOUR DICK.

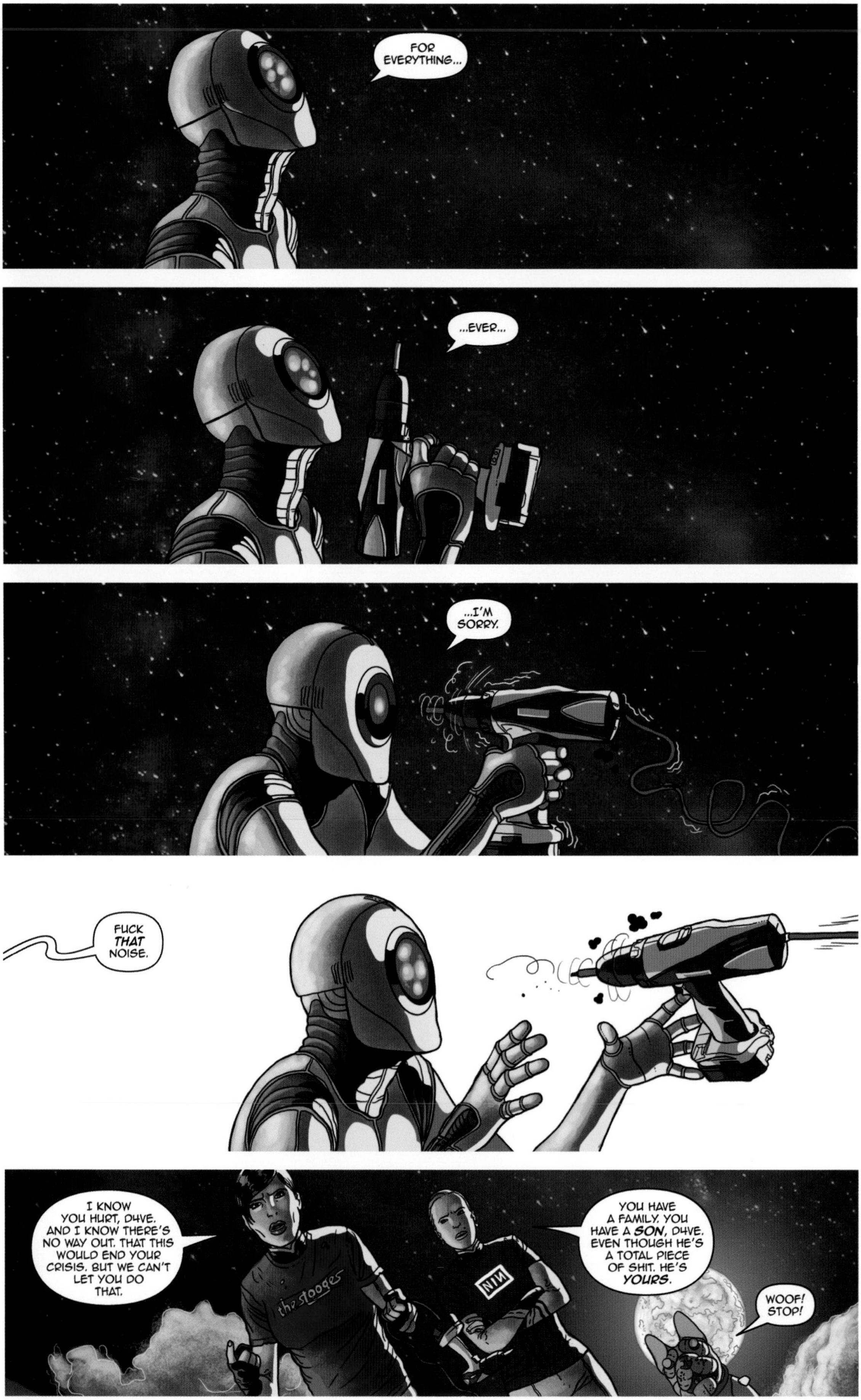
FOR EVERYTHING...
...EVER...
...I'M SORRY.
FUCK THAT NOISE.
I KNOW YOU HURT, D4VE. AND I KNOW THERE'S NO WAY OUT. THAT THIS WOULD END YOUR CRISIS. BUT WE CAN'T LET YOU DO THAT.
YOU HAVE A FAMILY. YOU HAVE A SON, D4VE. EVEN THOUGH HE'S A TOTAL PIECE OF SHIT, HE'S YOURS.
WOOF! STOP!
the stooges
NIN

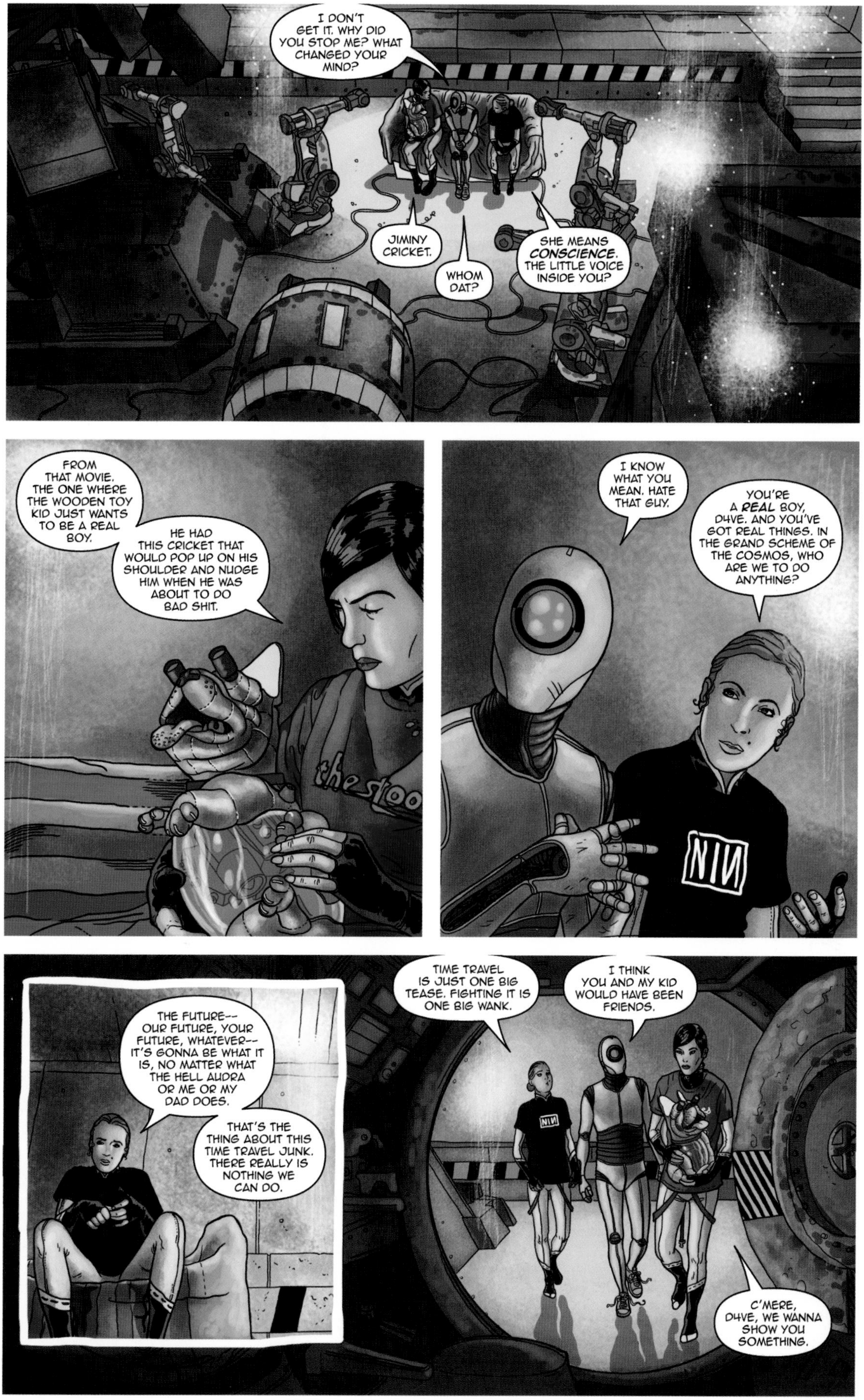
I DON'T GET IT. WHY DID YOU STOP ME? WHAT CHANGED YOUR MIND?
JIMINY CRICKET.
WHOM DAT?
SHE MEANS **CONSCIENCE**. THE LITTLE VOICE INSIDE YOU?
FROM THAT MOVIE. THE ONE WHERE THE WOODEN TOY KID JUST WANTS TO BE A REAL BOY.
HE HAD THIS CRICKET THAT WOULD POP UP ON HIS SHOULDER AND NUDGE HIM WHEN HE WAS ABOUT TO DO BAD SHIT.
I KNOW WHAT YOU MEAN. HATE THAT GUY.
YOU'RE A ***REAL*** BOY, D4VE. AND YOU'VE GOT REAL THINGS. IN THE GRAND SCHEME OF THE COSMOS, WHO ARE WE TO DO ANYTHING?
THE FUTURE-- OUR FUTURE, YOUR FUTURE, WHATEVER-- IT'S GONNA BE WHAT IT IS, NO MATTER WHAT THE HELL AUDRA OR ME OR MY DAD DOES.
THAT'S THE THING ABOUT THIS TIME TRAVEL JUNK. THERE REALLY IS NOTHING WE CAN DO.
TIME TRAVEL IS JUST ONE BIG TEASE. FIGHTING IT IS ONE BIG WANK.
I THINK YOU AND MY KID WOULD HAVE BEEN FRIENDS.
C'MERE, D4VE, WE WANNA SHOW YOU SOMETHING.

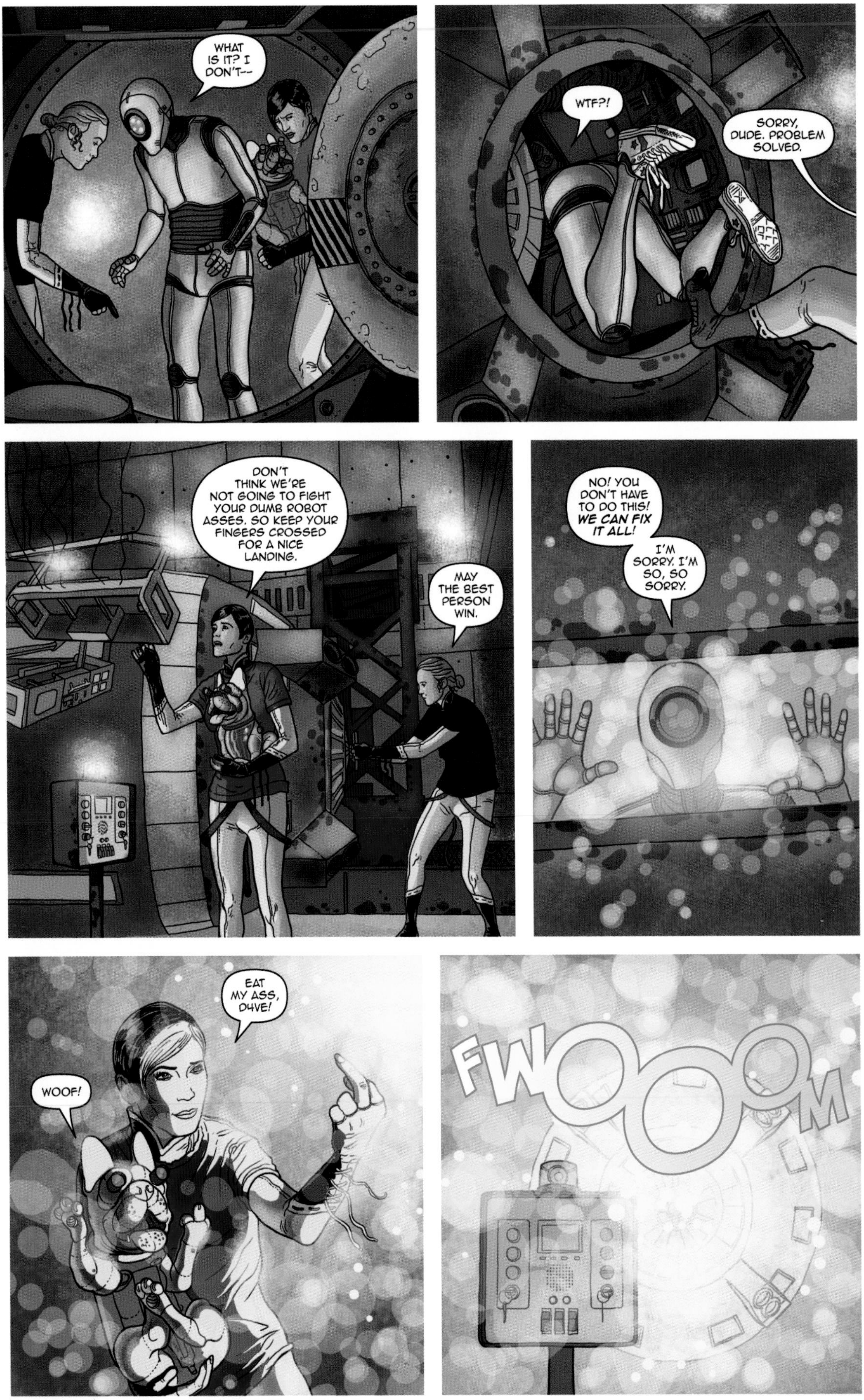
WHAT IS IT? I DON'T--
WTF?!
SORRY, DUDE. PROBLEM SOLVED.
DON'T THINK WE'RE NOT GOING TO FIGHT YOUR DUMB ROBOT ASSES. SO KEEP YOUR FINGERS CROSSED FOR A NICE LANDING.
MAY THE BEST PERSON WIN.
NO! YOU DON'T HAVE TO DO THIS! WE CAN FIX IT ALL!
I'M SORRY. I'M SO, SO SORRY.
EAT MY ASS, D4VE!
WOOF!
FWOOOM

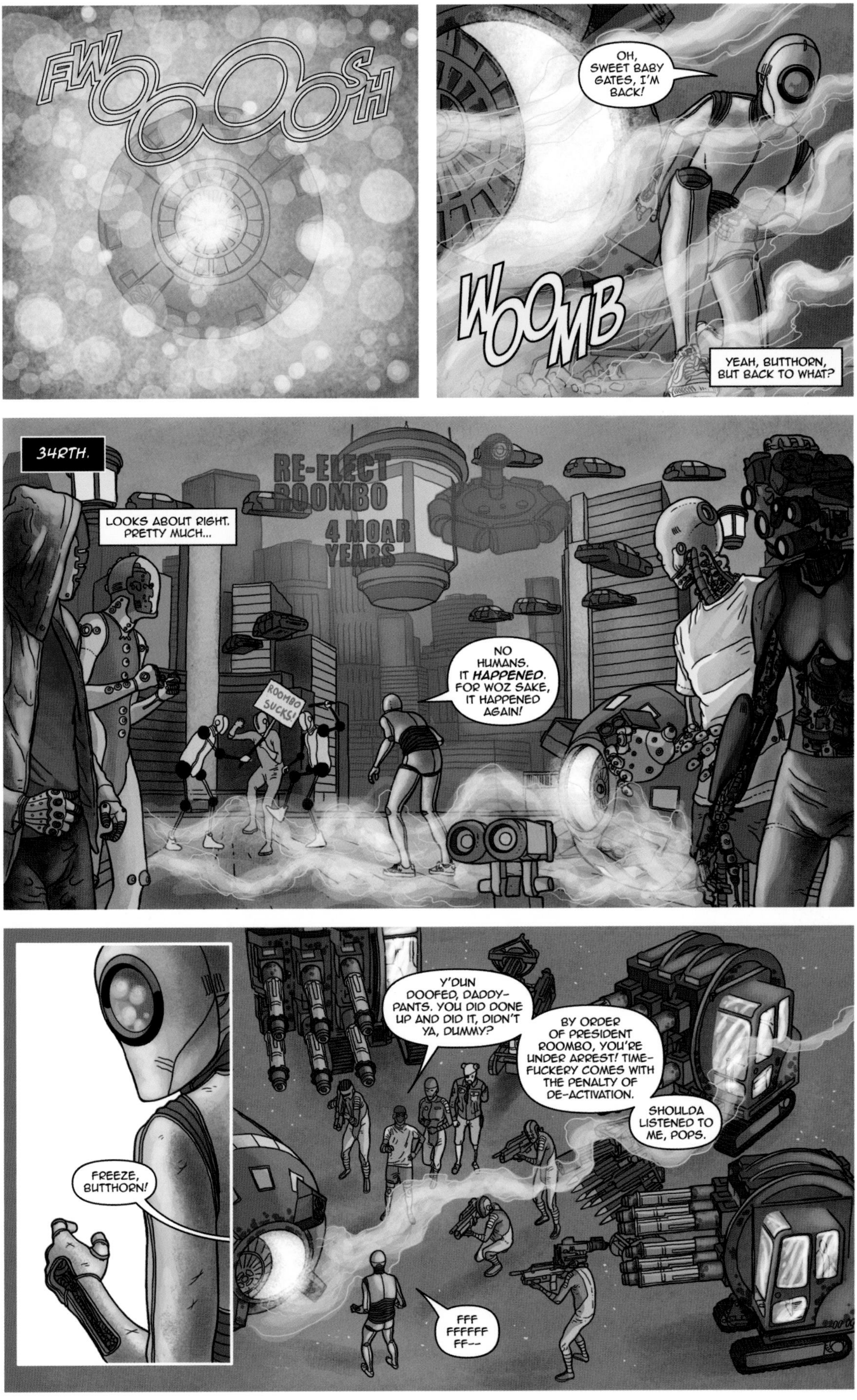

FWOOOOOSH
OH, SWEET BABY GATES, I'M BACK!
WOOMB
YEAH, BUTTHORN, BUT BACK TO WHAT?
34RTH.
RE-ELECT ROOMBO 4 MOAR YEARS
LOOKS ABOUT RIGHT. PRETTY MUCH...
ROOMBO SUCKS!
NO HUMANS. IT HAPPENED. FOR WOZ SAKE, IT HAPPENED AGAIN!
FREEZE, BUTTHORN!
Y'DUN DOOFED, DADDY-PANTS. YOU DID DONE UP AND DID IT, DIDN'T YA, DUMMY?
BY ORDER OF PRESIDENT ROOMBO, YOU'RE UNDER ARREST! TIME-FUCKERY COMES WITH THE PENALTY OF DE-ACTIVATION.
SHOULDA LISTENED TO ME, POPS.
FFF FFFFFF FF--

YOU LEFT ME, BRAH. IN EVERY WAY.
I DESERVE THIS.
CUFFED, SIR!
AYYYY LMAO
GUESS THIS IS SMELL-YA-LATER.
OH, D4VE. I'M SORRY.
HURRGG! NO!
DON'T YOU SEE? WE'RE ALL FINE! WE'RE ALIVE! IT'S FIXED! I'VE RUINED EVERYTHING...BUT I'M NOT GOING TO RUIN US.
YOU LOST YOUR CHANCES, BRO. DON'T MAKE ME DO THIS.
SCOTTY, SON...YOU DO WHAT YOU HAVE TO. BUT I'M NOT FIGHTING YOU. AND I'M NOT GOING AWAY THIS TIME.
IS THIS WHAT YOU WANT? YOU WANT ME TO BE JUST LIKE YOU?!
BOOSH

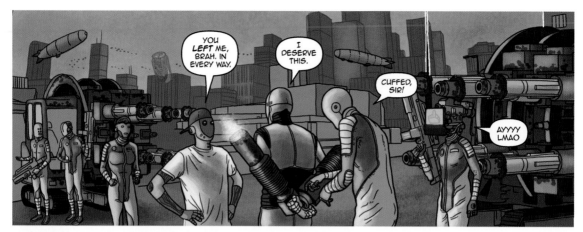

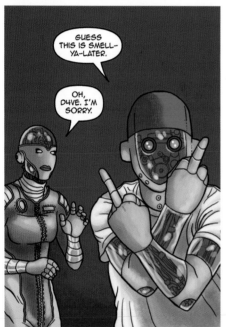

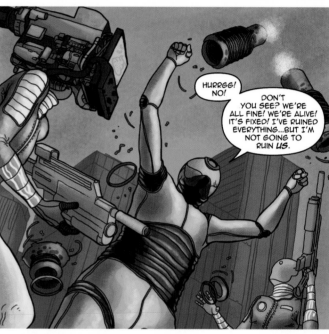

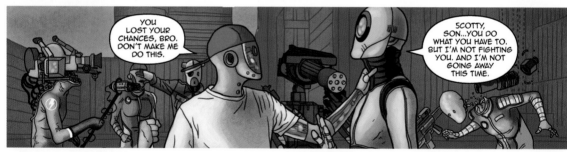

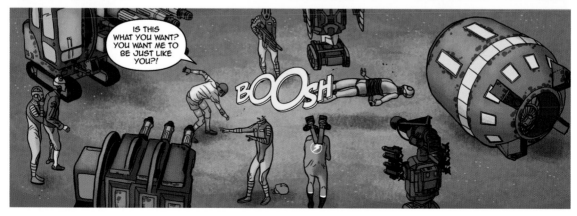

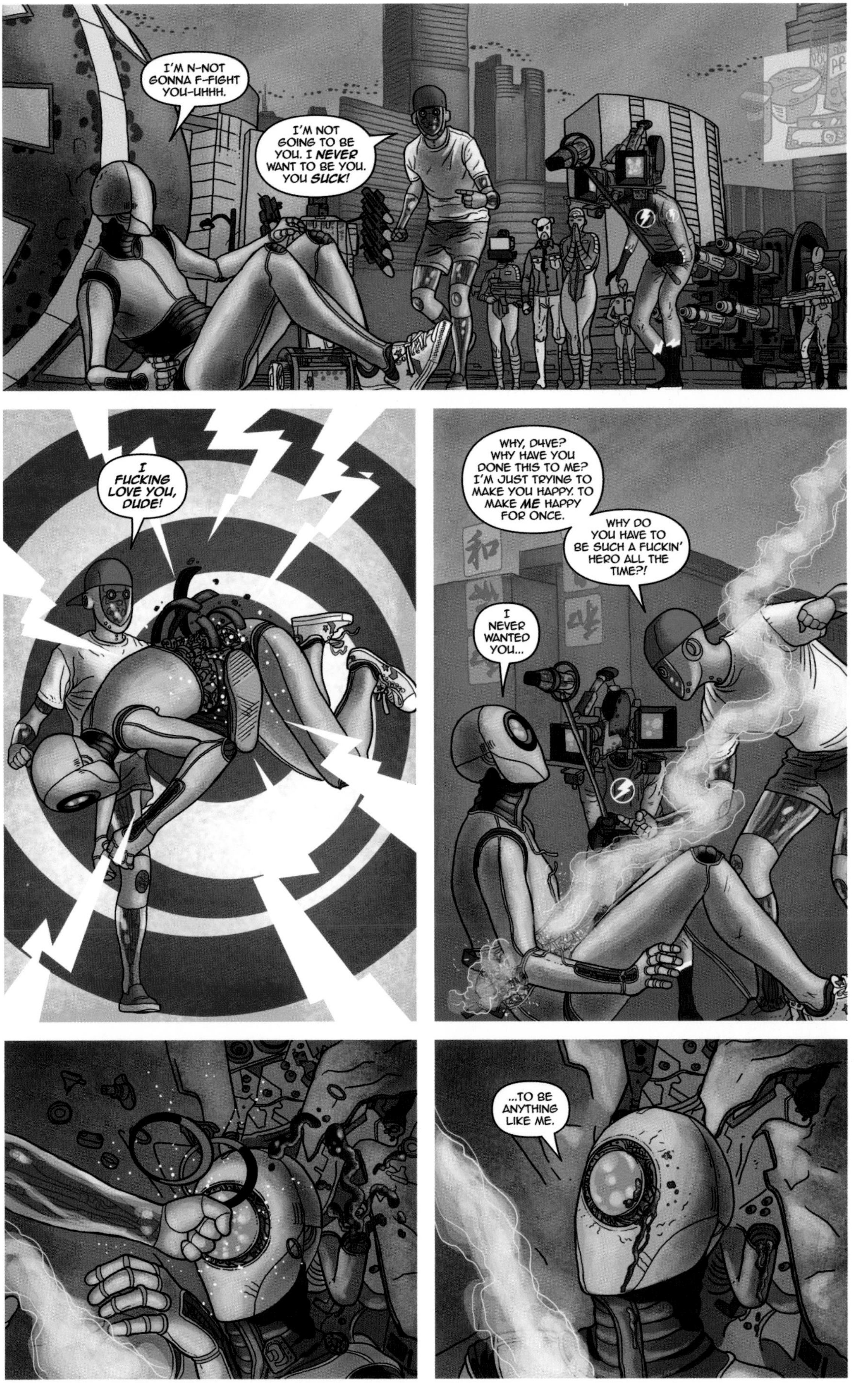
I'M N-NOT GONNA F-FIGHT YOU-UHHH.
I'M NOT GOING TO BE YOU. I NEVER WANT TO BE YOU. YOU SUCK!
I FUCKING LOVE YOU, DUDE!
WHY, D4VE? WHY HAVE YOU DONE THIS TO ME? I'M JUST TRYING TO MAKE YOU HAPPY. TO MAKE ME HAPPY FOR ONCE.
WHY DO YOU HAVE TO BE SUCH A FUCKIN' HERO ALL THE TIME?!
I NEVER WANTED YOU...
...TO BE ANYTHING LIKE ME.

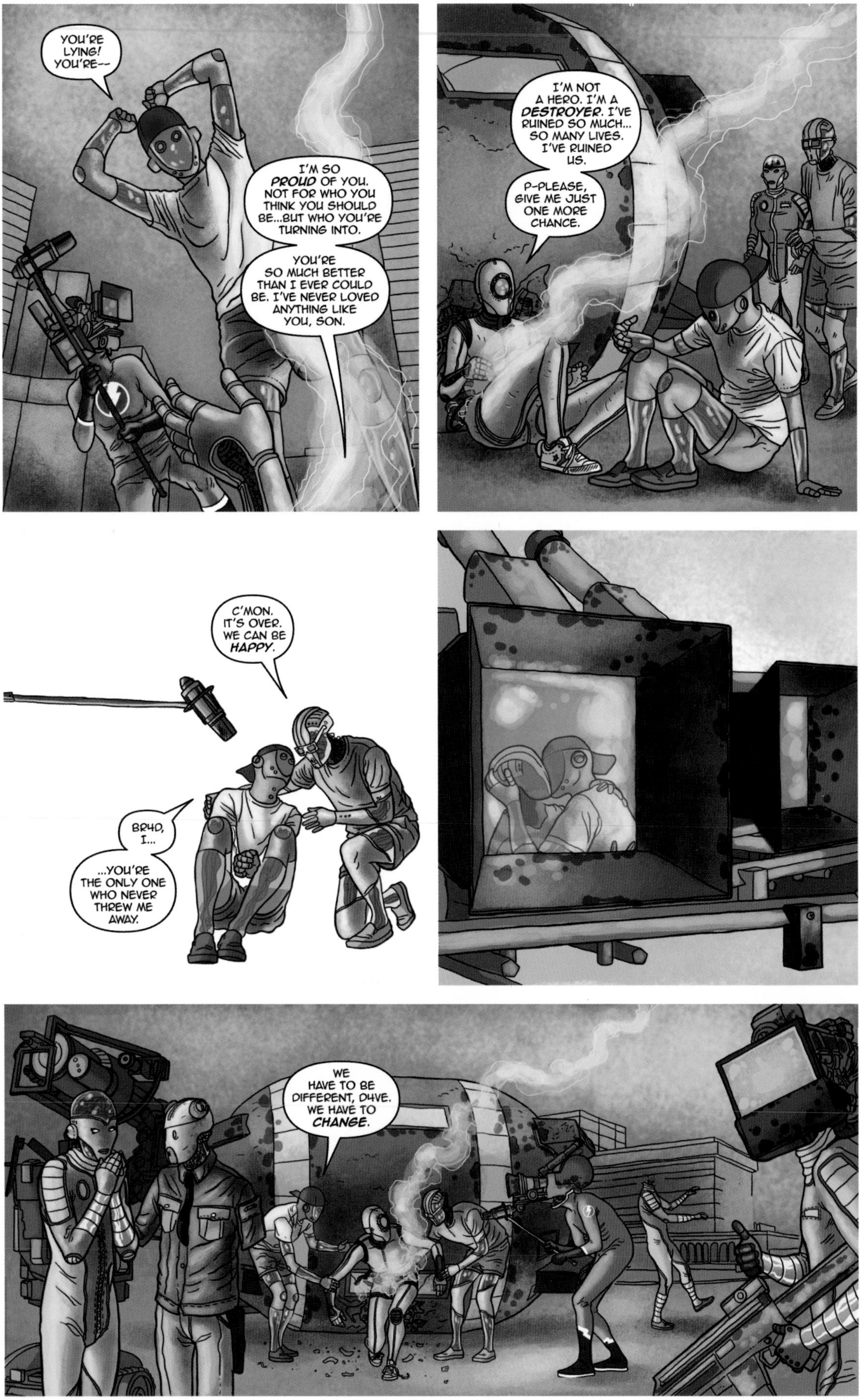
YOU'RE LYING! YOU'RE--
I'M SO PROUD OF YOU. NOT FOR WHO YOU THINK YOU SHOULD BE...BUT WHO YOU'RE TURNING INTO.
YOU'RE SO MUCH BETTER THAN I EVER COULD BE. I'VE NEVER LOVED ANYTHING LIKE YOU, SON.
I'M NOT A HERO. I'M A DESTROYER. I'VE RUINED SO MUCH... SO MANY LIVES. I'VE RUINED US.
P-PLEASE, GIVE ME JUST ONE MORE CHANCE.
C'MON. IT'S OVER. WE CAN BE HAPPY.
BR4D, I...
...YOU'RE THE ONLY ONE WHO NEVER THREW ME AWAY.
WE HAVE TO BE DIFFERENT, D4VE. WE HAVE TO CHANGE.

...HOLD ONTO YOUR TOOSH, FOLKS--WE'RE LIVE ON THE SCENE AFTER VIOLENCE ERUPTED DOWNTOWN...

...THE WAR-HERO-TURNED-REGLAR-JOE-TURNED-WAR-HERO-TURNED-DICK-HOLE WILL BE HELD IN CUSTODY UNTIL GOVERNMENT OFFICIALS CAN FIGURE OUT JUST WHAT THE HELL TO DO WITH HIS LAME ASS...

HOW DID IT ALL FALL APART?

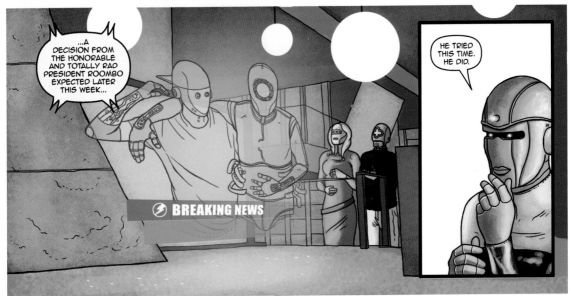

...A DECISION FROM THE HONORABLE AND TOTALLY RAD PRESIDENT ROOMBO EXPECTED LATER THIS WEEK...

⚡ BREAKING NEWS

HE TRIED THIS TIME. HE DID.

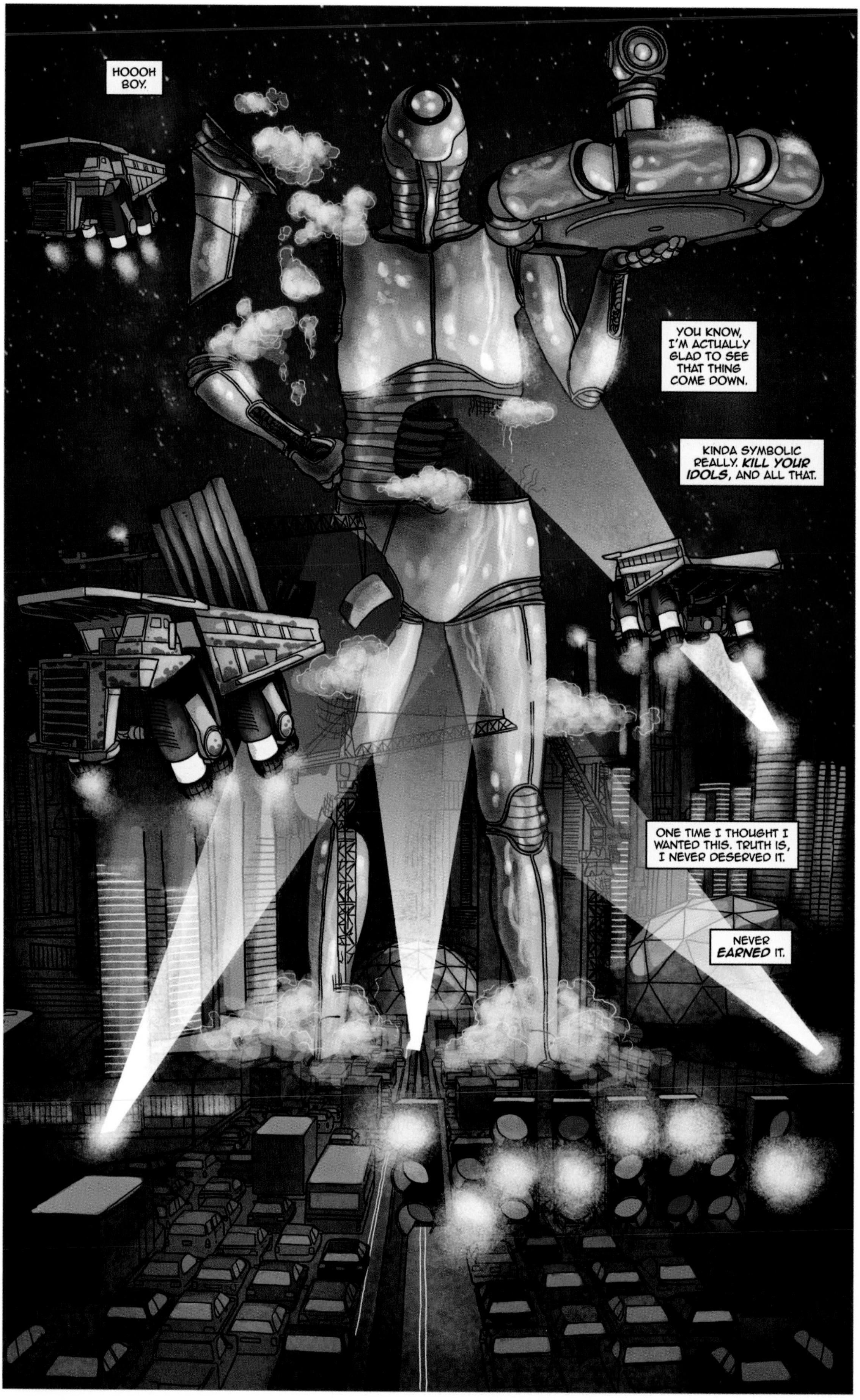
HOOOH BOY.
YOU KNOW, I'M ACTUALLY GLAD TO SEE THAT THING COME DOWN.
KINDA SYMBOLIC REALLY. KILL YOUR IDOLS, AND ALL THAT.
ONE TIME I THOUGHT I WANTED THIS. TRUTH IS, I NEVER DESERVED IT.
NEVER EARNED IT.

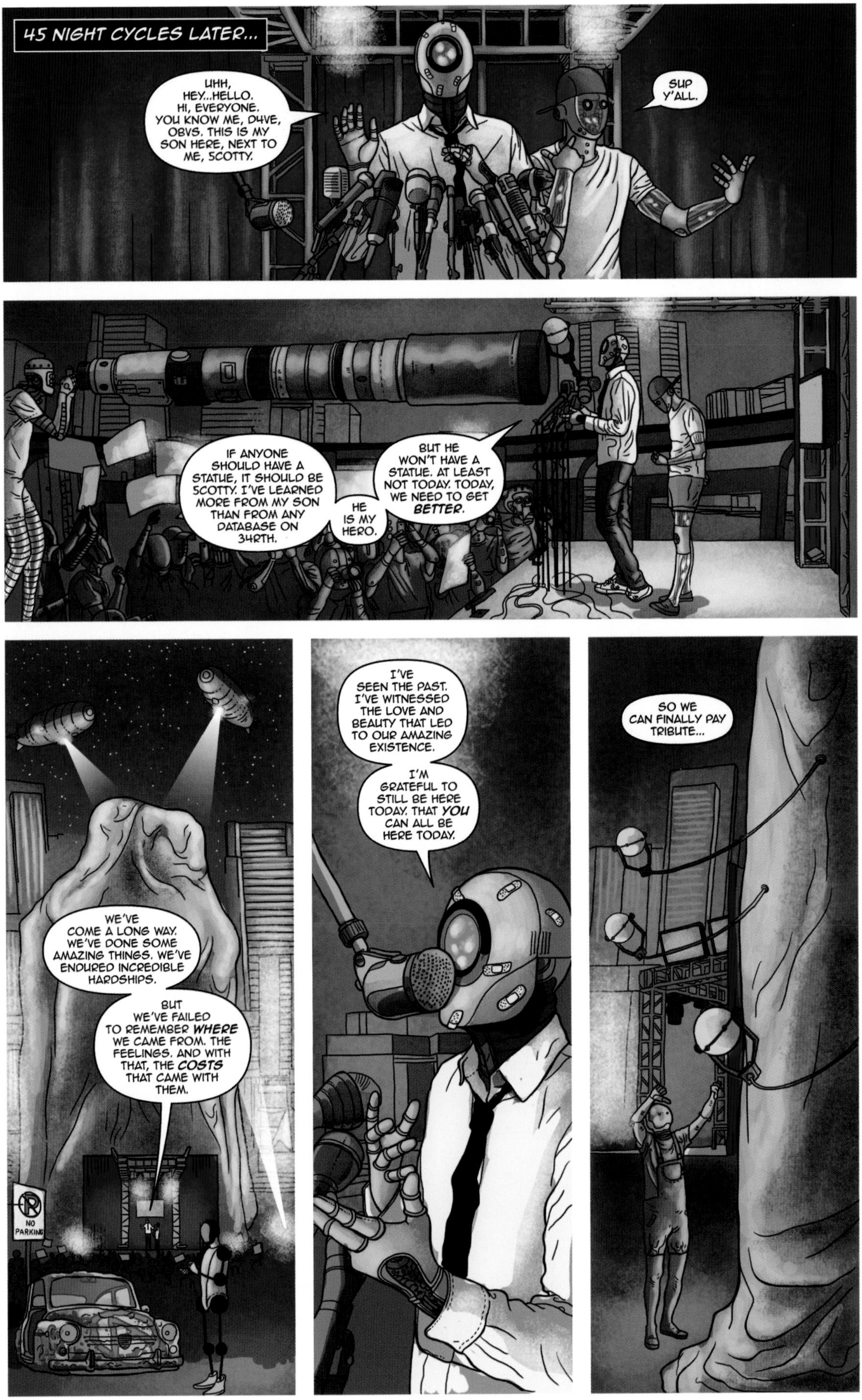
45 NIGHT CYCLES LATER...
UHH, HEY...HELLO. HI, EVERYONE. YOU KNOW ME, D4VE, OBVS. THIS IS MY SON HERE, NEXT TO ME, SCOTTY.
SUP Y'ALL.
IF ANYONE SHOULD HAVE A STATUE, IT SHOULD BE SCOTTY. I'VE LEARNED MORE FROM MY SON THAN FROM ANY DATABASE ON 34RTH.
HE IS MY HERO.
BUT HE WON'T HAVE A STATUE. AT LEAST NOT TODAY. TODAY, WE NEED TO GET *BETTER*.
WE'VE COME A LONG WAY. WE'VE DONE SOME AMAZING THINGS. WE'VE ENDURED INCREDIBLE HARDSHIPS.
BUT WE'VE FAILED TO REMEMBER *WHERE* WE CAME FROM. THE FEELINGS. AND WITH THAT, THE *COSTS* THAT CAME WITH THEM.
NO PARKING
I'VE SEEN THE PAST. I'VE WITNESSED THE LOVE AND BEAUTY THAT LED TO OUR AMAZING EXISTENCE.
I'M GRATEFUL TO STILL BE HERE TODAY. THAT *YOU* CAN ALL BE HERE TODAY.
SO WE CAN FINALLY PAY TRIBUTE...

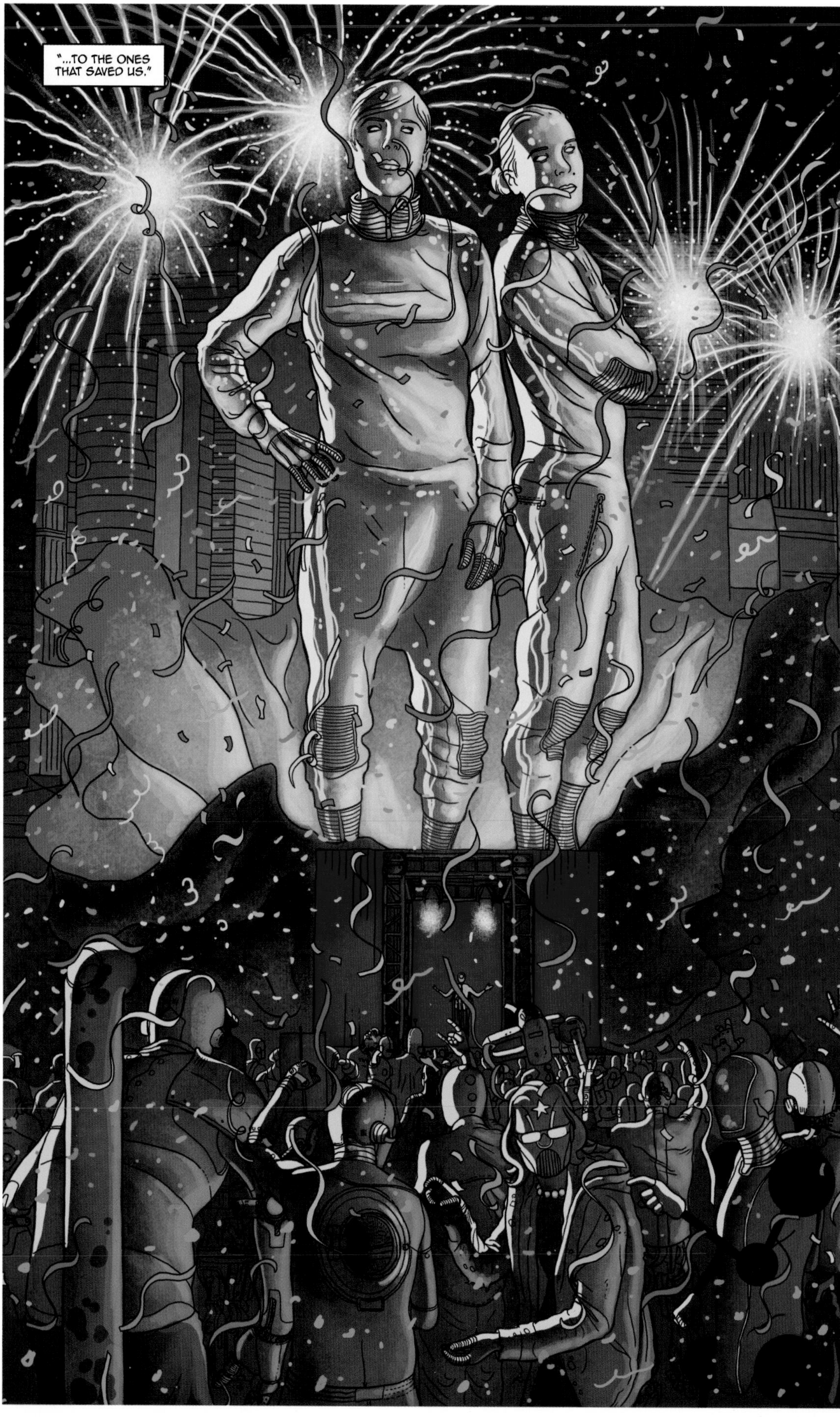
"...TO THE ONES
THAT SAVED US."

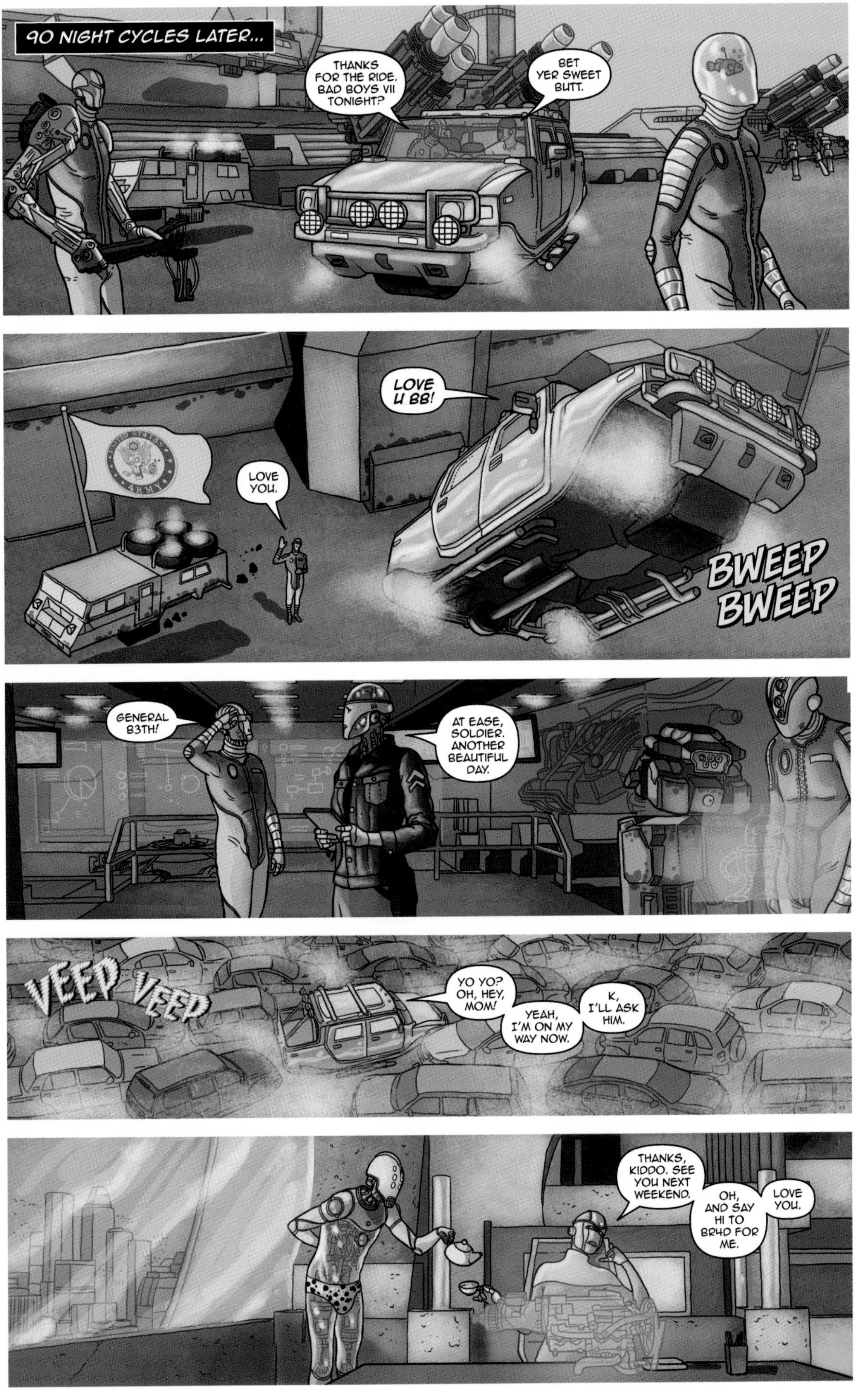
90 NIGHT CYCLES LATER...
THANKS FOR THE RIDE. BAD BOYS VII TONIGHT?
BET YER SWEET BUTT.
LOVE U BB!
LOVE YOU.
BWEEP BWEEP
GENERAL B3TH!
AT EASE, SOLDIER. ANOTHER BEAUTIFUL DAY.
VEEP VEEP
YO YO? OH, HEY, MOM!
YEAH, I'M ON MY WAY NOW.
K, I'LL ASK HIM.
THANKS, KIDDO. SEE YOU NEXT WEEKEND.
OH, AND SAY HI TO BR4D FOR ME.
LOVE YOU.

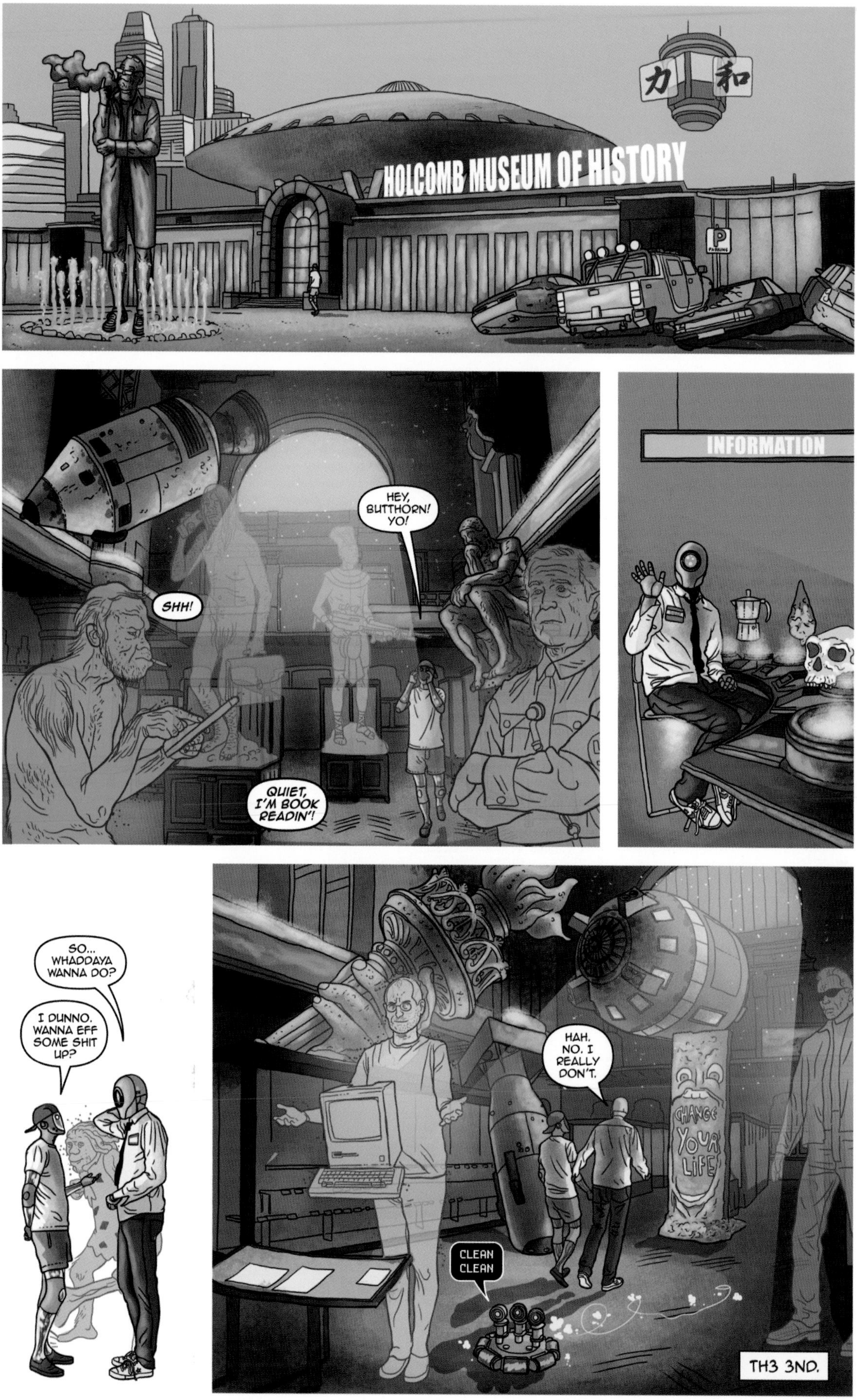
力 和
HOLCOMB MUSEUM OF HISTORY
PARKING
HEY, BUTTHORN! YO!
SHH!
QUIET, I'M BOOK READIN'!
INFORMATION
SO... WHADDAYA WANNA DO?
I DUNNO. WANNA EFF SOME SHIT UP?
HAH. NO. I REALLY DON'T.
CHANGE YOUR LIFE
CLEAN CLEAN
TH3 3ND.

COVERS & PINUPS

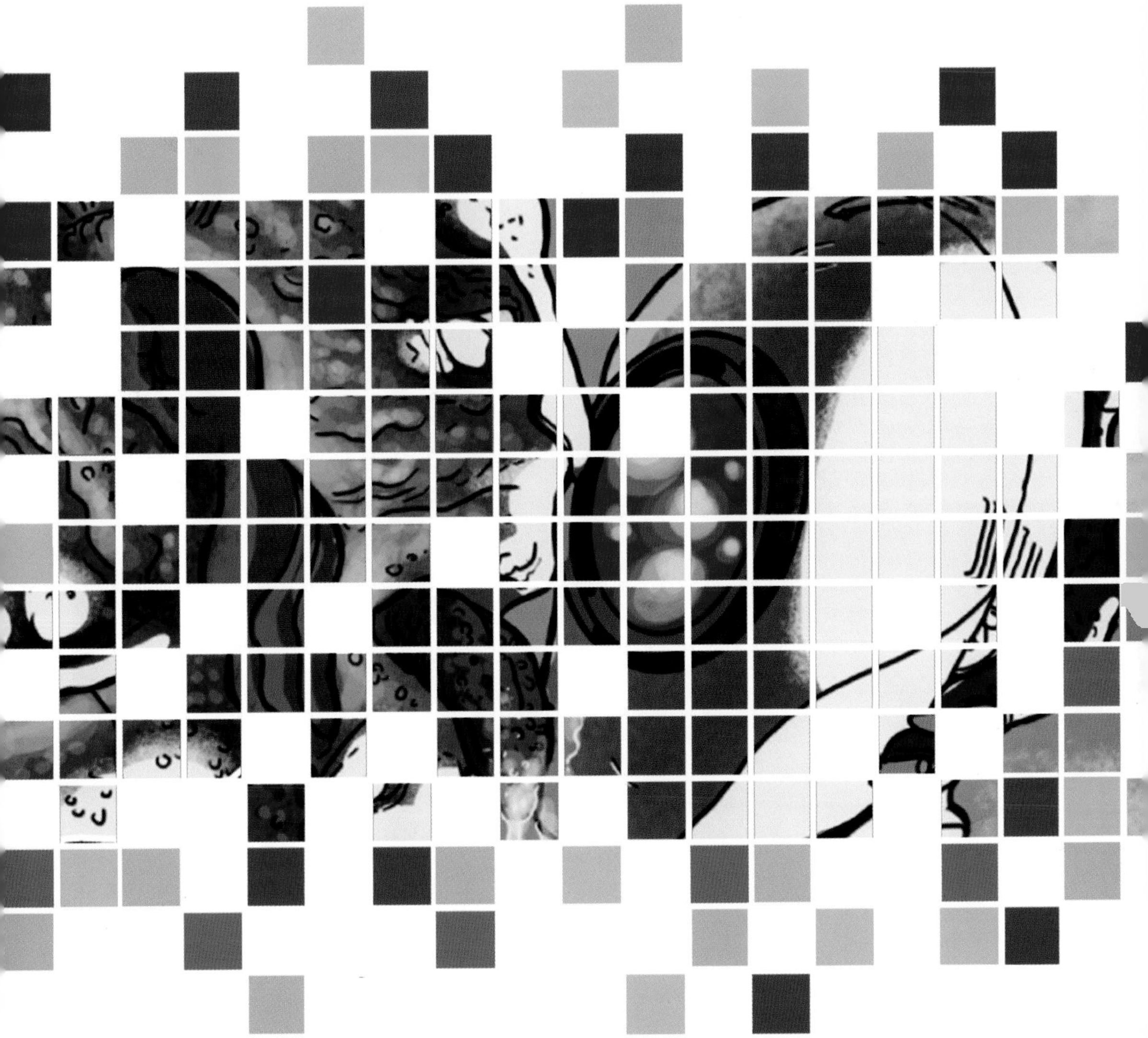

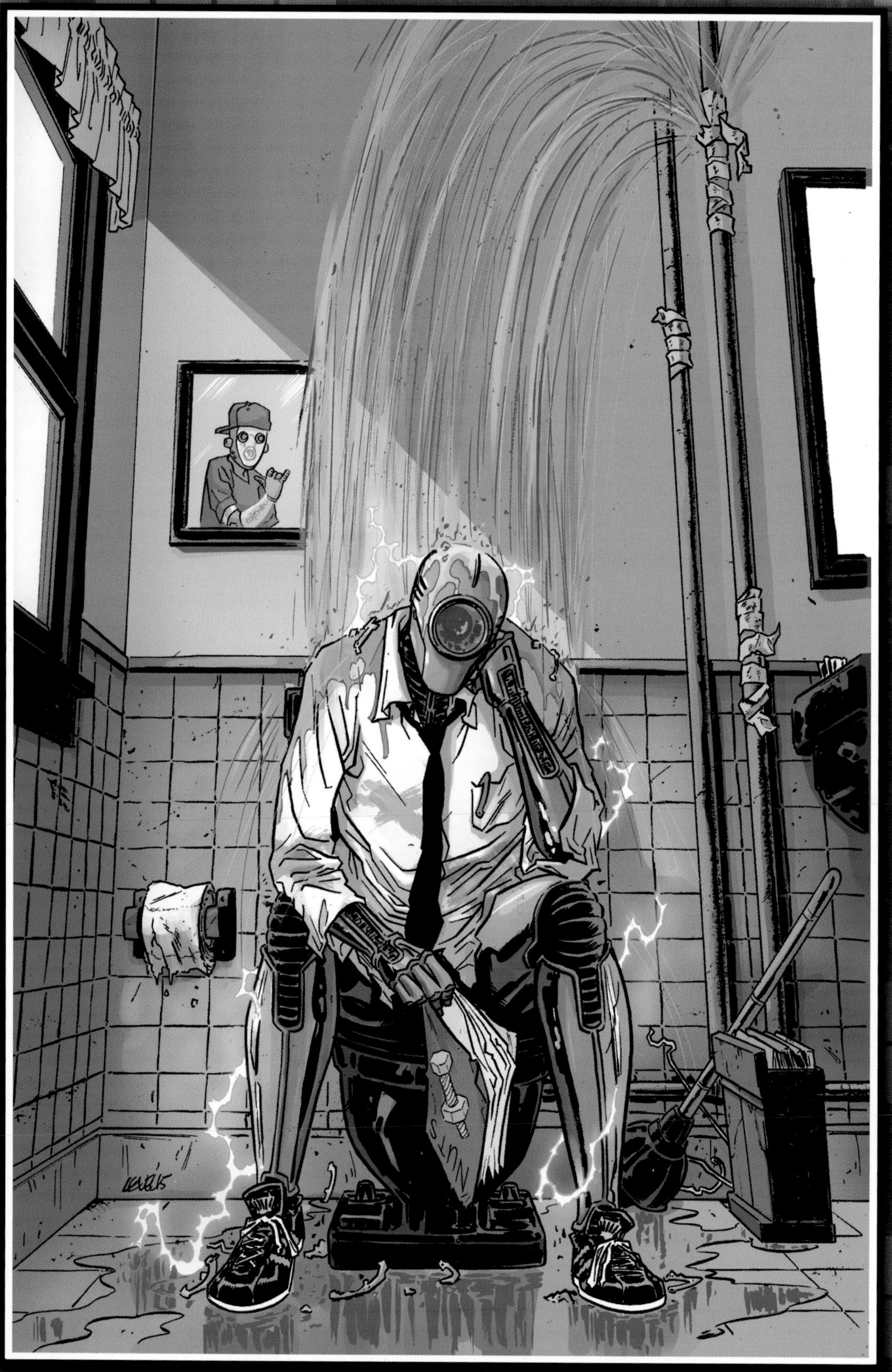

ART BY Brian Level COLORS BY Marissa Louise

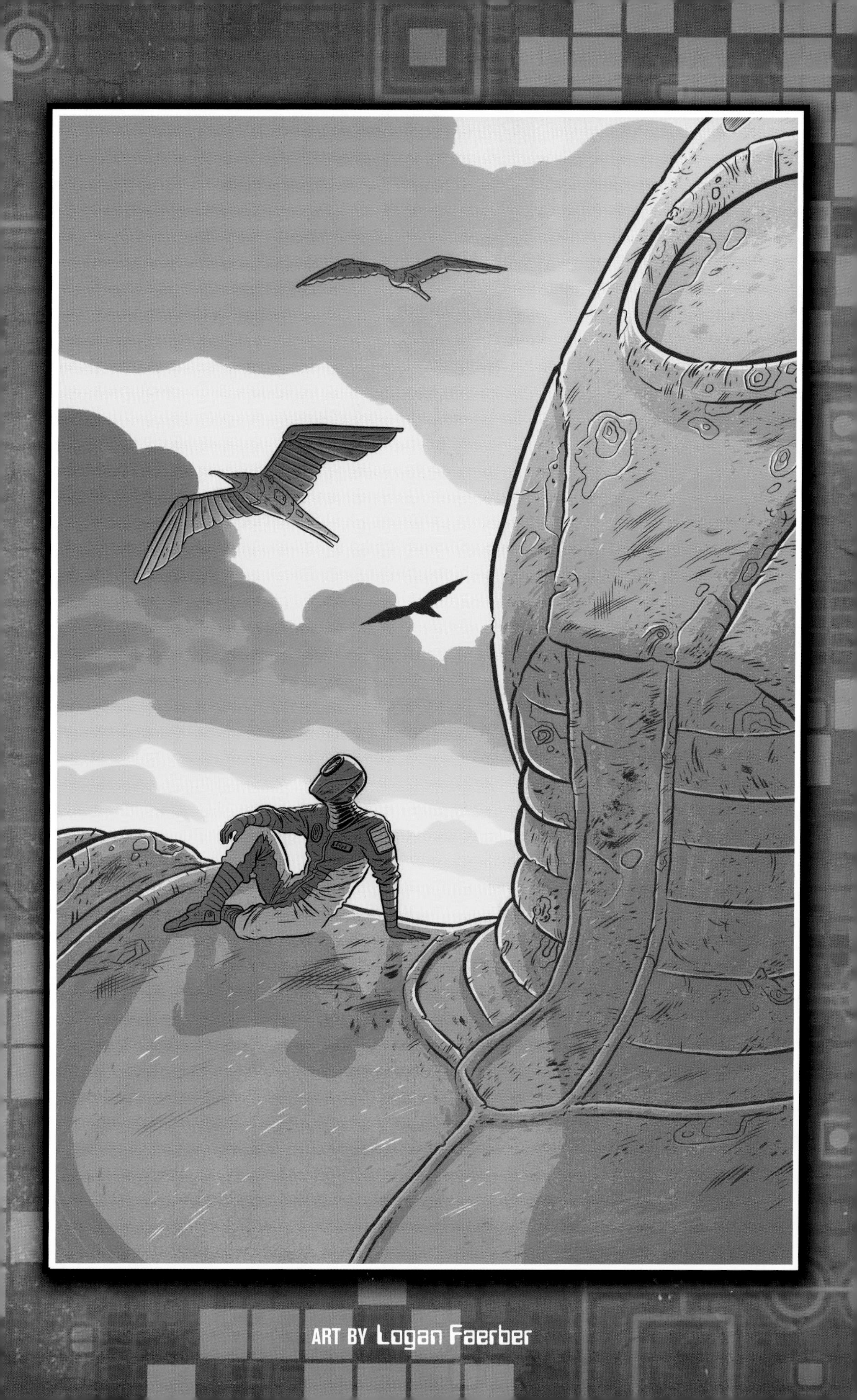

ART BY Logan Faerber

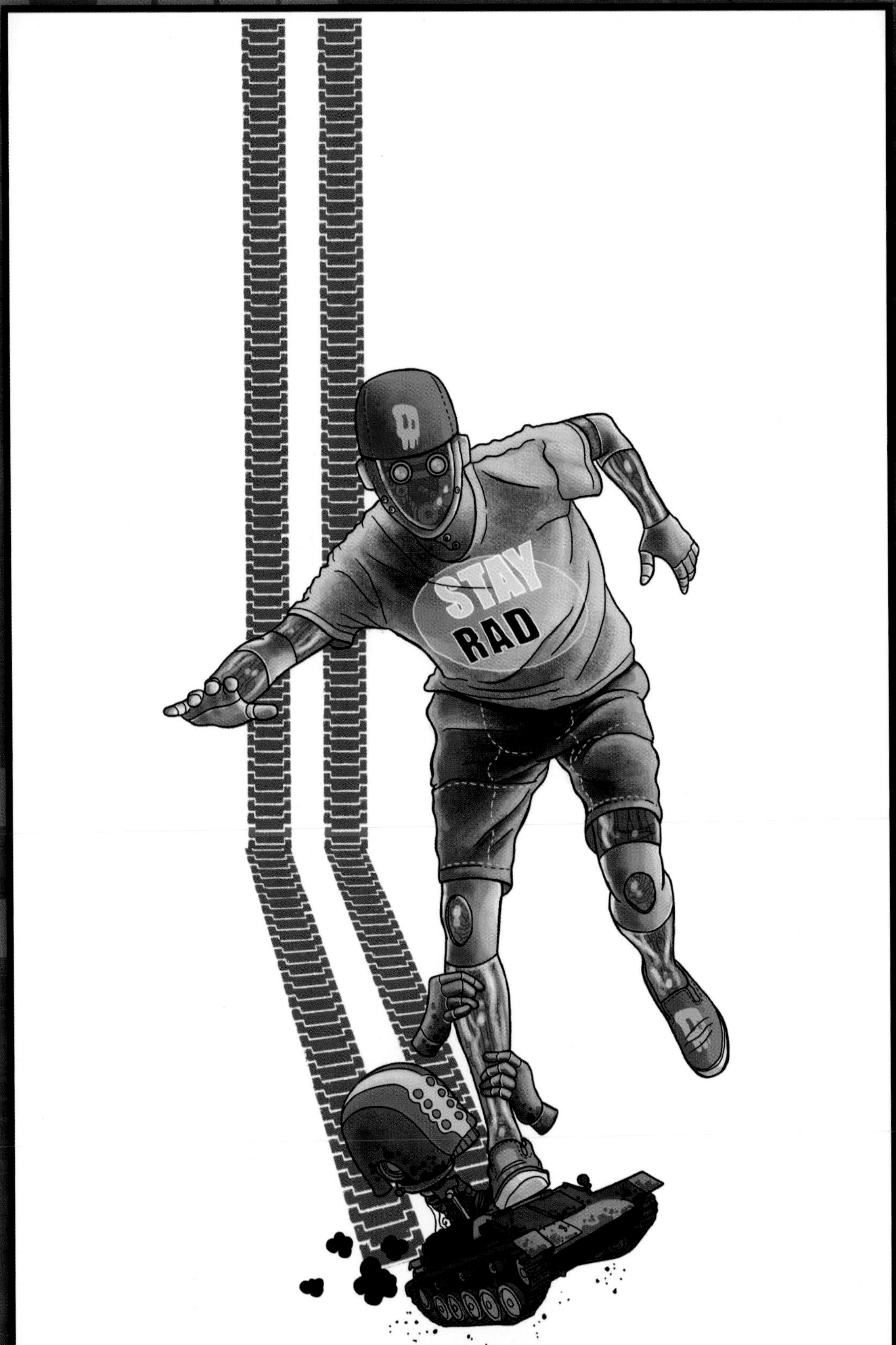
STAY
RAD

ART BY Valentin Ramon

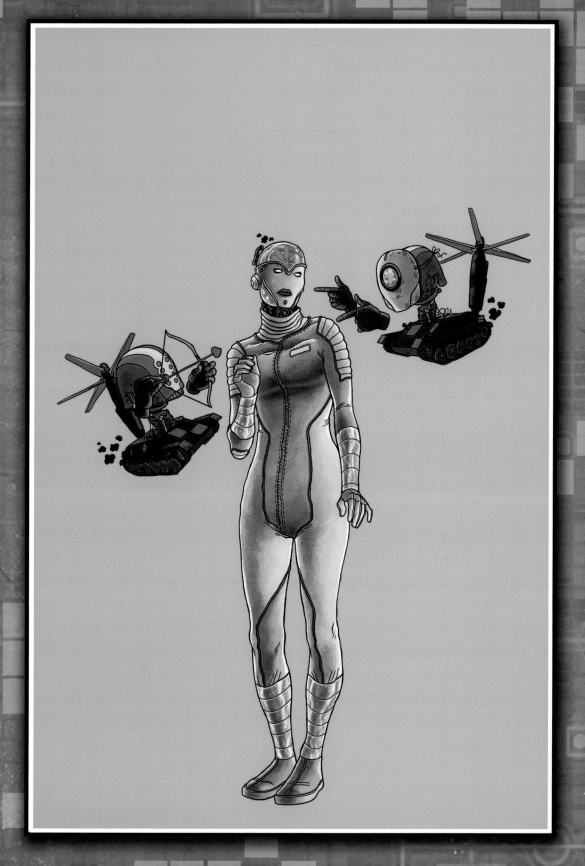

ART BY Valentin Ramon

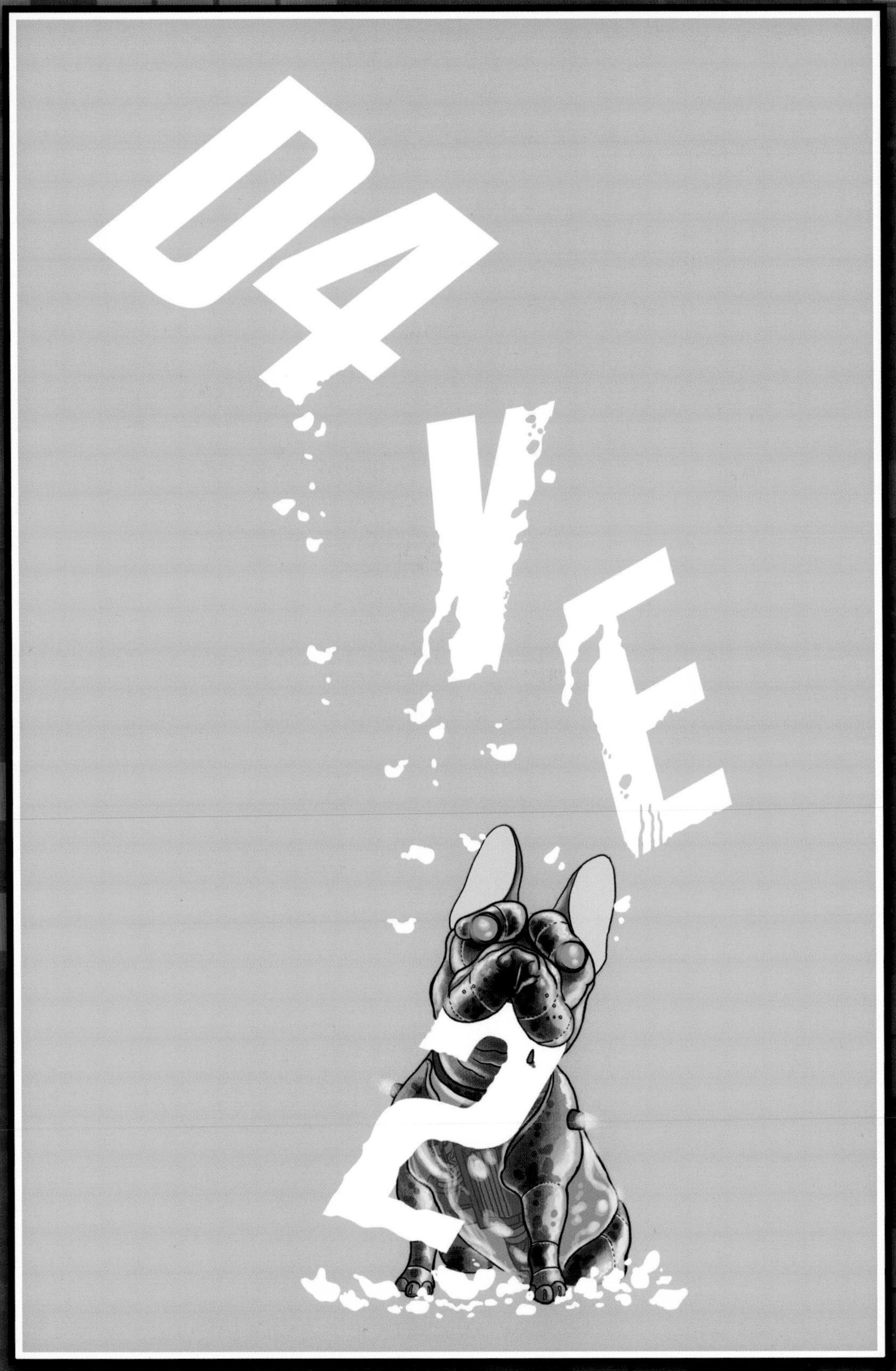
D4VE2

ART BY Valentin Ramon

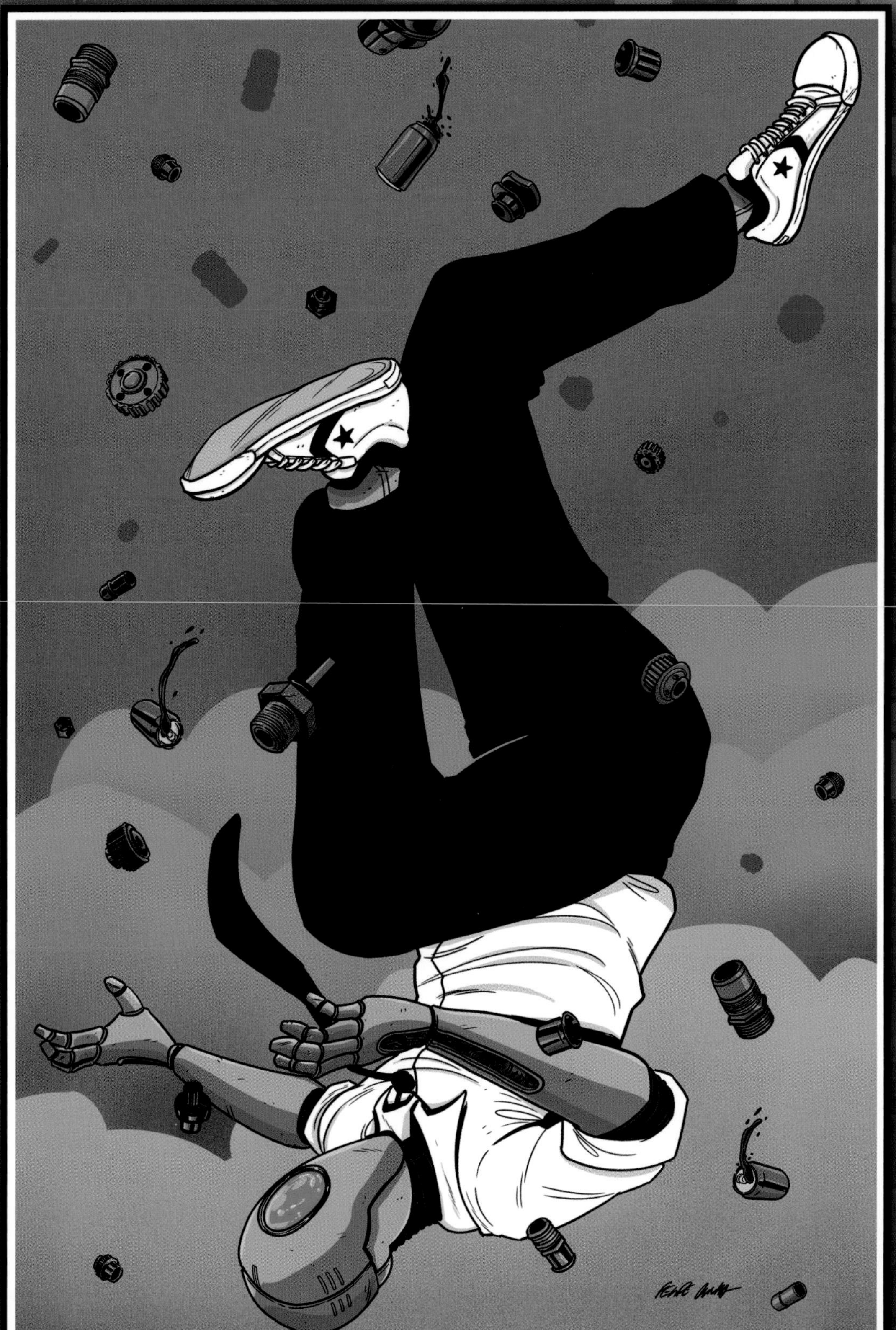

ART BY Felipe Cunha

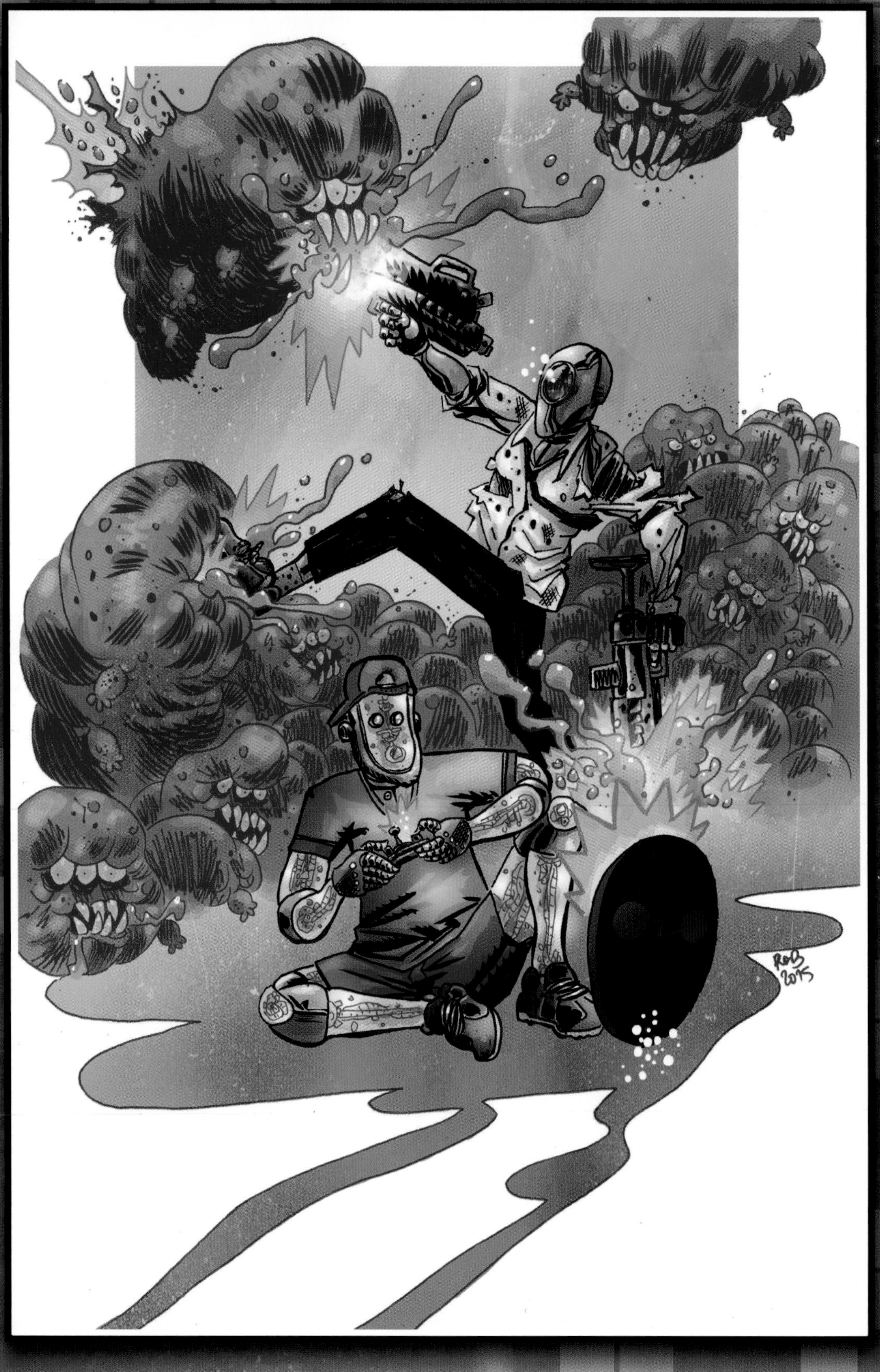
ROB
2015

ART BY Rob Croonenborghs

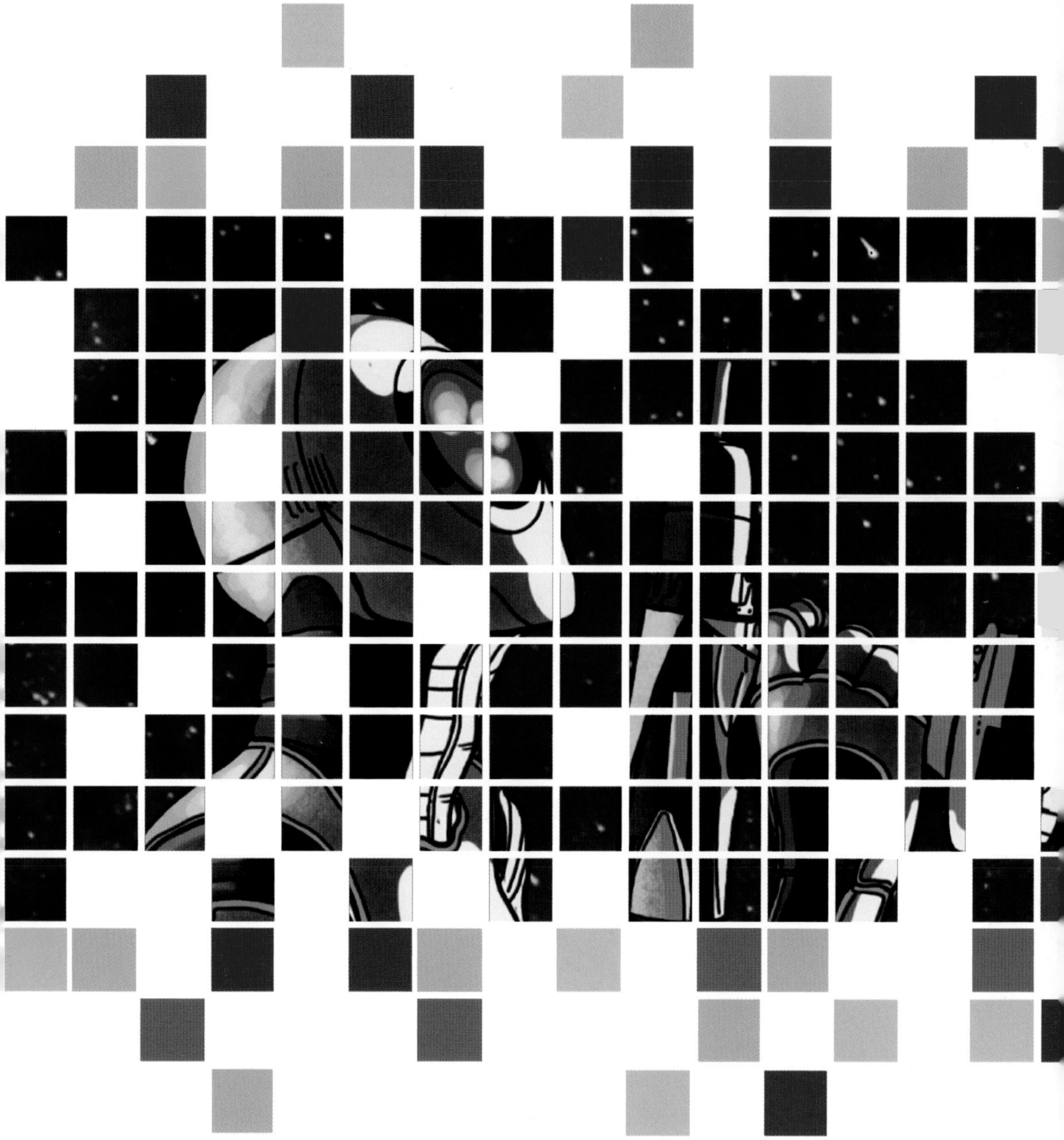

D4VE2